GOLD!

The Kincaid Saga, Book 1

By

THOMAS GREENBANK

ISBN: 978-0-6489611-4-7

This book is dedicated to my wife Linda, without whose encouragement (and occasional badgering) it might never have seen the light of day. Thank you for your love, patience, and unwavering support.

BEHIND EVERY GREAT FORTUNE, THERE IS A CRIME.

Honoré de Balzac. (1799-1850)

****

LIFE IS WHAT HAPPENS TO YOU WHILE YOU'RE BUSY MAKING OTHER PLANS.

John Lennon. (1940-1980)

Acknowledgement

Many thanks to Ross MacLennan of BookCoversAustralia.com for his brilliant work on the cover of this book. From only the simplest of briefs, he produced a cover that perfectly matched my vision.

Thanks also, to John Baselmans for kindly allowing us to use the drawing of the Aboriginal faces. (https://www.johnbaselmans.com/)

<u>Thank you for choosing to buy and read this book.</u>
You could have bought any book, but you bought mine. For that I'm grateful, and I hope you enjoy it.

Reviews are important for any writer, and especially so for a self-published author.
As a self-publisher, I don't have the resources the major publishing houses have at their disposal for book promotion. Your honest reviews will make it easier for other readers to find this and other indie works.
Please take a few minutes to register your opinion (after you've finished, of course) with one of the following links:

To leave an Amazon review, Try This First:
https://www.rpbook.co.uk/azr/B08N5ZVMZT
Although it's a UK link, it is designed to redirect you to your region's Amazon review page. Easy-peasy. I'm all in favour of that.

If you'd prefer to leave a review somewhere else, here are 2 options:

https://books2read.com/u/3yewpv
This covers most online book stores. Just scroll down the list until you see your preferred retailer and leave your review and comments.

Or this one:
https://www.goodreads.com/review/new/56165411-gold
Goodreads is an online forum for both readers and writers. You might just find your next favourite book here. (You're welcome to use both of these links)

Please visit my website, **thomasgreenbank.com/join-the-tribe,** and sign up for my newsletter to receive exclusive free stories, content, and other goodies from time to time including a FREE copy of my Short Story Collection; *The Ravine and Other Tales*.

In addition, I'll keep you informed of my progress with future books and other projects. Any feedback is always welcome.

Thanks again for choosing to read GOLD!

Thomas.

Preface

THIS STORY TAKES PLACE in Western Australia over an approximate 30-year timeframe, starting in 1975. Notwithstanding the earlier disclaimer, many of the locations and events mentioned are based on fact. Indeed, even some individuals mentioned in passing existed then, and possibly still do today. The story, as written, is fictional and should not be construed as anything else.

Perth, the capital of Western Australia, is located in the south-west of the state. Kalgoorlie, where much of the action takes place, is around 400 kilometres north-east of Perth. The Nullagine region and Port Hedland are approximately 1350 kilometres to the north.

Gold mining has been a major part of the history and economy of Western Australia since white settlement. Over the years, many fortunes have been won and lost, and there have been numerous documented reports of clashes between the new settlers and the indigenous land-dwellers. Most did not bode well for the native inhabitants.

Prologue

Monday, June 27, 2005

A SLEEK, BLACK MERCEDES KOMPRESSOR 200 glides to a halt outside the concrete and glass edifice that houses the corporate offices of Kincaid Mining Corporation; forty-four storeys of superb modern architecture near the western end of St Georges Terrace in Perth, Western Australia. The building is a fitting tribute to the huge conglomerate KMC has become. It's mid-morning. The sounds of a busy city fill the air along with the contrasting odours of exhaust fumes and fresh coffee.

Rain has been falling for most of the night and a slight drizzle persists, despite the bright rays of morning sunshine piercing the clouds and reflecting from the upper floor windows. A sign of better things to come, perhaps?

Lachlan extends his hand to Aretha, holding the umbrella over her as she climbs from the vehicle. He escorts her across the sidewalk and they stride purposefully through the entrance and foyer, acknowledging the greeting from the doorman, and enter the elevator. On the top floor, far above, the others will be waiting. As they are whisked smoothly and almost silently upward toward the boardroom, Lachlan allows himself to ponder the long and tumultuous history of the family business, one which now can truly be considered a force to be reckoned with in global mining terms.

It wasn't always so, however, and after today the company will never be the same.

But to tell the story of KMC, we need to go back some thirty or more years. Back to before Lachlan was even born, in fact. Back to the heady days of the 1970s. Heady days of miners, entrepreneurs, and shady wheeler-dealers. Back even before the days of what came to be known as WA Inc. with all its controversy and double-dealing in politics as well as in business. And back to the goldfields of Western Australia, where many a fortune was won or lost …

Chapter 1

MALCOLM KINCAID WAS AN HONOURABLE MAN. Ambitious; even ruthless by some standards, but honourable nonetheless. He told himself so regularly. But then, Malcolm Kincaid was a liar.

Mid-December, 1975.

Malcolm stepped from the comparative cool of the WA School of Mines building in Egan Street and squinted against the shimmering midday haze. A small crowd was emerging from within, and he took Rachel's arm firmly, drawing her sideways to the edge of the throng.

It was hot that day—even for Kalgoorlie. In a place where the heat didn't really start to bite until mid-January, Nature seemed to be forewarning of summer's impending advance. The searing east wind, straight from the heart of the Great Victoria Desert, gave the impression of standing before a blast furnace. A gyrating dust devil danced along the road and red dust swirled in eddies, stinging his eyes and leaving a gritty taste in his mouth.

To the west, heavy clouds loomed on the horizon, their elephant-grey forms wracked by occasional thunderclaps. There would be no rain today, however; anyone familiar with the local weather patterns would know that. All that the approaching front would deliver would be a change of wind direction and more humidity—along with the ever-present possibility of lightning-induced bushfires.

Not that any of this bothered Malcolm all that much. Nothing would spoil this day. Today was the start of a whole new life, one that he knew would be exceptional. Malcolm was on the way up. Under the ever-watchful eye of their father, Feargus Kincaid, he and older brother Jamie had applied themselves diligently to their studies, right up to graduating with honours from one of Australia's premier mining academies.

Malcolm recalled—with little fondness—their father's relentless bullying. He had to admit, though, the old Scot had done himself proud. Jamie had graduated with an Associate Diploma in Mining Engineering and Extractive Metallurgy just three years earlier. Malcolm, having completed his studies through correspondence from his home in Perth, now clutched his own graduation papers in his hands.

Feargus Kincaid's one driving ambition for both his sons was financial success; success he'd always felt was his birthright, but that the Fates had conspired to deny him. Malcolm wasn't sure about how much fate had to do with it, but he already had plans for his own immediate future.

A familiar voice boomed from behind, jerking him from his reverie. 'I suppose you feel pretty pleased with yourself. Top marks, hey?'

'Jamie!' exclaimed Malcolm, turning quickly. 'I thought you hadn't turned up!'

'That'd be the day,' grinned Jamie. 'As if I'd miss my new business partner's graduation. Well done, little brother.' He grasped Malcolm's right hand in both fists, pumping enthusiastically. 'I knew you'd ace it, Bro.'

At a shade over six feet, Jamie was taller than Malcolm—slim and wiry. Dressed in faded denims and a check sports shirt, and with a bushy black beard that Ned Kelly himself would have envied, he cast an imposing figure. He might have looked out of place in the well-dressed crowd, but he obviously didn't feel so. His tanned face and arms—a legacy of many hours under the Australian sun—and his callused hands, bore evidence of the years already spent working on the mines.

Malcolm, by comparison, appeared plump and urbane. The younger Kincaid was clean-shaven except for a neat ginger moustache and sideburns. He was a good five kilograms heavier than his sibling, and almost as far removed from Jamie in appearance as a brother could be.

'Little brother?' Malcolm chuckled, patting his paunch. 'Not unless I lose this, mate.'

'A month in the bush and you'll be a new man,' Jamie replied. 'Too much soft city living, that's your problem.

'And what's with the suit?' He eyed Malcolm up and down. 'Did someone miss the memo about the weather up here?'

They both laughed heartily. One thing these brothers had in common, which nobody could fail to notice, was their roaring, exultant laugh. When they laughed together, which they often did, they never failed to attract attention.

'A pity the old man couldn't be here,' Malcolm said after a moment. 'He was the one who wanted us both to graduate from the School of Mines. I reckon he'd be pretty pleased his browbeating has paid off.'

'That's for sure,' said Jamie. Then, turning his gaze to the petite, demure woman at Malcolm's side, he said, 'And I suppose you're the gorgeous young thing who's stolen my brother's heart?'

'Oh. Sorry,' said Malcolm. 'Jamie, meet Rachel. Rachel, this—as you've probably guessed —is my big brother Jamie.'

'Good to meet you, Jamie,' Rachel beamed. 'I've heard a lot about you. Nice to put a face to the name at last.'

She offered her hand, which Jamie squeezed eagerly. 'Likewise, Rachel. So what do you think of beautiful downtown Kalgoorlie?' He spread his arms wide to encompass the surroundings.

A smile flickered across Rachel's lips. 'Hot.'

'Better get used to it. It'll really start to warm up after Christmas.'

Jamie turned to face his younger sibling. 'So, the notorious Kincaid brothers are together again.' He nudged Mal with his elbow and added, 'I never thought I'd ever get you out of the big smoke, by the way. And starting Monday, we'll be working our own mining lease.'

'I still can't believe you tossed in your cushy, well-paid supervisor job with Hillfire Mines.' Malcolm said, shaking his head and ignoring Jamie's reference to the lease. 'You worked hard for that promotion. You were set for the long haul there, I thought.'

'Mal, just wait 'til you see these latest assay reports.' Jamie brandished a sheaf of papers. '*We* are going to be set for the long haul.' He put special emphasis on *We*. 'In fact, *we* are going to be rich, very rich.' He fixed Malcolm with his beaming grin, waiting for a response.

'You sure you really want to go down that track? Dad wasted most of his life scratching around his old claim, barely making enough to cover costs most of the time.' Jamie's grin still didn't waver as Malcolm continued. 'I still say the best plan is to target management positions and let someone else take all the risks.'

'And all the profits!' Jamie countered. 'And forget about that old school grubbing around like Dad did. Open cut! That's the way to go. We bring in dozers, scrape away a foot or two at a time, before sweeping it with detectors. Then we repeat the process.'

'Dozers?' Malcolm took a small backward step. 'Dozers, plural? And where is all the money coming from?'

'OK, OK, dozer. For now, at least. I have a D8 in mind, for starters.' Malcolm was shaking his head again, but Jamie continued. 'Belongs to a pal of mine. He's prepared to do us a special deal on a short-term lease. Mate's rates, you could say.' Jamie was clearly excited and obviously not ready to let it go. Malcolm grew silent—a resigned look taking up residence where doubt and incredulity had been a moment earlier.

'Come on, I'll buy us a beer or three and fill you in on the details,' Jamie said. 'Little brother, you are not going to believe these reports!' He waved the papers in Malcolm's face as they walked away toward the nearest pub.

They crossed to the shady side of the street, and Rachel felt Malcolm grip her hand in his. She glanced across at the two brothers. It wasn't just physical appearances that set them apart. How could this man—tall, rugged, good-looking, and so open and friendly—possibly be Malcolm's brother? Under different circumstances, the smile Jamie had given her might have melted her heart on the spot!

Malcolm had provided scant details, so she hadn't known what to expect. In the back of her mind, though, she'd had an image of simply a more senior version of Malcolm Kincaid. What she saw—and yes, felt, when she sized up the older Kincaid—made her just a little uncomfortable. Especially when she'd probed those penetrating hazel eyes …

As they walked, her mind drifted back over the events of the past three months; the events that had led her to accompany Malcolm Kincaid to Kalgoorlie.

They had met at a friend's dinner party and he had captivated her right away with his wit and charm. So much so, that she'd gone against her usually cautious nature and moved in with him after only a few weeks. Once their situation seemed permanent, however, Malcolm had changed subtly, becoming more demanding and less attentive. She'd considered ending the relationship more than once, yet here she was agreeing to relocate more than 400 kilometres with him! Rachel shook her head, wondering at the wisdom of her own actions.

What was it, she thought, this hold that Malcolm had over her? And what about Jamie? How could two brothers be so different? Malcolm was a calculated, ambitious optimist; it didn't take a genius to work that out. Jamie, on the other hand, seemed to turn optimism into an art form. He chatted away, oblivious to the fact that his brother wasn't paying the slightest attention to what he said, while Malcolm walked in stony silence.

The younger Kincaid was digesting the situation. When Jamie focused on an idea, there could be no reasoning with him. That's the way it always had been and, he supposed, always would be. He'd just have to let Jamie rave on for a while—nodding in the appropriate places—then say that he needed time to think on it. Tomorrow, he'd tell Jamie about the position he'd already decided to accept with Newmont Mining, a US corporation that was considering expansion into Western Australia. They had head-hunted him based on his recent performance at the School of Mines.

* * *

Later, the brothers were on their second pint, reminiscing about old times and Rachel was at the bar ordering lunch for the three of them, when Jamie turned to Malcolm.

'Rachel seems like a great catch, Mal,' he said with a grin. 'How did an ugly prick like you snare a looker like that? Was it witty Malcolmisms, or "Does this smell like chloroform to you"?'

'Very funny,' Malcolm answered. 'Just keep your hands off this one, hey? I still remember Bernice.'

Jamie furrowed his brow before answering, 'Bernice?' After a brief pause, he said, 'You mean Bernie Wainwright? Hell, Malcolm, that was years ago!'

'Maybe so,' Malcolm replied. 'But I still say keep your hands off.'

Jamie sat back, raising his arms in mock surrender. 'Sure thing, little brother. Consider me put in my place.'

In fact, Malcolm had long held a grudge against his older sibling over the Bernice Wainwright incident. Bernice, around a year older than Malcolm, was the most beautiful thing he'd ever seen. Malcolm had been smitten, and Bernice, despite the age difference, was fond of Malcolm and had done nothing to discourage his advances. Until she met Jamie, that was.

Malcolm had walked in on the two of them making out on the family sofa. The younger Kincaid completely lost control and attacked his brother with the first thing that came to hand—a brass statuette of Elvis Presley. Jamie received a cut to his forehead, and Malcolm a black eye and fat lip. Elvis was left with a permanently twisted right arm. Bernice had stormed out and refused to speak to Malcolm again from that moment onward.

This was the first time Malcolm had broached the subject in several years, and he actually found himself a little surprised that he'd mentioned it now. The two had long since agreed on a truce where Bernice Wainwright was concerned.

In the back of his mind, though, Malcolm knew the reason for his reaction. He and Rachel were having problems of their own. Nothing too serious, of course, but the relationship was on shaky ground.

Rachel had overheard him flirting with one of her work colleagues and created the usual female fuss. For fucksake, he was just being friendly, wasn't he? Why did some women have to make such a big deal of things? She'd confronted him, and threatened to leave him, but Malcolm put her straight. She hadn't mentioned the incident in over a week, and the bruises on her arms and back were clearing up nicely, thank you.

He also hadn't failed to notice how Rachel had looked at Jamie when they met …

'Well?' Jamie broke his train of thought. 'Are you going to look at these figures or not?'

'OK,' sighed Malcolm, 'show me what you've got.' He took the report from his brother and began to scan the pages with little enthusiasm. Malcolm was reading ore sample reports but not really absorbing the information, at least not at first. He stopped, reread a section, turned back two pages, ran his hand across his moustache, then looked up at Jamie, who was watching intently with that same broad smile.

'This … this can't be right. Are you sure there's not been a mistake?'

'Double checked and triple checked, little bro.' Jamie was beaming now. 'I said you'd be blown away.'

'But … Where is this lease, anyway?'

Jamie leaned toward his younger brother conspiratorially. 'If I tell you, I'll have to kill you.' He laughed before continuing—ignoring Malcolm's raised eyebrows at his clichéd attempt at a joke. 'It's actually just east of Dad's old mine. I reckon it's the mother lode Dad was looking for all those years. I went out there on one of my days off and walked around with a metal detector.' He held out a bronzed hand, with three nuggets, each bigger than a thimble. 'And look what I found—in under twenty minutes!'

Malcolm was staring, open-mouthed, as Jamie continued. 'I raced in to register a claim, and it turned out it was part of Dad's lease all along! Next day I dug some rock samples and took them to be assayed. You have the results there in your hands.' He waited for Malcolm's response, which wasn't forthcoming. 'So what do you say now, Mal old pal?'

Chapter 2

December 1, 1976

MALCOLM PAUSED, put down his tools, and reached for the water bag. Gulping thirstily at the contents, then splashing some of the precious, cooling liquid on his forehead, he stood to survey the scene. Malcolm had changed a lot, from the debonaire form he'd once struck. He now had a beard that almost matched his brother's, though the distinct ginger colour was more reminiscent of Henry the Eighth than Ned Kelly. He'd also lost considerable weight around his midriff, replacing it with sinewy muscles to his arms and shoulders.

The Two Brothers mine, some fifty-odd kilometres north of what would one day become the celebrated KCGM Fimiston Super Pit, had been in production now for nine months. During that time, the Kincaid brothers had extracted more gold from the small site than even Jamie, on his most optimistic day, would have dreamed.

Initially, they concentrated on the easy pickings, scraping the surface of loose rocks and earth with the D8 dozer and fossicking with the metal detectors. Now, they'd amassed enough collateral to start serious mining of the hard rock which, hopefully, would contain the gold seam their late father spent so much of his life pursuing. In a few more days, they'd have the newly purchased diesel-powered rock crushing plant and dry blowers in operation and could begin processing their first loads of ore.

'Come on, slacker,' Jamie called. 'No rest for the wicked, you know.'

Malcolm smiled over at his older brother and offered him the water bag. 'And you'd be the expert on that, I guess. Here, have a shot yourself.'

As Jamie swallowed, Malcolm said, 'This crusher is costing a fortune, and it'll cost another to run. I just hope the ore is as rich as the drilling tests show. 35 grammes to the tonne—I still can't believe it! If that's accurate, we'll be in the black in no time.'

'Yep,' agreed Jamie. 'And in the meantime, we just have to keep the bank happy,' he added with his usual impudent grin.

Keeping the bank happy was their biggest worry at the moment, Malcolm knew. It had taken a lot of smooth-talking and personal guarantees from both of them, including refinancing Jamie's home, to attain the necessary funding. This despite the fact that the manager, Joe Worthington, was a long-time friend of the boys' father, and was also Jamie's godfather. In the end, the results so far and the fact that both men were proficient at what they were doing were enough to swing things their way. Still, Joe had taken pains to point out, if profits weren't forthcoming …

'So Jamie, tonight's the big Birthday Bash. How does it feel to be twenty-nine? Just think, one more year and you're thirty. Practically an old man!'

Jamie laughed. 'You'll find out for yourself in three years,' he countered, before adding, 'Pretty much the same as yesterday, I guess, and no doubt the same as I'll feel tomorrow.'

'That's not allowing for the post-birthday hangover,' Malcolm said with a chuckle.

'Hopefully, a bit less weary than I am right this minute, in any case,' Jamie added.

He punctuated the last with a deep sigh before continuing. 'Is Rachel going to put in an appearance? You said things were a bit shaky between you two at the moment.'

'Oh, she'll be there. We had a long talk last night. She's been putting in a lot of extra hours at the Lucky Miner, and it's getting her down, that's all.

'I told her to tell them to shove it,' Malcolm continued. 'I can support her now, but you know how she is, always the independent one. She won't even give up her room at the tavern and move in with me.'

Jamie nodded. He knew how it was all right. Rachel had confided recently that she felt smothered by Mal's possessive and controlling nature. She liked living in Kalgoorlie and enjoyed her job at the Lucky Miner. Lately, though, she'd toyed with the idea of leaving him and moving back to Perth, even though she knew Malcolm would probably follow her and pester her until she relented and came back with him.

'She's a sweet girl, Mal. You're a lucky man to have her.'

Jamie immediately regretted that last comment. The last thing he needed right now was a jealous outburst from Mal. To diffuse the situation, he quickly said, 'We'd better finish up and head on home to get ready.' Then he added, shaking his head, 'Though I can't for the life of me fathom why I let you talk me into a birthday party, of all things. At my age?'

Malcolm shrugged. 'Best celebrate every milestone we can, I say. Besides, any excuse for a party, right?.'

Chapter 3

The Party

RACHEL WAS STILL WORKING when Malcolm arrived at the Lucky Miner tavern. She had taken it on herself to organise Jamie's party and was busy putting the final touches to the tables in the rear function room. Malcolm stole up behind her and put his hands over her eyes.

'Guess who.' he whispered at the nape of her neck.

'Ooh, Sean Connery?' Rachel said. 'No? Ah … Paul Newman?'

She turned to Malcolm, feigning surprise and disappointment. 'Oh, it's you. Oh well, better than Count Yorga the vampire, I guess.'

'And I don't bite,' Malcolm said. 'Well, maybe a little, but I don't leave marks.'

Rachel giggled. She gave him a quick kiss and made to return to her work when Malcolm grabbed her arm, pulling her back to him. 'Is that all I get?' He placed his mouth on hers and kissed her deeply, then added, 'There's a down payment on what's in store for you later.'

She struggled free from his embrace, glancing around to see if there were any spectators. Thankfully, they were alone. 'Mal,' she said, 'you're hurting me. My back's still tender from—you know …'

'Oh, come on, Rach. I hardly touched you. Anyway, that was days ago—you're not going to sulk over it all night, are you?' Then he added in a whisper, 'This is Jamie's birthday. I don't want you fucking it up, so let's play nice, hey?'

Rachel managed a weak smile. No, she would not spoil Jamie's party. Later, she decided, they'd have that discussion she had been putting off for the past week or more—if she could find the courage, that was.

Rachel gave the room a final once-over, and they walked through to the lounge bar. 'I need a drink,' announced Malcolm.

'Well, I need to pop upstairs and change,' said Rachel. 'You behave yourself while I'm gone, OK?'

'Me? What else would I do?' he replied, and added with a mischievous grin, 'I'd rather come up and help you out of those uncomfortable clothes, though.'

'Cool it, Buster,' she chided. 'I've had a long day—and it's not over yet.'

* * *

Later, as they sat in the lounge—Rachel nursing a Bacardi and Coke and Malcolm half-way through his second pint—she said, 'You never told me how you and Jamie became involved in gold mining. I mean, it's not exactly everybody's idea of a career path, is it?'

Malcolm took a long pull from his glass, finishing the contents before replying. 'Dad had a trucking business,' he began. 'He used to do a regular delivery run between Perth and the goldfields and was based here for a while.' Mal paused, recalling the way his father had told the story countless times. 'He got in the habit of frequenting the bush two-up school north of town and became pally with a Chinese guy called Chow Li Wong, or something like that. Around town, he was just known as Charlie Wong.'

'Some guys in the bar were talking about two-up the other day,' Rachel said, adding, 'Why on Earth do they call it a school?'

'I'm not too sure, could be something to do with suckers being taught a lesson in blowing their money.' Malcolm snickered at his own off-the-cuff attempt at humour. 'No, I reckon it's like a school of fish, maybe?'

'Or sharks!' Rachel interjected. They both chuckled at this.

'It's illegal, of course,' Malcolm continued. 'Some guy named Sheehan has been organising it since the '50s I believe. He moves the ring around regularly to keep the coppers off his tail, but I reckon some of them are on his payroll anyway and warn him when there's likely to be a raid.'

Malcolm waved a waitress over and ordered another pint before continuing his story. 'So, one day Charlie Wong's been having a bad run but, as usual, he reckons his luck's about to change and he bites Dad for a hundred quid. This was back in '54. A hundred quid was a lot of money back then. Anyway, he puts up his mining lease as collateral. Dad's pretty flush, having had a profitable day, and so he stakes Charlie. Within a half-hour, Charlie's broke again and Dad's the new owner of Charlie's gold lease.'

'Poor Charlie,' was all Rachel could say.

'Poor Charlie be buggered!' Malcolm cut in. 'Served the old chink right, I reckon.

'Charlie's mine turned out to be a waste of time, though. At least, it was the way Charlie had been working it. He'd fallen for the old myth about quartz being a guaranteed signpost for gold.' He took another long swig from his glass. 'A lot of the early miners thought quartz on the ground automatically meant gold deposits and his lease had a huge white quartz outcrop so Charlie wasted his entire mining life scratching around near this white monolith where he thought the gold was just waiting for him. There were no metal detectors in those days, of course.'

'Well, now we know just how close he came to making his fortune,' Rachel mused. 'What do you think became of him?'

'No idea.' Malcolm said with a shrug. 'Dad never talked about him. I just know that's how he came to own the mine. I reckon Charlie just moved on.

'Charlie's mine was a curse to Dad, though. He became obsessed, and wasted countless weekends fossicking around on it for years. Got to where he'd spend every spare moment on the lease, even neglecting his business. Dad was convinced, just like Charlie, that the so-called mother lode was there somewhere. In the end, he died never having found as much as a dozen ounces.'

'And now it looks like becoming one of the richest mines in the district,' Rachel said. 'Sad in a way ,though, isn't it?'

Her voice trailed off, as she visualised first the old Chinaman, and later Feargus Kincaid, determinedly tunnelling away at the base of the quartz talus, oblivious to the rich gold-bearing rock buried less than 500 metres to the east. So near—and yet so far.

Malcolm scoffed. 'That's the way it is with mining. Some win, some lose. Knowledge and research is the real key to success. Dad eventually realised that and pressured Jamie and me to study at the School of Mines, and the rest, as they say ...' He shrugged.

'What about your mother?' Rachel said after a pause. 'You've never mentioned her to me.'

Malcolm fell silent for several seconds before replying. 'Jamie and I are actually half-brothers. His mother died in childbirth.' He paused again before continuing, 'Dad met and married my mother a couple of years later.'

Rachel considered the revelation. This was the first time she had managed to get Malcolm to open up about his family history. 'Well,' she said, 'I guess that explains a few things. I mean, you hardly look alike, yet sometimes the bond between you is uncanny.'

What she chose not to say was how much it explained the *differences* between them.

Over the past several months, Malcolm had seemed to become more and more self-obsessed the more she came to know him. In more modern times, people might have called him a borderline sociopath. This term wasn't part of Rachel's vocabulary, but if it had been, it would probably have been her first choice if asked to describe Malcolm's true nature.

'And your mother?' she asked.

'She left when I was about five,' Malcolm replied. 'Dad never gave much of an explanation, but he drank a fair bit and had a decent temper, so maybe that had something to do with it. Personally, I reckon we were better off without her. I mean, what sort of woman pisses off and leaves her kids?'

'And you never heard from her at all?' Rachel raised her eyebrows.

'Not a word. In fact, she seemed to have just disappeared from the face of the earth.'

Rachel was about to say more when Jamie arrived, accompanied by a young woman Rachel recognised immediately. Julie Watkins was probably the last person she would have expected to see on Jamie's arm. A regular at the Lucky Miner on Saturday nights, Julie mostly arrived by herself or with a casual friend. She rarely went home alone, however. Jamie spotted them as he entered the room and made a bee-line for their table.

'Hi there, Birthday Boy!' called Malcolm, as they drew closer. 'I see you've scrubbed up well.'

'Mal, Rachel,' replied Jamie, nodding to each. 'You've met Julie, haven't you?'

After the usual pleasantries, the two brothers adjourned to the bar for a round of drinks for all. 'I didn't realise you knew Jamie,' Rachel said to Julie. 'He's not part of your usual crowd, is he?'

Julie checked herself in her compact mirror. She seemed pleased with what she saw, as she chose not to make any adjustments. Julie Watkins was the type of woman who never went unnoticed, whether at a bar, a party, or the local greengrocer's. She dressed to impress, and tonight was no exception. Julie wore a tight-fitting, low-cut dress in a red and green print that should have clashed violently with her fiery auburn hair, yet somehow didn't. She capped the ensemble off with bright red stiletto heels and matching lipstick and nail polish. Rachel suddenly felt more than a little underdressed.

'Friend of a friend, you could say,' Julie said in reply to Rachel's question. 'No, he's not exactly my type, but hey, a party's a party, right? We may end up together for the night, or we may not.' She gave a laugh, and continued, 'So you're Malcolm's other half? He's cute, but a bit intense for my blood. Still, I believe there's a good deal of money on the horizon—or so I hear, anyway. Best we play our cards right, hey?'

Rachel smiled and shrugged—preferring not to reply directly—and changed the subject. Within minutes, the Birthday Boy and his brother returned with drinks and some snacks.

* * *

Later, while Julie was cruising the dance floor and Malcolm was ensconced at the bar, Rachel broached the subject of Malcolm's mother—and her disappearance—with Jamie. Jamie explained that as he was three years older than Malcolm, he still had coherent memories of his stepmother.

She was a gentle soul, he recalled, with a sweet nature, but totally dominated by her overbearing husband. There were occasional beatings, though not so severe as to require medical attention. Mostly, she explained to any who noticed that she was just accident-prone. It seemed doors had a way of jumping out on her when she least expected it, and chairs would collapse beneath her diminutive weight.

Friends and acquaintances alike would exchange knowing glances and 'tut-tut' sympathetically.

When she disappeared, it surprised few. But none could explain why she would abandon the children. And yes, she considered both boys to be her own and treated them equally in every respect.

There were rumours, of course. Emily Kincaid wouldn't have been the first person to mysteriously disappear in the goldfields, and probably not the last. Most folk, however, were happy to accept Feargus Kincaid's explanation; an argument followed by Emily storming out and vowing never to return. A bit of marital argy-bargy wasn't exactly rare in those days, and a good many men considered it a husband's right—no, duty—to *keep the little woman in line* that way.

In any case, no official enquiry ensued, and Malcolm grew up believing in his mother's abandonment. A belief their father did nothing to discourage, and a major factor, Jamie felt, in explaining Mal's attitude to women in general.

'Don't get me wrong,' Jamie said as clarification. 'Mal's my brother—and my best mate. I love him dearly, but I accept that he has issues.'

'But didn't you ever talk about it?' Rachel asked. 'He must have heard the gossip.'

'Only once, when he was around twenty-two,' Jamie replied. 'It was the day after Dad's funeral, actually. Mal flew off the handle at the suggestion that Dad could have been in any way responsible.'

He paused for a few seconds before continuing. 'He reckoned the sun shone out of Dad's arse, and wouldn't hear anything different.'

Rachel sat quietly, digesting this new information. Yes, Malcolm Kincaid did have a definite misogynist streak. At least she now had an inkling of the reasons behind his attitude—not that it made it any easier to accept.

There was something else, though—something in Jamie's voice as he recounted the tale. Rachel couldn't quite put a finger on it, but …

'Thanks for explaining,' she said. 'He's discussed none of this with me before today.' She inhaled deeply before continuing. 'To be honest—and I'd really like you to keep this to yourself—I don't know how much longer I can put up with his attitude. I'm sorry, Jamie, if this makes you the proverbial meat in the sandwich. You're a great guy.' She swallowed hard, and added, 'This may be the drink talking, but I really wish I'd met you first.'

She realised she was blushing, surprised by her own candour.

Jamie's reply caught her even more off-guard.

'You're not the only one, Rachel. When I see how he treats you sometimes, I want to punch his lights out!' He fixed her with those clear, hazel eyes, and she felt the redness growing even more.

'I need to visit the little girls' room,' she said, quickly rising and almost running toward the nearest exit.

As fate will sometimes have it, the events which would forever change all the relationship dynamics happened just two hours later.

Chapter 4

STILL SEATED AT THE BAR, Malcolm had by now switched from beer to single malt whisky. Rachel had attempted to get him onto the dance floor, but without success. Dancing and merriment were not his scene, he insisted.

Julie Watkins flopped onto the stool alongside the younger Kincaid with a sigh. Nodding toward the crowd, she said, 'Seems like your girlfriend is having a splendid time.'

Rachel was dancing with two of the bar staff; a waitress named Debbie and the bar manager, Jerome.

Jerome was around 25; trendy, outgoing, and good-looking. Everyone at the tavern knew Jerome didn't have a girlfriend—and was never going to have one. In the mid-70s such things weren't usually talked about in mixed company, but few could misinterpret Jerome's sexuality.

Rachel liked him immensely, even though she didn't quite understand how a man could prefer a relationship with another man to a traditional relationship.

Jerome also had what was known as 'a touch of the tar brush'. In other words, he was part-Aboriginal. His skin was dark, though not overly so, and he had deep, dark, penetrating brown eyes.

Malcolm hated him. On so many levels, Malcolm hated him.

'I can't stand that Jerome prick,' he told Julie. 'Just something about him. I mean, I know he's a coon, but it's more than that. He makes my skin crawl.'

'You don't know?' Julie answered, 'He's as gay as they come.'

'Gay?' Malcolm raised his eyebrows.

'You know,' Julie explained. 'Queer—bats for the other team—a raging fag.'

Realisation dawned on Malcolm's face. Julie leaned in and whispered, 'Yeah, he's a homo.'

She watched his changing expression with amusement. He really had been living under a rock, it seemed.

Malcolm downed the last of his Scotch and strode toward the dance floor.

'Oh boy,' Julie Watkins murmured to herself. 'This *is* going to be interesting ...'

The band had just launched into Nutbush City Limits and the three were lining up with a larger group to dance the Madison when Malcolm shoved his way onto the dance floor.

Elbowing Jerome aside with a cursory 'Piss off, pretty boy,' Malcolm fronted Rachel. 'Come on, we're leaving!'

When Rachel failed to reply immediately, he yelled over the music. 'Come on, Rachel! You will not embarrass me any longer. Doing this stupid dance is bad enough, but I won't have you dancing with this queer.' He jerked his thumb in Jerome's direction, before giving him another dismissive push and made to grab Rachel's arm.

Rachel saw at once how drunk he was. Another time she might have yielded, but not this time. She pulled her arm away from his grasp and fixed him with a determined glare.

'Malcolm, I'll dance with whoever I want, and to whatever music I want. Jerome's my friend. Get used to it!'

Malcolm stared at her for several seconds before turning his attention to cute, pretty-boy Jerome; the epitome of all he despised in queer, effeminate men. And a coon, to boot!

Without saying a word or giving any warning, he swung a crashing right cross into Jerome's cute, pretty-boy face. The young man careened across the floor—skidding into several dancers and knocking them off their feet—before coming to rest, semi-conscious, against the stage.

Blood was oozing from Jerome's split lip—and he'd definitely be needing to visit his dentist tomorrow. Despite the damage he'd already inflicted, Malcolm strode to where the hapless Jerome struggled to get to his feet and was preparing to deliver a mighty kick to finish the job when Rachel intervened, pushing him off balance.

'Stop, Malcolm,' she yelled. 'Stop it! Now!'

Malcolm staggered. Regaining his balance, he turned his attention to Rachel. 'You fucking bitch!' he screamed at the top of his lungs, 'You fucking ungrateful bitch!'

He took one unsteady step toward her, sized her up, and swung his fist.

Unfortunately for Malcolm—but fortunately for Rachel—the blow never connected.

Jamie grabbed his brother's arm, wrenching him off balance. He shoved his younger sibling away from Rachel and growled: 'If you ever lay a hand on her in my presence, I'll take you apart, brother or not!'

By now, Malcolm Kincaid was totally out of control. He glared at his brother for a millisecond and swung a haymaker at Jamie's face.

Jamie just had time to evade the full force of Mal's swing, but still caught a glancing blow to his cheek. He reeled and barely regained his balance before there was another on the way.

Rachel forced herself between them. 'Enough, Malcolm!' she screamed. 'Back off!'

Malcolm's swing already had momentum. It caught Rachel above her left eye, mostly because she was shorter than the intended target. She staggered backwards, stars spinning in her head.

Jamie stepped forward and delivered a blow that might have finished Malcolm for good if it had fully connected. Instead, Jamie's fist caught Malcolm across his left temple and sent the younger brother reeling across the room to where he also landed in a heap against the stage. Luckily, Jerome had by now staggered to the edge of the dance floor, else Malcolm would have landed fully on top of him.

Not that Malcolm would have known it. He was by now losing consciousness even as he fell.

Jamie swung to grab Rachel, who was also on the verge of passing out.

'Rachel! Rachel! Are you OK?' Jamie's voice echoed as if coming from the end of a long tunnel. Rachel struggled to maintain her balance, opened her eyes briefly, then closed them again. A blinding light seemed to burn into her very being.

Jamie guided her to a nearby table and sat her down gently.

Rachel groaned. The stars in her vision spun more slowly, but nausea threatened to overwhelm her.

'Jamie?' she mumbled. 'What happened?'

The realisation of the last few minutes became clearer. Had she really confronted Malcolm like that?

Jerome—where was he? How was he? And Jamie? Her head still spun, and a loud buzzing filled her ears. The answers would not be coming any time soon.

As her vision cleared, she was aware of Jamie holding her tightly. She put her arms around him as best she could and held on as if her life depended on it.

'Jamie,' she whispered. 'Oh, Jamie.'

Jamie lifted her and carried her out to the saloon bar, where he sat her gently on a chaise longue in the room's corner. 'I told you I'd punch his lights out,' he said. 'And I promise you this: he'll never raise a hand to you again so long as I'm around.'

Gazing into Jamie's hazel eyes, hearing his reassuring words, Rachel knew where their future lay. 'I love you, Jamie,' she whispered.

He kissed her gently, more gently than she had ever been kissed before, and held her close for the longest time. This, she realised, was the embrace she wanted to feel from now until forever. No guilt. No doubts. No recriminations. Malcolm had at last shattered the remnants of any affection she had felt for him.

'And I love you, Rachel,' Jamie murmured. 'Since the day I first saw you.'

Chapter 5

AT 10:30 THE FOLLOWING MORNING, Malcolm was hammering on the door of Rachel's room. 'Rachel,' he called. 'I know you're in there. We need to talk—now!'

Debbie, the waitress Rachel and Jerome had been dancing with the night before, poked her head through the doorway of her adjoining unit. 'She's not in, Malcolm,' she said. 'And I really don't think she'd be too keen to see you today.'

'Whaddya mean, "not in"?' he bellowed. 'Where the hell is she?' His head was hurting—along with his pride—but Malcolm Kincaid wasn't ready to take any lip from anyone, let alone a bloody waitress.

'She's in hospital. And I'm not surprised after what you did to her.'

'What I ...?' he stammered. His memories of the previous night were returning, albeit slowly. Images of Rachel taunting him—that fag Jerome—Jamie stepping in to take Rachel's side. There had been a fight, that much he could remember. He recalled with smug satisfaction having given nancy-boy Jerome a decent slapping, but little else. Had Jamie punched him? Had he hit Rachel?

He gave Debbie a dismissive wave and lurched off toward Hannan Street, where he set out to walk the mile or so to the hospital. The long hike helped to clear his head, and by the time he reached his destination, memories of the previous night's events were a little more lucid. Malcolm arrived as Jamie was helping Rachel into a cab. On seeing him approaching, she slammed the door shut and thumped the lock button down with her fist.

'Rachel, I'm so sorry,' he said, his face pressed against the glass. 'I didn't mean to hurt you.'

'You never do,' she said evenly, without unlocking the door. 'You say you never mean to hurt me, yet you always do. Not again, though. It's over Malcolm. I never want to see you again. Now leave me alone.'

Malcolm opened his mouth to speak, but Jamie laid a hand on his shoulder. 'Leave her, Mal. You've hurt her badly this time. Better if you let her be.'

Malcolm spun to face his sibling. 'And since when did you become Rachel's keeper?' He gave Jamie's chest a shove, causing the older Kincaid to take a step backwards. 'This is none of your business, big brother, so fuck off!' There was venom in Malcolm's voice, venom the like of which Jamie hadn't heard in a long time. Jamie's fists clenched as he struggled to maintain control.

'Mal,' he said eventually. 'Can't you see you're only upsetting her more? Give her some space. I'm taking her back to her place, and I suggest you stay clear for a while.'

'Oh, you'd love that, wouldn't you, big bro? This is just like Bernice, all over again. Jamie, the hero, coming to the rescue. Well, we don't need your interference!'

Their faces were so close now that a fine spray of saliva settled on Jamie's beard. Rachel wound down the window enough to say, 'Please, Malcolm, go. Give me space, like he said. We can talk later. I need …' Her voice trailed off. Her head swam, and she tapped the driver's shoulder, saying, 'Please, get me out of here.'

The cab driver didn't need a written invitation. He jerked the T-shift into Drive and sped off, leaving about ten dollars' worth of rubber in twin streaks on the hardstand.

The two brothers stood facing each other. It was Malcolm who spoke first.

'You are the worst arsehole of a brother a man ever had. I hope you fucking die!'

He spun on his heel and stormed off, leaving his brother open-mouthed.

They left the carpark in opposite directions; Jamie heading inside to call another taxi, and Malcolm setting off for the walk home. Home, thankfully for him, was only a block away.

* * *

The following day, Malcolm gingerly tapped on Rachel's door. She peered through the gap, keeping the security chain in place.

'Mal, I told you we're finished, and I meant it.' Her head still hurt, and a purple bruise showed the outline of Malcolm's signet ring on her forehead. 'I'm not taking any more of your crap. You've hurt me for the last time.'

'All right,' he replied. 'I guess we need a break. I'm going down to Perth for a while. I've got friends there I can stay with. Will you tell Jamie?'

'I will,' she said, nodding. She stifled the urge to tell him again that it would be more than a break. He'd get the message eventually, she reasoned.

Rachel watched with a mixture of relief and, yes, a little pity, as he walked to his car. When he turned to look back, she quickly pulled the door closed, hoping he hadn't seen her face. When next she risked opening the door a little, he was gone.

Chapter 6

February 1977

TWO MONTHS AFTER the birthday party incident, Malcolm was jolted awake by the persistent ringing of his phone. 'Malcolm?' a voice said. 'It's Jamie. We need to talk.'

Mal clenched his jaw, inching himself into a sitting position. 'So talk.'

Jamie paused before continuing. 'Look Mal, I know you probably aren't in a good place still, but we need to sort things out.'

He waited for a response, and when none was forthcoming, he continued. 'The mine. I can't run this whole thing on my own. We're still partners, and we're still brothers. I don't ...'

'I'm coming back to Kal this weekend,' Malcolm cut in. 'I just needed some time to get my shit together.'

'Mal, what the hell have you been doing these last two months, and why haven't you returned any of my calls?'

'Like I said, I needed to sort myself out,' Malcolm replied. 'I know I acted like a total prick to Rachel and to you, and I guess I'll have to live with that. How is she? She won't answer when I call her.'

'Rachel's OK.'

Jamie and Rachel had both decided not to rush things. After their mutual confessions of affection, they both knew where things were heading, yet the spectre of Malcolm's presence in both their lives was something they could never ignore. They saw each other almost daily, yet it had been two weeks before their first actual date.

Should he tell Malcolm about their relationship? Jamie thought discretion was probably best for now. 'I'm not sure if she'll want to see you right away, but give her time, hey?'

'Tell her I'm truly sorry for what happened. Tell her I hope we can patch things up.' Malcolm's voice was almost plaintive.

'Mal, you really hurt her. I mean physically. She still has headaches and blurred vision sometimes. Doctor Servino has her on medication and she may have to take it permanently.' Without thinking it through, he added, 'We've been seeing each other a bit.'

Jamie waited for a response. Eventually, it came. 'OK, I guess I can't blame either of you. Thanks for being honest about it.'

'So we'll see you in a few days, then?' Jamie pressed. 'Are you driving up, or taking the train?'

'Driving,' Malcolm said. 'Well, riding, actually. I bought myself a Harley last week. Can't wait to get her out on the open road.

'I'll be there sometime Saturday,' he added. And with that, he hung up.

* * *

Once Malcolm returned to Kalgoorlie, he and Jamie came to an uneasy truce. Despite some initial awkwardness, they both worked to restore their relationship and rebuild their old bond.

By August, the Two Brothers mine was showing good profits and was well on its way to putting the company in the black. The rock crusher, bought second-hand from Hillfire Mining, was churning out as much loose ore as the dry blowers could manage, and the gold output was exceptional.

The mine was still largely a two-man show. Jamie and Malcolm shared the operational work, and Rachel ran a small on-site office they'd constructed. Rachel's headaches came and went. Doctor Servino told her she'd probably have to be on medication long-term, and warned her to avoid alcohol.

Malcolm seemed to have accepted the new situation with Jamie and Rachel. He even helped move Rachel's belongings from her room at the Lucky Miner to Jamie's home and professed to being pleased for them both.

Chapter 7

Mid-September 1978

'THANKS FOR AGREEING to stay over, Mal.' Rachel said as she put the final touches to the meal she'd prepared for them both. 'Jamie's turned into something of a worrywart lately. Honestly, I would have been fine for two nights while he's away.'

It was now almost a year to the day since Rachel and Jamie had formalised their relationship by moving in together, and their romance had blossomed.

Rachel was relieved that she and Malcolm were back on friendly terms, though she knew there would always be a veil between them. It had taken some time, but for Jamie's sake, more than her own, she welcomed the new status quo. When Jamie suggested Malcolm stay overnight, she'd been hesitant at first, but the brothers, Jamie in particular, had been adamant and Rachel capitulated.

'No problem, Rachel,' Malcolm assured her. 'If there's been a prowler reported in the street, I guess it's best to be safe. At least I get a home-cooked meal, and I've brought us a couple of bottles of good shiraz.'

'I'm not sure about the wine,' Rachel countered. 'The doc says to take it easy with alcohol while I'm on medication. Still, I guess a glass with dinner shouldn't hurt.'

* * *

The meal went well, and they chatted amiably to the accompaniment of some light classical music—Rachel's latest passion. One bottle turned into two, followed by a couple of margaritas. By nine o'clock, Rachel had drifted off and Malcolm found himself alone with his thoughts and the delicious view of Rachel's long legs and shapely thighs stretched before him on the couch opposite.

How could he have been so stupid as to drive her away like he did? Would he ever have the chance to win her back?

Sure, he'd said all the right things to her, and to Jamie, even pretending to be pleased for them, but deep down he still ached for her. He always would—this, he knew. Now, looking at her sleeping form, he felt those same stirrings she had always invoked in him.

He rose, strode to the kitchen, and splashed his face with cold water. Walking outside, he stood for some time staring at the moon. Fine tendrils of cirrus clouds drew spidery webs across its face, reminding him of a night long ago, when he and Rachel had first made love on a secluded beach. Malcolm returned to the lounge and, scooping Rachel's petite frame in his arms, carried her upstairs to her bedroom.

His right hand caressed her buttock beneath the satin skirt she was wearing. Rachel murmured softly and snuggled into his neck. Once again, he experienced that familiar stirring in his loins. Was she feeling the same? Surely she knew it was he, Malcolm, who carried her up the stairway? Had she engineered this situation to reignite their love for each other?

Upstairs, he lay her on the bed and stood over her for several minutes. The satin skirt had ridden up, and he could plainly see the outline of her body beneath her underwear.

As though having a mind of its own, his hand reached and touched that gentlest part of her. He stroked her tenderly, allowing himself to savour the memory of how he would sometimes wake her that way, not so long ago.

Rachel didn't stir. Her deep, rhythmic breathing suggested she was in a deep sleep.

Malcolm traced the outline of the soft mound behind her panties. He noted with satisfaction that she was not wearing pantyhose. She knew he hated them. 'Passion killers,' he called them.

Rachel stirred, rolling fully onto her back, and her legs opened slightly.

He halted. Was she really sleeping? Did she know what he had been doing? The cheeky minx—she was foxing! Pretending to be asleep, as she had done sometimes in the past, in happier times.

Slowly, tenderly, he resumed stroking her, and then gently removed her underwear.

Rachel began to wake. Jamie! He was home at last! Through the fog produced by the soporific combination of alcohol and her medication, she remembered dinner with Malcolm, but not much afterwards.

She felt his beard brushing across her thighs and sensed what was coming.

What was it with these Kincaid brothers? Had they compared notes?

He was kissing her now, in that special way Mal had done so many times. The realisation came to her that one of the few things she had enjoyed about her time with Malcolm was his love for cunnilingus. Could that really be the reason she put up with his behaviour for so long?

She recalled suggesting it to Jamie once, but he expressed disgust, so she turned it into a joke.

And yet, now, here he was, gently running his tongue up and down her soft, secret parts while his hands behind her buttocks held her close, so close to him, as if she might escape.

She moaned, softly at first, then with more intensity. Rachel fought to remain in that half-sleep state where all inhibitions ceased to exist. It wasn't much of a fight, the alcohol saw to that.

The probing tongue had found its target. Rachel knew she was nearing the point of no return; that delicious slippery slide of emotions and sensations that she now craved so much.

She was writhing now, as if attempting to escape and yet submitting completely. Then came the climax. The hot, thunderous climax.

Suddenly he was on her, driving himself deep within her and kissing her mouth aggressively. She could taste herself on his tongue, and in his beard, and it heightened her excitement even more.

Then, all at once, an alarm seemed to sound inside her head. This wasn't kind, gentle Jamie, the man she had come to know and love. This was Malcolm! The realisation came to her in an instant. She struggled to wake, and to extricate herself from his pressing weight.

Malcolm emitted a low groan, one she instantly recognised, as he poured himself into her.

She pounded him with her fists, to no avail. 'No! No!' was all she could manage.

Malcolm's body fell limp. She knew the sequence well; he'd be asleep within a minute and she would have to struggle out from under his weight while he drifted into dreamland.

Summoning all the limited strength she was capable of, she shoved him as hard as she could. He flopped over onto his back on the other side of the bed and lay immobile. The alcohol in his system finally took control, and he was asleep immediately.

Rachel lay for several minutes, not yet able to rise, and not daring to allow herself to drift back into sleep.

Eventually, she dragged herself to the bathroom, where she washed her face and stared at her reflection in the mirror. Her head spun, her stomach churned, her blurred vision had returned with a vengeance.

How could she have allowed that to happen? How could she possibly have mistaken Malcolm for sweet Jamie? Her mind drifted back over the past several minutes, and she was suddenly nauseous. She ran to the toilet where she kneeled, vomiting, then retching until her stomach ached.

As soon as she was able, Rachel discarded her clothes and climbed into the shower. She washed, scrubbing her private parts until the skin was raw, then fell into a crouch in the cubicle's corner and wept.

She must have dozed off, as when she opened her eyes, the water had run cold. How long had she been there? She had no idea.

Towelling herself dry, Rachel wrapped herself in a blanket she took from the closet and stumbled downstairs. She could hear Malcolm snoring loudly in the bedroom; the bedroom she had shared with Jamie—and which would now forever hold a secret, terrible memory.

She collapsed onto the couch and plunged into a deep, thankfully dreamless, sleep.

* * *

The sun was shining when Rachel woke. The light hurt her eyes, and she turned her face to the back of the sofa.

From the kitchen came Malcolm's voice. 'Welcome back to the land of the living, Sweetheart. Breakfast's almost ready. How does scrambled eggs and bacon sound? I can add a grilled tomato if you like.'

Rachel struggled to clear her head. Gradually, the whole terrible nightmare came back to her. And there was Malcolm—as large as life and twice as bold—asking her about breakfast!

She sat up, clutching the blanket tightly around her, and stood to face him.

'Malcolm. You have to leave—now!' she snapped with as much strength as she could muster.

'But I've fixed you breakfast. I thought we ...'

'Malcolm!' Rachel screamed, trying to ignore her pounding head. 'Listen! You have to leave! I don't want you here anymore!'

Malcolm stared open-mouthed. But surely things were back to where they were between them?

Rachel added, as firmly as she was able, 'And I don't want Jamie to ever learn what happened last night—it would kill him.'

She swallowed hard before continuing. 'Please, Malcolm. Promise me you'll never breathe a word of this to him. I'll keep it to myself. I just don't want Jamie to hear of it—ever.' She was sobbing now. 'It wasn't all your fault. I blame myself as much as you.'

This was true, despite logic dictating otherwise. She should never have allowed herself to be alone with him under any circumstances, she told herself, never mind getting drunk with him!

Malcolm slid the meal he had been making onto a plate and stared at her fixedly. 'OK,' he said. 'If that's the way you want it, but ...'

'Promise me, Malcolm! Promise me!'

'OK, it's a promise,' he said. Without saying more, he spun on his heels and left.

Rachel waited until the rumble of his motorcycle faded into the distance, then emptied the meal he had prepared into the kitchen waste bin and collapsed once more onto the couch.

She rose again around noon and spent the rest of the day tidying up and washing the bed linen, attempting to obliterate any signs or memory of Malcolm's presence—with limited success. The clothing she had been wearing quickly found its way into the trash bin as an accompaniment to Malcolm's breakfast offerings.

Chapter 8

Friday, November 4th, 1978

JAMIE AND RACHEL were deep in conversation as Malcolm walked into the mine site office. He strode to a timber and glass cabinet containing several gold nuggets of varying sizes. In pride of place, on a purple satin square, lay the ones Jamie presented to Malcolm on that scorching December day three years ago. From time to time, the brothers supplemented the collection with any unusually shaped nuggets they found.

'I've got a fresh addition for the display,' Malcolm announced. 'Check out the odd shape of this one.'

Rachel and Jamie looked up quickly and broke off from what they were saying.

'Oh, sorry,' said Mal. 'Am I interrupting something?'

Jamie glanced first at Rachel, then back to Malcolm.

'I guess you may as well hear it now. Rachel and I are getting married.'

'Wow! That's great!' Malcolm replied. He didn't actually feel all that great about it, but he knew that was the only acceptable response. 'When's this happening?' he asked. 'Have you set a date yet?'

'Next month or so,' was Jamie's reply. Rachel was silent.

'You don't believe in wasting time, hey? I have to say you caught me by surprise there.'

'Yeah, there's a certain amount of urgency involved.' Jamie shared another quick glance with Rachel, and continued, 'You're going to be an uncle, Mal, old pal. What do you think of that?'

'Wow,' was all Malcolm could manage. 'That's, ah, unexpected.' He paused before continuing, 'Is, er, this what we'd call good news? I mean, I didn't expect you'd be planning a family just yet—what with the company still finding its feet and all.'

Rachel rose and headed toward the door. 'I'll attend to that business with the samples, Jamie. Catch you later, Mal,' and she quickly left the room.

Jamie turned to Malcolm. 'Rachel had to stop taking the pill. It was causing problems with her medication. We've been taking precautions, but you know what they say—nothing's foolproof.'

'Still,' Malcolm countered, 'I guess it's not all that bad, is it?'

His thoughts were spinning as he mentally processed the dates. Could it be? And even if his suspicions were correct, what could he possibly do about it?

Of course, there was absolutely nothing he could do—or say. He'd made a promise to Rachel, hadn't he? And he knew he would keep it.

Slapping Jamie on the back, he said, 'Well, big brother, I didn't think you had it in you. Wow, Uncle Malcolm. How about that?'

Then he added, 'I reckon this deserves a drink or three. Why don't we all head in to town and I'll buy the bar?'

'Rachel's still sworn off alcohol. She hasn't elaborated but something put her off drink altogether, so I guess she'll pass,' said Jamie, then he added. 'Sure, let's do it! It must be beer o'clock somewhere.' He grabbed the keys to the Land Cruiser and led the way out to the compound. They both climbed in, Jamie behind the wheel, and sped down the access road and southward toward Kalgoorlie.

Chapter 9

JAMIE AND RACHEL were married on December 10th, just over a month after the announcement. Rachel's parents came up from Perth, and her high school best friend made the trip from Queensland to act as bridesmaid.

Malcolm stepped up as Jamie's Best Man, and even Jerome attended, much to Malcolm's disgust.

'It's a wonder you didn't have him as a flower girl,' Mal whispered to Rachel surreptitiously as they took their seats at the bridal table.

She shot him a look that might have frozen the Red Sea but said nothing. In fact, she'd hardly spoken more than a few words to Malcolm since the incident the previous September. Perhaps one day, she thought, she may be able to exchange pleasantries with him again. That time remained a long way off, however.

For his part, Malcolm had kept to his promise and Jamie was blissfully unaware of the deep secret his wife and brother shared.

After the nuptials and celebrations, the happy couple went on their way. Malcolm adjourned to his apartment, after visiting a brothel on Hay Street. He'd become quite a regular there in recent times.

* * *

The mine was doing well. What had once been a prominent ridge of quartz and rock was now replaced by an ever-increasing hole. Once a week the brothers would lay charges and blast huge volumes of rocky soil and then the dozers—there were three now, working twelve hours a day—scraped the debris away and an excavator and two dump trucks delivered it to the ore crusher.

Yes, the Two Brothers Mine was a success. Open cut mines were still a rarity, and many saw it as an expensive folly to invest so heavily in it. Underground mining remained very much the norm, and it wouldn't be until near the end of the 1980s—when the KCGM Super Pit came into existence—that open-cut became widely recognised as the future in mining.

Chapter 10

June 15, 1979

Lachlan

'HE CERTAINLY HAS the Kincaid nose, doesn't he?' said Malcolm, bouncing the latest addition to the family in his arms. It was true there could be no disputing the baby Lachlan's bloodline. The deep blue eyes were his mother's contribution, but the nose, with its small hook at the tip, was definitely Kincaid. Even at this tender age, that one family feature was patently obvious.

Rachel smiled. 'Oh yes, he's a Kincaid, all right. There's no doubt about that. My mother calls it the fish-hook nose.' She chuckled lightly, adding, after a pause, 'So what's so important that my husband is too busy to come and visit his wife and son? He only stayed for an hour yesterday, too.'

'We're still having problems getting the crusher back in operation,' Malcolm replied. 'He asked me to pop in to town for some parts.

'I really wish we'd been able to afford a completely new setup from the start,' he added. 'Sometimes buying second-hand just means buying someone else's problems.'

'So what are you doing here, then—shouldn't you be back at the mine?'

'Mmm, yeah,' Malcolm answered. 'Actually, there's something I wanted to talk to you about. Without Jamie being here.'

Rachel looked closely at her brother-in-law. She knew only too well what was on his mind. It was surprising, she thought, that he had waited so long to bring it up. Rachel had thought long and hard about how she would handle it if and when the subject finally surfaced. She decided to tackle things head-on.

'Yes,' she said after a moment. 'He is your son. He's not as premature as Jamie thinks he is. I'm sure you've worked that out for yourself already.'

Malcolm gazed at the infant in his arms for a moment, then spoke evenly without lifting his gaze, 'But we're still not going to say anything about it, are we?'

'Are you crazy?' she hissed through clenched teeth. 'No! We will not be saying anything about it!' Rachel looked around to make sure nobody was within earshot. 'You really don't think either of us is going to do that to Jamie, do you? We spoke about this, Malcolm. I agreed not to take it further, and you agreed we would never mention it. Ever!'

She glared at Malcolm, who was still gazing fondly at the baby Lachlan. 'Malcolm? Are you listening?'

Malcolm lifted his gaze to meet hers. 'Rachel, you know how I've always felt about you. After that night last September, and now this …' He looked back at Lachlan.

'Malcolm,' Rachel spoke determinedly, 'last September was nine months ago, as you are well aware. I don't know how you remember it, but I know what happened. I'm sure you do too, even though you seem to have twisted the story in your own mind.'

Gently, Malcolm placed Lachlan back in his crib and looked at Rachel. 'We had something once, Rachel. We really did. That night I realised I still felt the same, and I think you did too.'

'Mal,' she hissed again, 'you raped me!'

'What?' he spat. 'Rape? You must be joking. I wouldn't …'

'But you did!' she almost screamed. 'You did! I was drunk. I passed out and woke with you inside me. If that's not rape, I don't know what else you'd call it.'

'But … you were as keen as I was. You came. I know you did.'

'I thought you were Jamie,' she said angrily. 'I thought you were Jamie!' She burst into tears then, sobbing uncontrollably while Malcolm stared open-mouthed.

The memories of that fateful night came flooding back to him. Yes, they had been drunk, that was never in dispute, but Rachel had welcomed him into her, he was sure of that. The morning after had been awkward, and Rachel had pressed him until he promised never to reveal the incident to his brother, but rape? No! He couldn't have done that, could he? Could he?

Malcolm was struggling to find the right words to reply when the door opened and a nurse entered with the observations trolley. 'Oh, sorry,' she said. 'I didn't know you had a visitor.' Then, moving over to Rachel, 'Is everything all right?'

'Yes, I'm OK,' Rachel replied, dabbing her eyes, then gently blowing her nose into a tissue. 'Just the baby blues, I guess. I'll be all right.' Then, looking at Malcolm, 'So I'll see you later then, Mal. Don't forget to tell that husband of mine how much I love him and miss him. And remember our agreement.' That last comment carried just enough emphasis to convey her meaning, and although the nurse would have missed it, Malcolm was acutely aware of Rachel's intention to hold him to their pact. He also sensed, finally, that his hopes for a reconciliation with Rachel might well and truly be over.

He left the hospital with mixed emotions, his mind a blur. The only woman he had ever loved, maybe the only woman he ever would love, had finally sent him packing, once and for all. Malcolm had always hoped against hope that one day she would accept that they belonged together. Even though he didn't know how he would reconcile this with his brother, he'd held on to that dream. And dream it was, for now, she had jolted him into wakefulness by her accusation of rape. Rape? The woman was crazy, surely. How could he, Malcolm Kincaid, do something like that to the woman he loved?

There was one other thing his mind was struggling to process. He had a son! Sure, he had suspected as much, as soon as he had given the timing of her pregnancy some thought, but now she had confirmed it. A son! He wanted to tell the world, scream it from the rocky hillsides, but knew he never could.

He drove back to the mine site as if in a dream. He was halfway there before he realised he had forgotten to collect the replacement parts he had driven in for. Oh well, he'd tell Jamie they weren't available, and make the trip back in again tomorrow. One thing he did do, though, was stop off at the Broad Arrow Tavern for a bottle of his favourite single malt. Tonight, he'd celebrate—and drown his sorrows at the same time.

Alone in her room, Rachel sat quietly, ruminating over their conversation. How could Malcolm be in such self-denial? Why couldn't he see they were finished forever? And how could he genuinely believe she had willingly allowed him to do what he did?

She hated the idea of lying to Jamie. Hated herself, and Malcolm, for the secret they were now forced to keep. Their new son, Lachlan, whilst truly a Kincaid, must never know the shocking truth behind his parentage. Besides, she reasoned, Jamie would be a far, far better father than his brother could ever hope to be. Lachlan would grow up surrounded by love. With Jamie's help, Rachel would see to that. She knew she could rely on Malcolm to keep the truth to himself, if only to keep his own nose clean.

The brothers had much in common; that was true. Jamie, though, had empathy and kindness in his heart, whereas Malcolm had only self-interest. The attraction between her and Jamie was mutual, and as much as they both had fought it, Malcolm's actions the night of Jamie's birthday had finally made up Rachel's mind for her.

The brothers, always close friends as well as siblings, had sorted things out in their own way. Eventually, Malcolm seemed to accept the new status quo. Perhaps, thought Rachel in hindsight, a bit too easily. As time passed, though, she had accepted him, and he her—or so she thought—as family. Until the previous September, that was.

After feeding her new infant and settling him for the night, Rachel drifted into an uneasy sleep. She dreamed of Jamie, as he had appeared at their first meeting, and saw him holding his new son. She dreamed of her home and family in Perth. Then the dream gave way to nightmare.

She saw herself with her husband, walking along a deserted road and wheeling baby Lachlan in a large English pram. It was dark, the ground underfoot soft and wet, making progress difficult. A figure approached from the darkness, and she saw it was Malcolm. As he drew nearer, she realised he was holding Lachlan, who now appeared to be about a year old. Alarmed, she looked into the pram and saw that it was empty. She raised her head again to see Malcolm smiling. Not a friendly smile, but a smile more malevolent than any she had ever thought him capable of. He stared at her for a long time, then turned and walked off into the darkness, leading a still older version of Lachlan by the hand, as she and Jamie watched helplessly, their legs and feet held firmly in a boggy mire. Rachel tried to call to Lachlan but found herself unable to cry out or move. She turned to Jamie and realised he had disappeared completely, leaving only his muddy work boots embedded in the sticky, black soil. Struck completely mute and immobile, Rachel felt panic setting in. With a scream and a jerk, she tore herself free from the terrifying vision and into wakefulness.

Her heart pounding, almost breathless with fear, she lay panting for several minutes before she regained some semblance of control. Her mind spun, trying to make some sense of what had surely been just a bad dream? And yet somehow it seemed so real. Unable to shake the growing feeling of unease—no, dread—she rang for the night nurse and insisted on being taken to the nursery where she watched Lachlan sleeping peacefully for fully fifteen minutes before agreeing to return to her room.

Back in the ward, and despite the sedative the nurse insisted she take, Rachel lay awake for over an hour before sleep finally claimed her again just before dawn. This time, though, she did not dream.

Chapter 11

Monday, November 17th, 1980

'JAMIE, MALCOLM. COME THROUGH,' said Joe Worthington.

Joseph Charles Worthington was the CEO of Worthington Lang Finance Brokerage, and Jamie's godfather. The former manager of Kalgoorlie's largest bank, he had brought the Two Brothers Mine with him as a client when he and his son-in-law, Mark Lang, set up their new business just three months earlier.

Joe was an imposing figure. He stood a little over six feet and must have weighed at least 110 kilos in his underwear. He sported a pair of small wire-rimmed glasses that accentuated his tiny piggy-like eyes and gave his face the look of having a perpetual squint.

His dark blue suit jacket was straining to contain his girth and his tie was already loosened, despite the air conditioner whirring noisily in the office window.

'So what can I do for you boys today?' he asked with a hearty smile. 'You looking to buy out someone's lease?'

Jamie swallowed before speaking. 'You remember that ore crusher we bought when we were starting up?'

'The one I told you to stay away from?' said Joe. 'The old banger Hillfire was so glad to be rid of?'

'Yeah,' sighed Jamie. 'That's the one.'

Joe Worthington waited for the older Kincaid to continue. After a brief pause, he offered, 'You want to replace it.' It was a statement, not a question.

'We *need* to replace it!' Malcolm chimed in. 'It's costing us a fortune in downtime, not to mention spare parts.'

'How's your bottom line at the moment?' Joe queried. 'Can you service a loan of this size?' He studied both men as he waited for a reply.

'Yes, if we were to get back to full production!' It was Jamie this time.

He passed a folder across Joe Worthington's desk. 'Rachel's put this together for you. Profit and loss statements and production figures for the last three months. Of course, they'd be better if we could get seven days out of every week instead of wasting half our time playing amateur mechanics.

'You've still got last year's figures on file, so you'll see just how much it's costing us every day.'

'OK,' Joe replied. 'I'll play with them for you and lodge an application with one of the big banks. Ten days? I can't get approval that quick, of course, but I should be able to get a verbal OK.'

'Do what you can,' Jamie said with a sigh. 'We're dying a slow death, as things are.'

'I'll see what sort of price I can get you for the old banger,' said Joe. 'Might have to be scrap value, though.'

The brothers nodded resignedly. At least they'd be finally rid of the old piece of crap. Still, at the time of startup, they would never have been able to raise the required amount for a new machine. When it worked, it worked well. The only problem was that the breakdowns had been more and more frequent. When the crusher isn't working, everything grinds to a halt. No production means no income, while most of the expenses continue to mount up.

The drive back to the mine was uneventful. Jamie offered small talk about the weather, but Malcolm seemed in another world. Back in the office and each nursing a can of Hannans beer, Malcolm finally revealed what was on his mind.

He was standing before the display case, showing the brothers' accumulation of nuggets —large and small—and stroking his beard idly.

'You're not thinking we should sell off our collection, are you Mal?' said Jamie. 'There'd be quite a few thousand bucks' worth there I'll grant you, but not enough to pay for a new crusher.'

'Mmm, not exactly,' Malcolm replied. 'But there just might be a way for these babies to buy us some time, at least.'

'What's that devious mind of yours cooking up now, little brother?'

'You remember that news item a while back about some Yank millionaire buying a nugget for double its gold value?' Jamie remembered the report. 'Well, I reckon if we take these three here,' Malcolm pointed to three finger-sized and elongated nuggets, 'and weld them to this bit,' he indicated another, 'using these little fellas and the oxy welder,' he pointed to two more,' we could make a new nugget weighing around eight kilos. That's about two hundred and seventy ounces. And, coincidentally, looking remarkably like a human hand.

'At today's prices of around two hundred and fifty an ounce, that'd be worth close to seventy grand. To a wealthy collector? More like a hundred and fifty, or even more!'

He turned his gaze to Jamie, whose response was immediate. 'And end up in jail for fraud! What the fuck, Malcolm? You can't be serious!'

Malcolm opened the display case with the key on his watch chain.

'Check these out,' he said, handing two nuggets to Jamie. 'You probably don't recognise them.'

Jamie looked closely at the lumps of precious metal in his hand. No, he didn't recognise them, he admitted.

'Grab your loupe,' his younger brother offered. 'Tell me whether either of them is a fake. And if so, which one?'

Jamie thought for a moment, then took the small eyepiece from his desk drawer. He examined the objects for several minutes before looking up at his brother.

'Did you make this?' he asked, holding up one curiously shaped nugget.

'I don't know, did I?' Malcolm was grinning. 'I put both in there yesterday, but did I find them on the lease, or did I manufacture them?'

'This one has a few discrepancies in the crystalline structure. The other looks genuine, but I'd be dubious about buying this as a natural nugget,' said Jamie, holding up the oddly shaped piece of gold.

'Even if I hadn't told you it might be fake?'

'If I were a gold buyer looking at a supposedly unique nugget for a collector, then yes,' Jamie replied.

Malcolm's face fell slightly, then he burst into laughter. 'Well, big brother, that one *is* a natural nugget. That's what got me thinking. It's such a strange shape, almost like a human thumb. I had to see if it could be done—whether we might fool an expert. Well, I reckon you'd know more about gold in all its forms than almost anyone else. And you couldn't pick the fake. This one!' he said jubilantly. 'This one's the ring-in!'

He stabbed the second nugget still nestled in Jamie's palm. 'I took three small ones, added a bit of sand and quartz, and combined them into that. It took me about an hour, all up.'

He stepped back and surveyed his older brother's expression. Jamie replaced his loupe against his right eye and again examined the second nugget, this time even more closely.

'You're shitting me, Bro,' he said after another two minutes of intricate examination. 'You're having a laugh, aren't you?'

'Am I?' said Malcolm, with raised eyebrows. 'Are you willing to put money on it?'

'We'd be putting more than just money on it if we did what you're suggesting. The risks, Mal. Is it really worth it?'

'If we do it right, we'll pull it off,' Malcolm responded. 'We don't offer it through a dealer. We find some rich tourist with more money than sense and tell them it's all hush-hush.

Other than that, one of us can smuggle it out of the country and sell it to some high-roller in Vegas or Hong Kong. They'll be getting what they want, and we'll have enough funds to keep us solvent for a few months. Win-win—everybody grin.'

Malcolm fixed Jamie with a self-satisfied stare and waited for his brother's response.

After another hour of heated discussion punctuated by several more Hannans each, the brothers finally reached a compromise of sorts.

Malcolm would create his masterpiece; a roughly eight-kilogram gold nugget shaped to resemble a human hand. Not too closely, of course. It had to look as though Nature herself had crafted it millions of years ago.

They even agreed on a name for it; the Hand of God.

At this point, Malcolm suggested a Plan B.

Jamie's principal objection to the plan was the risk of the buyer bringing in an independent assayer. This wouldn't happen, though, if they never actually tried to sell the nugget.

Malcolm proposed that they have it valued by an assayer they both knew and add it to their company insurance policy. Then they would place it on display in a securely locked cabinet from where it would be 'stolen' in a ram-raid on the company offices. Malcolm assured Jamie he'd be able to arrange all this with little fuss, thanks to some dubious acquaintances made during his frequent trips to Perth. They would file a claim with the insurance company, and the gold would eventually find its way back into the crusher, bit by bit. No doubt the authorities all over the country would search for years for a clue to the whereabouts of the legendary 'Hand of God' nugget without success, Malcolm predicted gleefully.

Jamie was still unconvinced, and told Malcolm so. However, after much haggling, he finally capitulated—not to the actual insurance scam part of the plan, but to the manufacture of the nugget. He was by now curious to see if Malcolm could pull off such a fraud.

If Malcolm failed to produce a bogus nugget that Jamie couldn't find fault with, they agreed that they'd consign the gold to the smelter along with all the other mine produce. 'Fair enough,' Malcolm agreed. 'Nothing to lose except my time and a bit of oxy and acetylene. There's bugger all happening now anyway, without a working crusher.'

With that, they toasted each other with the last of the beer in their cans and opened two more.

* * *

It was after 6 pm—and close to sundown—when they finally called it a day. Malcolm announced he'd stay at the mine, as he often did lately. He'd fix himself something to eat in the camp kitchen and sleep on a stretcher in the back of the office. Jamie, against his better judgement, decided to risk the drive back to Kalgoorlie. Rachel would be beside herself if he wasn't home before dark, and in any case, he was missing her and their new son. One last thing he pressed Malcolm into agreeing to before leaving was that Rachel should never know of their plans to create the fake nugget. She would never go along with it. Besides—he thought to himself—it would probably come to nothing, anyway.

Malcolm had no problem with another secret. It seemed his life was becoming one long intrigue. Rachel? She was already having far too much say in the mine operations, and he saw no reason for her to know anything about these plans.

Malcolm had already opened another can of beer by the time his brother started the Land Cruiser and headed down the access road toward the Goldfields Highway. He stood on the verandah, watching as the receding taillights glimmered in the deepening twilight.

As Jamie neared the mine turnoff, he popped a cassette into the Cruiser's player. John Lennon launched into 'Beautiful Boy', Jamie's current favourite song, and he cranked up the volume as he swung onto the bitumen. Thirty minutes and he'd be home. Home to Rachel and his own Beautiful Boy, 17-month-old Lachlan.

Chapter 12

WARREN BURROUGHS—Rabbit, to friends and coworkers—couldn't remember a longer, more frustrating day. What started out as a routine run from his depot in Coolgardie to Kambalda—a mining town 60 kilometres to the south—and then up to Menzies with a 'hot shot' delivery before returning home, had turned into an epic comedy of errors.

Delays and unexpected problems were a fact of life in the transport industry, but today had been one to take the cake.

A round trip of a little less than 400 kilometres, the whole thing should have been done and dusted by mid-afternoon. When dealing with mining company hierarchy, however, things rarely went to plan. Although he had been on the road by six am, and arrived at his Kambalda destination before seven, it would be well past midday before he was on his way north again. The mine site office had not been aware he was even coming, let alone prepared his load.

Communication glitches like these were common. He settled himself in a corner of the office to wait while the staff located the replacement pump he was to deliver. Then, of course, they had to complete a stack of paperwork and finally arrange someone to load it onto the back of his ageing Kenworth for the next leg.

Next came the news that the low-loader organised to bring the pump out to him had broken down. He was welcome to drive on-site to collect his load, but first, he'd have to do a short induction course. Once he completed this, it was time for lunch, so there was another hour's wait before he got the OK to proceed onto the mine site and collect his cargo.

After leaving Kambalda at a little after 1:30, he eventually reached his drop-off point around 4 pm.

Fortunately, things went more smoothly this time. Probably because they had been champing at the bit waiting for the pump, the breakdown having halted production for the past twenty-four hours.

Then, at 5:30 pm, he was at last on his way home. All he had to worry about now, he thought, was dodging kangaroos.

He was just passing Lake Goongarrie, a sprawling salt lake on his left side, when a voice called over the two-way radio.

'G'day there, Rabbit, you old bugger!' It was a voice he knew well.

'How you doin', Ralph?' Rabbit replied, 'Havin' a good run? How's the new rig going, by the way?'

The north-bound road train, its three trailers loaded with supplies bound for Menzies and beyond, thundered noisily past. Rabbit's unladen rig swayed as it did so.

'Oh, you know,' Ralph said, 'same old shit, different shovel. I'm having a better day than you, apparently. I hear they held you up a bit down at the Kambalda site.'

The bitumen grapevine was working to its usual standard, Rabbit thought. 'Yeah, you could say that,' he replied. 'Sometimes I swear that if I had a duck, it'd bloody well drown.'

Ralph laughed, though Rabbit didn't hear it and continued with a sigh, 'Yeah, you know the drill. This is WA, after all; 'wait-a-while'.'

'You got that right,' Ralph replied. 'Oh well, you keep it safe and stay upright Rabbit. I'll catch you on the flip-side.'

'Roger that. You too, Ralph.'

The radio was already breaking up, so there was no time for any in-depth conversation. Still, it was good to hear a familiar voice now and then. Rabbit wondered how the old-timers had coped in the days before CB radios came into being. For that matter, spare a thought for the old bullockies and camel drivers who'd often go for weeks or even months without seeing another soul.

Rabbit reached down and upped the volume on his cassette player. A familiar Slim Dusty tune filled the air, and he sang along, grateful there was no one else there to suffer his discordant rendition. He noticed a light-coloured four-wheel-drive approaching the highway on his left, about a kilometre away. Someone had been working late, it seemed. The land around here was dotted with many small and medium-sized mines. As desolate and uninviting as it looked, this was a genuine gold mine of opportunity, this barren land.

As he approached the mine access road, Rabbit eased back on the accelerator. Was that clown going to stop? Surely he'd seen the truck coming. His rig was hardly invisible!

Before he knew it, the Land Cruiser veered straight onto the road not fifty metres in front of him.

Rabbit jumped on the brake and clutch simultaneously, and as the tyres shrieked in noisy protest, he braced himself for impact.

Jamie knew he should have stopped before driving onto the highway. He knew because he had driven out of this access road so many times before. He also knew that had he not consumed so much beer in the last few hours, he *would* have stopped.

But now it was too late for recriminations; too late for anything but to hold on and hope for the best.

The Kenworth's bull bar caught the four-wheel-drive on the right front side, spinning it around like a toy. The rear of the Toyota then collided with the leading edge of the big rig's trailer, which sent it careening off the roadway and straight into the large quartz rock with *Two Brothers Mine* painted on it in bold, red letters.

Although the Land Cruiser was barely doing over thirty, the force from the impact was enough to drive the engine block through the firewall and into the driver and passenger area. The steering column struck Jamie square in the middle of his chest, breaking several ribs and squeezing his lungs to around half their volume.

Immediately after the collision, the scene was eerily quiet. Rabbit's eighteen-wheeler remained upright, but the driver himself was unconscious and would be for several minutes. Few truckies in those days, and even these days, bothered with seat belts. A trickle of blood snaked its way down his forehead and dripped onto the dashboard.

In the wrecked Land Cruiser, Jamie struggled to stay awake. A vain struggle, however. His heart, fuelled by adrenaline, was pumping hard; pumping his lifeblood out of his body from severe crush injuries to his legs and onto the floor.

Strangely, the cassette player was still working. As Jamie drifted into unconsciousness, John Lennon was singing, "Life is what happens to you while you're busy making other plans."

* * *

Back at the site office, Malcolm stood in the doorway sipping his beer and watching the setting sun as it disappeared behind the saltbush. His thoughts were on his plans for the Hand of God nugget—and how he would go about creating it—when he heard the crash. Stunned, and frozen for an instant, he dropped the can where he stood and raced for his keys.

Malcolm mounted his motorcycle and sped toward the highway. Halfway down the access road, he realised he'd forgotten his helmet. What the hell, if that crash meant what he thought it did, and involved Jamie, nothing else mattered.

He reached the site in minutes, recognising the vehicle immediately, and dropped his Harley without bothering with the stand. Wrenching the driver's door ajar, he found his brother pinned to the seat by the steering column. Blood pooled around Jamie's feet from injuries to his lower legs, and his breathing was shallow. Malcolm struggled with the seat adjustment and finally rolled it rearwards a little. Jamie always drove with his seat well back, so Malcolm wasn't able to move it far. He took Jamie's head gently between his hands and pleaded, 'Jamie, Jamie, speak to me. Speak to me, Mate.'

He heard a sound behind him and turned to see a figure silhouetted against the setting sun. A strange, lurching shape that seemed to radiate light from within its very being. Malcolm's first thought was of the Angel of Death.

'Fuck off!' he screamed. 'Fuck off, you can't have him! It's too soon, too soon.'

'Shit, I'm sorry mate,' mumbled Rabbit. 'I couldn't avoid it. He just pulled out right in front of me. Do you know him?'

'He's my brother, you arsehole!' Malcolm yelled. 'What the fuck have you done?'

Rabbit's mind began to clear, And with it, his vision. 'Holy crap,' he managed, seeing Jamie. 'We need help. Fast!'

'Can you ride a motorbike?' Malcom asked.

'Sure,' Rabbit answered. 'I got a Trumpy at home. You want me to go?'

'I can't go,' Malcolm replied. 'I've got too much grog in me. Grab my Harley back there,' he gestured toward where his machine lay in the dust. 'and get to Broad Arrow. Call for an ambulance. Go! Go! I'll stay here with Jamie.'

As Rabbit turned to go, Malcolm called after him. 'The brake is on the right, not the left.'

'No worries, mate,' said the big truckie. 'I've ridden a few Hogs in my time.'

Without another word, Rabbit sprinted toward the motorcycle. His head still pounded, but his vision was clearing. Yes, he could do it. He knew how to handle a Hog all right. He stood the machine upright and looked around for a helmet. Not seeing one, he decided not to waste another second and kicked the engine into life.

On the highway, he gunned the XL-1000 and quickly disappeared southward.

Malcolm cradled his brother's head on his shoulder and realised just why people resorted to prayer at times like these. He would have prayed himself had he known how. Feargus Kincaid was not one for religion and had brought his sons up the same way.

He suddenly remembered his parting words to Jamie that day, so long ago, after the fight.

How could he have wished Jamie dead? How could he wish any sort of harm on his brother?

'I'm sorry, Jamie, I'm sorry,' he sobbed. 'I never meant it. You know that.' Looking skyward, he pleaded, 'Please, God, if you're there—please save my brother. Please save him.'

Coming from a man such as himself, the words had a hollow ring to them. He knew this, but what else was there to do?

He didn't dare move Jamie, for fear of compounding whatever injuries he already had. All he could do was stay with him, listening to his ever shallower breathing, and wait.

Why hadn't he paid more attention at that first aid course he'd attended last year, instead of trying to chat up the instructor? He knew there was no way he could do chest compressions without causing further damage. He did, however, know enough to administer mouth-to-mouth if Jamie stopped breathing altogether. He also knew this may, or may not, keep his brother alive.

It was an hour before the ambulance arrived. Malcolm, by then giving the Kiss of Life to Jamie, readily accepted the offer to relinquish responsibility.

* * *

Rachel looked anxiously at the kitchen clock. 7:15; ten minutes since the last time she checked.

Jamie was never this late. She wished again that the telephone they had arranged for the mine office was installed and working. Why did some things have to take so long?

She resolved to give him ten more minutes, then she'd bundle Lachlan and herself into the station wagon and drive out to meet him.

The Toyota had been giving trouble lately. Perhaps Jamie was stuck by the roadside somewhere. Maybe he'd had a puncture. Either way, he'd be pleased and relieved to be rescued, she told herself.

On the other hand, though, Jamie always said she was a panic merchant. If everything turned out to be OK, she'd have to put up with his teasing for a week at least. Rachel decided that 7:30 would be the deadline. If he didn't arrive home by then, she was coming to get him, no matter what!

By the time Rachel drew within a kilometre of her destination, she was growing ever more worried. There had been no sign of the Land Cruiser anywhere on the way. He wouldn't still be at the mine, would he?

When she saw the flashing red and blue lights ahead, panic truly set in.

Rachel pulled the Kingswood wagon over to the left and jumped out, leaving Lachlan asleep in his booster seat. Two ambulance officers were loading a stretcher into their vehicle.

Rachel barely recognised the Land Cruiser. It was a write-off. The front was crushed back to the doors, and the rear wasn't much better. The driver's door was missing, presumably removed by the rescue crew. She spotted Malcolm standing in the light from the ambulance interior and ran to him.

'Mal!' she cried. 'Is Jamie all right?'

Malcolm put his arms around her, holding her back from seeing too closely just how bad Jamie looked. 'He's alive, that's something,' he assured her. 'And in the best of care for the moment.'

He would have added more, but his throat suddenly became too dry. He tried to swallow, but there was nothing there.

Rachel's head swam. Her world turned white, her ears buzzed, and she collapsed into Malcolm's arms, almost pulling him to the ground.

Ten minutes later, Rachel woke, laying on the back seat of a police patrol car. An officer held a damp, cooling cloth to her forehead as Malcolm looked on from outside.

Seeing her awake, the constable said, 'Your husband is on his way to Kalgoorlie Regional Hospital. If you feel up to it, my partner can drive you and your brother-in-law there in your vehicle.' His voice remained steady and formal, but Rachel could sense concern there. Concern for her, or for Jamie? She feared the latter.

'Lachlan!' Rachel jerked and struggled to rise, suddenly remembering her son in the station wagon. The rapid movement made her head hurt, and she fell backwards again, groaning slightly. The damage from Malcolm's blow the night of Jamie's birthday still lingered. Perhaps it always would, as a constant reminder to her of what he could be capable of.

'Lachie's fine,' Malcolm said. 'He's still asleep. Take it easy. We can go straight there as soon as you're OK.'

She nodded, and after a moment she said, 'I'm good. Let's get going.'

At the hospital, they both sat in the waiting area while the medical team worked on Jamie. Malcolm paced, and Rachel sat in stony silence—alternately chewing her nails and wringing her handkerchief.

Julie Watkins had arrived to take Lachlan home with her. Julie and Rachel had become unlikely friends of late—the attraction of opposites, perhaps, Rachel reasoned.

After what seemed an eternity, Doctor Servino appeared. His solemn look said it all.

Rachel sprang to her feet. 'Please say he'll be all right.'

The medico shook his head. 'I'm sorry, Rachel. He'd lost too much blood. The ambos kept him on resuscitation all the way in, and we did our best here, but I'm afraid he's gone.'

He took one of Rachel's hands and placed his other arm over her shoulder. Rachel swayed again, and he guided her back to her chair.

Malcolm sat beside Rachel, placing his arms around her, and they both wept unashamedly.

Chapter 13

JAMIE KINCAID'S FUNERAL was a big affair. During the time the brothers were resident in Kalgoorlie, they made many friends and acquaintances. Jamie, in particular, had proved very popular. The accident, and tragic aftermath, made the front page of the Kalgoorlie Miner and the obituaries filled two full columns.

'Rabbit' Burroughs had spent two days in hospital and was fit for work within the week. His trusty Kenworth, though, did not fare quite so well. Fortunately, his insurance company agreed he was not at fault and by the end of the month, he would be back on the road. The emotional trauma, however, would stay with him for a long time.

Malcolm had spent the time since the accident either at the mine or riding his motorcycle. There was scarcely any work to be done until the new ore crusher could be installed. Aside from making the necessary arrangements, he and Rachel had spoken very little until the funeral.

As they stood staring into the deep, dark grave, Rachel clenching Lachlan's hand, Malcolm finally broached the subject that had been on his mind for the past few days.

'What are you planning to do? Will you be staying here in Kal?'

'I'm going home to Perth with my folks for a week or two,' Rachel answered. 'Long term, I'm not sure. They want me to move back for good, but this really feels like home now.' Then she added, 'I need time to decide.'

'Well, for what it's worth, I think you should come back,' Malcolm said. Then he added quickly, 'Not for my sake. I've come to terms with how you feel.'

Rachel didn't speak, so he continued, 'Look, I've got no illusions about how I stuffed things up between us. You now own half the mine though, and as for Lachlan ...' he looked fondly at the young Kincaid by Rachel's side, 'I really want to be a part of his life.'

'Whatever I decide, you'll only ever be Uncle Malcolm to him. You know that, right?' She spoke softly and evenly, so as not to attract Lachlan's attention. Her voice, however, was grim with steely determination.

'Agreed,' he said resignedly. 'Uncle Malcolm it is.' After a pause, he continued, 'He'll be the first of the next generation of Kincaids—assuming there's going to be more, that is.'

'I don't expect there'll be any more, unless you finally settle down,' Rachel cut in.

Malcolm continued. 'Well then, eventually Lachlan will inherit the whole shebang. He'll have to learn the business one day. Wouldn't it be better if he learned it from the ground up? From us?'

Rachel wasn't in the mood for such a conversation and told him so. She did, however, add that she thought she would 'most probably' return to Kalgoorlie and her job as Office Manager of the mine. Anything more they could discuss later. In the back of her mind, however, was still that lingering uncertainty about her and Malcolm being able to work together successfully.

Rachel's mind was swimming with many uncertainties. She'd always imagined she and Jamie would grow old together; that Lachlan would have a brother or sister, and eventually children of his own. Jamie would have made a wonderful grandfather, she mused. She pictured him now, bouncing a new baby boy or girl on his knee; his beard flecked with white, and his hazel eyes brimming with pride.

As she led her son toward the carpark, she felt the tears returning but refused to wipe them away. What was she to do? One thing she was sure of; she would learn to manage for herself. From here on, she would be her own person. Every future decision she made would, of necessity, involve Lachlan's welfare. She had lost her husband, and the love of her life, but Lachlan had lost the only father he'd known. No matter what else came to pass, she determined, Malcolm Kincaid would not wield any influence over her son—now, or ever.

Yes, she may well return to Kalgoorlie, and her job with the Two Brothers mine—she knew that was what Jamie would have wanted. She may even need to work in tandem with Malcolm—the man she now realised she hated—but she would isolate her son and herself from him as much as possible. In time, maybe the bitterness would fade, but it would never disappear. Of this, Rachel had little doubt.

Chapter 14

Tuesday, Nov 25th, 1980

RACHEL WAS SITTING in the neat kitchen, gazing from the window into the back garden of the Claremont home of her parents, Simon and Marita Rose. Her coffee was long gone cold and a burnt-out cigarette lay like a fat, grey worm in the ashtray. She appeared not to notice when her mother entered the room.

'You're up early, Love,' Marita said. 'Anything on your mind?'

Rachel continued staring out of the window. 'The dream is back,' she said flatly.

The dream, the one in which she saw Malcolm leading Lachlan away, leaving her and Jamie immobile and helpless, had been a regularly occurring apparition for over a year now. Details changed, but in essence, it was the same horrible nightmare. On her last visit the previous December, Rachel had woken with a scream and Marita pressed her until she confided the details.

'It's just a dream,' Marita whispered. 'Dreams can't hurt us. People hurt us. Sometimes, dreams are just our way of coping. Is it Malcolm again?'

Rachel nodded. A small tear snaked down her cheek. 'Why did Jamie have to die?' she pleaded. 'Why?' then, after a few seconds' pause, 'Why the fuck couldn't it have been Malcolm? Jamie was so sweet, so kind ...' she swallowed hard. 'And Malcolm is such an arsehole!

'I'm sorry Mum, I shouldn't talk like this, especially to you. I can't help it. But it's true! And he won't leave me alone, even when I'm asleep!' she began to sob uncontrollably.

Marita placed an arm around her daughter and held her close. 'Let it out, Dear. You haven't really cried since the funeral. You let it out.'

Rachel let it out. For fully five minutes she wept like a baby, her tears soaking the older woman's blouse. When she regained control, she lifted her head and looked into her mother's eyes.

'Mum, I need to tell you something. I want you to promise me, though, on everything you consider holy, never to repeat what I say. Can you promise me that?'

Marita thought for a moment and agreed she would. Whatever her daughter had to say couldn't be worse than some things she had seen or heard throughout her lifetime. Rachel needed to tell her something—something terrible, Marita suspected—and she had a mother's duty to listen and understand.

Over the next half hour or more, Rachel poured out everything that had happened between herself and Malcolm, including his physical and psychological abuse. Things she'd kept to herself for far too long. She detailed the fight at Jamie's party and the rape several months later. At the time of her injury, Rachel told her parents she had tripped and fallen down a step. Why she covered for Malcolm, she couldn't say. Perhaps she was afraid they would insist on pressing charges—she wasn't sure.

Finally, Marita spoke, 'And Lachlan? Are you going to ...?'

'No! And you mustn't ever tell him!' Rachel almost screamed. 'I don't want Malcolm Kincaid having anything to do with his upbringing. I made a pact with Malcolm not to say anything on the condition that he keep out of Lachie's life. In fact, I don't even want Lachie to work at the mine, although I'm not sure how I'll get around that.' She paused, then added, 'If he ever finds out, I ...' Her voice trailed off.

Marita held her daughter close, stroking her hair gently for several more minutes. When she finally spoke, it was with a sadness Rachel had never heard in her mother's voice before.

'I know how hard it must have been for you to tell me all that, Rachel,' she said, then added, 'I'm glad your father's away—I can't think what he might say right now if he were here. You, my girl, are his reason for being, and I couldn't be responsible for what he'd do to Malcolm Kincaid if he learned any of this.'

Both women were silent for several minutes before Marita spoke again.

'Perhaps, in the light of what you've said, I need to tell you a story in return. Something I've always thought I should share with you, but never knew how to begin.'

She made them each a fresh coffee and began her own tale:

* * *

Marita Zimmer was born in rural Germany in 1930. She remembered little of her early childhood, or her mother, who died of consumption when Marita was three years old. She was the youngest of three children, the next youngest being thirteen at the time of their mother's demise.

Adolf Hitler had recently come to power, and Jewish families, particularly in urban zones, were becoming the targets of racism and violence. Many moved to rural areas to escape what they hoped would be a passing trend.

One such family was the Baumanns. They lived and worked on the Zimmer family allotment and when Marita's mother passed away, her father entrusted her care to Eva Baumann, who had no children of her own.

Eva Baumann was a kindly individual. She readily took on the responsibilities of her young charge and for several years, life for Marita was happy and peaceful. Things changed, however, with more and more Jewish families disappearing overnight and their homes and possessions being looted or destroyed.

Living in anonymity at the Zimmer farm, the Baumann family avoided the attention of authorities until an observant citizen reported them in late 1944. They were arrested and transported to Buchenwald concentration camp. Marita's life might have ended there, if not for one young German officer.

On being unloaded from the train and sorted into various groups, some younger, prettier girls were selected by well-connected personnel for "special duties." Marita found herself among them. Her particular "sponsor" was Leutnant Karl Schumann, the officer in charge of the main guardhouse. Despite his relatively low rank, Schumann enjoyed the privilege of having private quarters near the camp entrance.

The plan was for the girls to spend one or two nights with the German guards before being returned to the camp huts. Karl Schumann, however, found himself deeply attracted to the young Marita Baumann, as he knew her. Especially when he discovered she was not actually Jewish. At serious risk to his own welfare, he concealed her in his quarters, smuggling in for her whatever food he could. As payment for her 'protection', Karl Schumann demanded that Marita satisfy any and all of his desires and fantasies. With no other choice, the young girl complied, knowing that resistance would likely have resulted in an untimely death—possibly at the hands of less merciful individuals.

This subterfuge—if discovered—would no doubt have led to a disastrous end for them both, if not for the arrival of the 6th U.S. Armored Division on April 11, 1945. The German guards fled, leaving the few surviving inmates in the care of the US soldiers.

No trace was ever found of the Baumann family, nor of Marita's father or siblings in Germany, and Marita eventually found herself taken in by a Jewish welfare agency and repatriated to Australia as an orphan.

* * *

Rachel had listened to the tale in silence. Eventually, she said, 'This officer, Schumann, did you ever hear any more about him?'

'That animal didn't deserve to live. I hope he's rotting in Hell by now.' Marita responded icily. The determination in her mother's voice took Rachel by surprise. 'Yes, he could have been more brutal, like his fellow officers,' Marita went on. 'But rape is rape, no matter how you dress it up.'

Rachel nodded. Marita continued, 'When you first introduced Malcolm, I almost fainted. The similarity to Karl Schumann was unnerving. Take away the moustache and give him blue eyes, and he might have been Schumann's brother. That's why I never warmed to him. And it seems I was right about him from the very start.'

They sat in silence for several minutes, each digesting the other's revelations. 'It's so strange how fate has a way of stringing together the events in our lives,' mused Rachel. 'Is this what they mean when they say things are sent to try us?'

'Well, they certainly do—try us, that is,' replied Marita.

They sat for a few more minutes, both staring into the distance, each deep in their own thoughts, until Marita abruptly stood and asked, 'Well, what shall we have for breakfast, then?'

'Anything,' Rachel replied. 'Except scrambled eggs and bacon.'

Chapter 15

RACHEL STAYED WITH HER PARENTS for two weeks. She and her mother didn't discuss their shared secrets again, but the bond between them had strengthened imperceptibly. Rachel, however, couldn't shake the feeling that, as bad as her story was, Marita was leaving something out. Something even darker, and more sinister, lurking in her past.

Rachel's father, Simon, had returned home the following day from his business in the north, where he worked as an engineer for Main Roads WA. He'd arranged for several days of compassionate leave, and the four of them, including young Lachlan, went on a road trip in the Roses' motorhome. After a week on the road, including a few days at Albany, on the south coast, Rachel was well and truly ready for the return home.

Her parents meant well and doted on Lachlan as most grandparents do. But Rachel had moved on, and the ways of her parents were no longer her ways. She sensed that eventually there would be a clash of ideals within the household, and she'd be forced to move out, anyway. Better to do so on good terms, she reasoned, and keep the relationship intact.

*   *   *

Rachel returned to the goldfields a few days before Christmas of 1980. As the Prospector train pulled in to the platform, Malcolm was there waiting, with a bunch of flowers and a wooden toy fashioned after a dump truck.

Rachel accepted the bouquet, eyeing Malcolm suspiciously.

'Don't worry,' he said quietly as they exchanged the obligatory hug. 'No ulterior motives. I just want you to feel welcome.'

He stooped and picked up Lachlan as Rachel hugged each of the small group of friends there to meet her. Jerome, carefully maintaining a respectful distance between himself and Malcolm, seemed almost likely to burst into tears—or song—Malcolm couldn't be sure which.

Malcolm carried his young charge to the Nissan Patrol, bought to replace the wrecked Cruiser, while Rachel and her entourage followed with her luggage. After dropping

Lachlan and his mother at their house, he made his exit, telling Rachel to come in to work when she was good and ready, and not before.

Malcolm had started work on the 'Hand of God' the previous day and wanted to get it finished before Rachel had a chance to veto the whole plan. Without Jamie's expertise, he'd have to be a lot more fastidious about his workmanship, but he was confident he could still pull it off.

Rachel decided she was good and ready the following day. Malcolm announced he would set up a cot and playpen in the back of the office so that Lachlan could be with them.

He carefully concealed the fake nugget under some crates at the rear of the workshop and figured he'd finish the job when he knew she wouldn't be around. If Rachel asked where the nugget collection was, he would tell her he'd sent them to the smelter.

After a short while, Malcolm and Rachel settled into a routine that suited them both, more or less.

Rachel immersed herself in the business affairs of the mine and spent most of her free time with friends.

Malcolm spent most of his time either at the mine, or at the pub, or riding his motorcycle. Gradually, each of their lives took on its own version of normality.

Chapter 16

The Hand of God

IT WAS THREE WEEKS before Malcolm presented Rachel with the news about the huge nugget he'd found on the site. She was incredulous, of course, and wanted to know exactly where he'd unearthed it.

He recounted the story, just as he had painstakingly rehearsed it:

On one of the lengthy walks he included in his daily routine, he told her, he'd spotted some promising signs of a new gold deposit in a far-flung corner of the lease. Returning with a recently purchased detector—much more accurate than the ones he and Jamie had used in the early days—he'd been astounded to find a nugget of around eight kilograms or more buried deep below the surface. This had to be providence, surely! And the shape—who would credit that Nature could create something like this?

'I still can't believe it!' Rachel exclaimed. 'You and Jamie must have literally walked right over this when you were first scanning the area.'

'Yeah, but to be honest, we didn't spend a lot of time in that spot. The funny thing is, I did a few more passes around the general area and got absolutely nothing.' Malcolm didn't want Rachel expecting more of the same from that corner of the lease. Better if she saw it as a one-off. In the meantime, though, Malcolm proposed, the new find could go on display until they found a buyer for it.

He delivered the nugget to his preferred assayer the following day and subsequently obtained a certificate of authenticity and purity.

That week, first the Kalgoorlie Miner, and then the worldwide press in general, were trumpeting the news of the discovery of the Hand of God nugget at an undisclosed location near Kalgoorlie, Western Australia. Eight kilograms of high-grade gold, with a smelted value of approximately $80,000, and a private valuation of around twice that.

Malcolm placed the nugget in a safe deposit box at a secret location and waited for the offers from rich collectors to come flooding in.

He had no intention of selling it, however. He definitely preferred Plan B.

Malcolm rode down to Perth and started negotiations to arrange the next phase. For a price still to be negotiated, the nugget would disappear after a late-night break-in.

The Two Brothers Mine would then be assured of smelting at least eight extra kilos of gold over the following months, and their insurance company would have a considerable claim to handle. Malcolm Kincaid would see to that.

*   *   *

Rachel had finished work and left for home. Malcolm was almost ready to leave the office himself when he heard the familiar throb of two Harley Davidson V-Twins rumbling up the access road. He walked to the door and watched as two men parked their cycles in front of the building and dismounted. They stretched and removed their helmets, barely acknowledging his presence.

Both were over six feet in the old money, solid and muscular, and had that arrogant air of seasoned club bikies. The first, slim and fair-haired, and with a beard to match his own, sported shoulder-length blond hair that gave him the appearance of how Malcolm assumed a Viking warrior might have looked.

The other was much more heavily built. He was clean-shaven, and his skin had the colour of a South-Sea Islander or Maori. Neither wore any club colours, though both sported matching Death's-head tattoos—small but significant, Malcolm thought—below the left ear.

Despite having never met them, Malcolm knew at once their reason for coming to the mine.

He gave a quick wave, immediately wondering just what sort of greeting they expected. Although he had instigated the meeting, a surge of apprehension swept over him. This was it. No turning back now.

'You Malcolm?' the slim guy asked as they stopped a metre in front of him. Apparently, he would be the spokesman. Malcolm recognised a chain of command when he saw it. Maori Guy walked behind and a little to one side.

'That's me,' Malcolm replied. 'I didn't expect you today. I was just about to head off.' He extended his hand, which both men ignored. 'Were you sent by …?'

'Apparently, we have some business to conduct,' Slim Guy said. 'Is there anyone else here right now?'

'Just me,' Malcolm replied. 'In another five minutes, the place would've been deserted.'

The leather and denim-clad visitor nodded toward the door. 'Let's talk inside.'

Once through the door, Malcolm spoke again. 'I thought you'd be coming late at night.' then added, 'You're not planning to drag the safe down the road with your bikes, are you?' He attempted a smile.

'Where's the gold?' Maori Guy remained silent. He studied Malcolm's face with an amused expression.

'Gold? What ...?'

'You know, that yellow stuff you guys dig out of the ground by the truckload?'

'I ... I don't have any gold for you. That's not part of the deal,' Malcolm replied nervously. 'You're supposed to break in and take the safe. That's all.'

'He said you might give us a hard time,' Slim Guy replied. 'He also said we might need to use a bit of persuasion.' He stretched his arms out in front of him and interlocked his fingers, pulling backwards as he did so. The joints in his hands popped noisily. Reaching into his jeans pocket, he produced a brass knuckle-duster.

'I don't have any gold!' Malcolm was aware of how absurd this sounded. There they were, standing in the office of a successful, operational mine in the middle of one of the richest gold mining areas in Australia, and he was saying, "I don't have any gold." He was also becoming more than a little worried.

Slim Guy moved a step closer, looking Malcolm squarely in the eyes, and said, 'We're here to collect a big nugget. Biggest fucking lump of gold you ever saw, or so I've been told. Now, do we get the goods with, or without, causing you a world of pain?'

Malcolm swallowed hard and tried to speak. His throat was suddenly very, very dry.

Maori Guy couldn't contain himself any longer. He burst into uncontrolled laughter, doubling over and holding his stomach.

Slim Guy tried his best, but soon he, too, was laughing uncontrollably. Malcolm could only stare open-mouthed. *What the fuck?* he thought.

'We're shittin' you, Bro,' said Maori Guy eventually. 'Man, you should see your face.' With that, he broke into laughter once more, as did his compatriot.

Relieved and a little embarrassed, Malcolm himself was soon laughing, though still a little nervously.

When they had all regained their composure, Slim Guy extended his hand, which Malcolm shook readily. 'Sorry, man, couldn't resist it. I'm Robbo. This here's Moose.' He jerked a thumb in Maori Guy's direction.

Moose shook Malcolm's hand and said, 'Got any beer, Bro? I'm as dry as a wooden god.'

Malcolm handed each a can of Hannans from his personal bar fridge and they drank thirstily, emptying their cans in two long gulps. He offered them another, opening one for himself also, and they moved through to the office to discuss their plans.

Three weeks later, the following articles appeared in the local newspaper:

The Kalgoorlie Miner

Tuesday, 17 February 1981

MINE SITE BREAK-IN: CELEBRATED NUGGET FEARED STOLEN

Thieves who staged a brazen robbery at a gold mine north of Kalgoorlie over the weekend may have escaped with one of Australia's most famous gold nuggets. Police representatives are remaining tight-lipped about the incident, but informed sources revealed the recently discovered Hand of God nugget might have been the focus of the break-in.

The theft was not discovered until Monday morning when Two Brothers Mine office manager Rachel Kincaid arrived for work.

Police Superintendent Sidney Marshall said the perpetrators had apparently smashed their way through the front door of the mine office building and stolen a safe and other items. The safe appeared to have been loaded onto the back of a light truck using a forklift, both taken from the mine's workshop. The truck was located on Monday afternoon—burned out—on a dirt track near Ora Banda, a small mining town south of the crime scene. The safe has so far not been recovered.

Two Brothers Mine co-owner, Malcolm Kincaid, was away at the time, having left Kalgoorlie on Friday bound for Perth and an overseas trip.

Contacted by phone, Mr Kincaid is quoted as saying the theft is 'a great loss' to the company. There were plans in place, he said, to loan the nugget to the WA School of Mines as a promotional display, before offering it for sale on the open market, where it was expected to attract offers of over $160,000.

The Kalgoorlie Miner

Monday, 23 February 1981

NO BREAKTHROUGH IN 'HAND OF GOD' THEFT

Investigations are continuing into the recent break-in at the Two Brothers Mine, north of Kalgoorlie. A local truck driver discovered the missing safe last Friday, dumped in a parking area south of Merredin. According to a police spokesman, explosives had been used to open the safe, and no contents remained.

As a result of the theft, and damage to infrastructure, the Two Brothers Mine would be forced to suspend operations for three weeks, according to Malcolm Kincaid, mine co-owner. This would cause a significant loss of earnings, Mr Kincaid said. He was confident, however, that the mine's insurance would cover the theft, damage, and loss of income. This blow comes just two months after Mr Kincaid's brother, Jamie, tragically died in a motor vehicle accident on Goldfields Highway.

Investigations are continuing, and Goldfields Police are confident of a breakthrough in the near future.

No trace was ever found of the Hand of God nugget. Authorities assumed it had been sold on the black market and melted down.

The Hand of God theft has since become a part of Aussie folklore. There have been many theories as to the identity of the perpetrators, including some who claim it was an inside job, but no solid evidence has to date been forthcoming. The Two Brothers Mine was back in production by mid-March, having installed a new ore crusher and rebuilt the mine office.

In the months that followed the break-in, Malcolm learned just what it meant to live under pressure.

Television stations in Perth picked up on a story concerning a group of outlaw bikies that police suspected may have been involved in the Two Brothers break-in. Two or more members had been sighted in the area around the time of the theft, and screen footage showed two men Malcolm immediately recognised, being escorted to Police Headquarters for questioning.

They were both released without charge, but at one of many press conferences, the police spokesman announced they remained 'persons of interest' in the case.

Over this time, Malcolm found it increasingly difficult to sleep and avoided answering the phone whenever he could. Police vehicles in his rear-view mirror took on a completely new perspective, and more often than not, his motorcycle rides ended with him standing at Jamie's grave. One such occasion found him in an unusually self-recriminating mood.

'Fuck me, Jamie, I should have listened to you,' he said between cans of beer. 'You always were the smarter one. Sure, I seem to have gotten away with it, but now I think I'm going insane!'

He paused for another drink, and scanned the area before continuing, 'Hand of Fucking God! What was I thinking?' He suddenly saw the irony of the situation and began to chuckle.

'I bet you're pissing yourself laughing at me, mate. Well, here's to you and your fucking Big Brother superiority. Rest in peace, Jamie, old mate.'

With that, he finished his beer, opened another, and emptied the contents onto his brother's grave. Having completed this last act of what had become something of a ritual, he turned and strode to his Harley and gunned the big V-Twin into life before roaring away without a backward glance. *Fuck the cops*, he thought. *If they had anything, I'd have heard by now. Fuck them, fuck everyone! "A life lived large", as the Old Man used to say. That's me from now on, and God help anyone that gets in my way!*

And with that thought, Malcolm finally resolved to put his paranoia to bed.

In time, the TV and newspapers found other interests, and the Hand of God theft became consigned to history.

Chapter 17

'MORNING, MR KINCAID,' said Julie Watkins, as Malcolm entered the mine reception area. 'Lovely day, don't you think?'

'Is Rachel about? We have a meeting arranged.'

'She's in the main office. You can go straight through.'

Rachel looked up as he entered. She was never thrilled to see Malcolm, even on her best days, and this day was no exception. 'Give me a few minutes,' she said, returning to her work.

Malcolm waited impatiently while she completed totting up several columns of figures. 'How's Julie working out?' he asked, attempting to break the ice. 'How long has she been here now, three months?'

'Six.' Rachel didn't look up. 'And yes, she's working out fine.'

Over the previous three years, the Two Brothers mine had continued to prosper. Rachel had completed a degree in business management and taken over the operation of the mine completely, as well as another smaller lease nearby that Malcolm had acquired. The addition of Julie Watkins to the office staff had eased her workload considerably.

Rachel closed the folder she was working on and turned her attention to her brother-in-law. 'And to what do I owe the honour of this visit?'

Malcolm returned her gaze before replying. 'You realise it's three years tomorrow since ...'

'Yes. You don't really imagine I'd forget, do you?'

Rachel's mood always took a downward spiral as the anniversary of Jamie's death approached. Tomorrow, she would probably spend the entire day at home, mostly curled up in bed—as she had last year and the year before. Malcolm's presence did nothing to improve her frame of mind.

'No, I don't suppose you would,' he replied, then continued, 'That's not why I'm here, though. You remember Sam Bronson?'

Malcolm explained how Sam Bronson, a friend from his days with the WA School of Mines, had contacted him and suggested a joint venture to exploit an iron ore deposit about a hundred kilometres west of Kalgoorlie. Sam assured Malcolm there was 'a fortune just waiting to be taken.' Malcolm knew of the existing hematite deposits at Dowd Hill, near the Koolyanobbing Range north-east of Merredin, and agreed to look into it.

'Iron ore? That's a little out of our field of expertise, isn't it?' Rachel sat back in her chair, waiting for the rest of the spiel.

Malcolm shrugged. 'Mining is mining. Anyway, we can subcontract the operation of the plant once it's established. Iron ore's very profitable. It's the future of mining, some say. We'd be silly to pass up the opportunity.'

'Seems like you've already given this more than a little consideration,' Rachel said.

'The Dowd Hill mine delivers ore to Esperance by rail,' Malcolm continued, ignoring the interruption. 'I've already made some preliminary enquiries and we could easily grab a piece of the action. If this deposit is as rich as Sam says it is, we could end up making even more from iron than we will from gold.'

Rachel wasn't totally convinced, but agreed to let Malcolm investigate the idea some more. If nothing else, she thought, it would keep him out of her hair for some time. And if it turned out to be a viable proposition, they'd work on the details later.

* * *

Initial testing validated Sam Bronson's findings, and so by mid-1984 Kooly North No 1 Mine had commenced the first stages of establishment.

Iron ore mining was a lot different from gold mining, however, as Malcolm soon came to realise. The new venture was going to be a substantial drain on their finances, as it was likely to be a long time before it would show a profit. He arranged another meeting with Rachel to discuss some options.

'A holding company?' Rachel said when he had made his pitch. 'Are we really getting big enough for all that corporate wheeling and dealing?'

'It's got bugger all to do with size,' Malcolm replied. 'We need to attract some corporate investors.

'Besides,' he continued, 'it just means we keep full control of a subsidiary without being responsible for its debts.'

'I'm aware how a holding company works, Mal,' she said, leaning back and folding her arms. 'I'm not dumb. I just wonder if the legal costs and extra work—which I will have to do, by the way—would be worth it.'

Malcolm elaborated. 'As it stands, we have three mines being run as proprietary companies and operating independently. I propose we float a public company, with control over all the operations we have so far, plus anything else we might branch into in the future.

'We'll issue stock, but with limited voting privileges. That way, we'll still keep the upper hand.' Malcolm paused. Rachel waited for the rest of the spiel. She knew him well enough to realise he would have put a lot of thought into this before mentioning it to her. When she didn't interject, he continued, 'We'll make sure we keep a controlling interest, anyway. I reckon if we issued shares to cover forty to forty-five percent of our current value, we'd easily be able to fund the new iron ore mine and still be more than solvent.'

'Well, I reckon you've been spending too much of your time hob-nobbing with Alan Bond and his high-flying mates,' Rachel offered. 'This sounds like the sort of scheme he or Laurie Connell might dream up.'

'Actually, you're correct about that last part,' Mal agreed. 'Those guys know a thing or two about raising establishment funds. In fact, Dallhold, Bondy's personal investment company, is ready and willing to buy into the deal.'

Rachel was unconvinced and told him so. She did agree, however, to discuss Mal's proposal with their recently engaged firm of corporate solicitors in Perth. She accepted that it seemed to make sense to have one central organisation responsible for the running of what was fast becoming a disparate collection of smaller companies.

She'd been looking for an excuse to visit Perth for a while. Her father hadn't been well, and she could use a break from the mine—and from Malcolm.

Rachel hated driving long distances, so she took the Prospector train the following Monday, relishing the thought of the relaxing journey. School holidays had begun, so it was also the perfect opportunity for Lachlan to visit with his grandparents. He was five now and had started first grade that year. They could spend some quality time with her family, and she'd consult with the lawyers mid-week.

Chapter 18

Monday, December 24, 1984

MALCOLM HAMMERED his newly bought gavel on the table. 'I hereby call this inaugural meeting of the board of Kincaid Mining Corporation Pty Ltd to order,' he announced.

Rachel actually laughed; something she rarely did in Malcolm's presence these days. 'You're enjoying this, aren't you?'

'I certainly am,' he replied with a grin. 'Now, what's the first order of business?'

'I propose we send a fax to Santa, reminding him of our new business address,' Sam Bronson offered. 'He missed me last year, and I want my train set.'

Rachel laughed again. Malcolm banged the table several more times. 'You're not a shareholder,' he told Sam. 'You don't get a vote.'

Sam feigned a disappointed look. 'I want my train set,' he said with a pout.

'OK, boys,' Rachel said, deciding to end the tomfoolery. 'Enough's enough. We have work to do, and I've still got gifts to buy.'

* * *

Kincaid Mining Corporation, publicly listed in November, was now operating from its new headquarters at the western end of St George's Terrace in Perth. The company offices took up about a third of the second tier of the building, but Malcolm had already announced he aspired to loftier goals.

'One day,' he'd told Rachel as they inspected the modest suite prior to signing the lease, 'KMC will own this entire building. We'll have our boardroom on the top floor, and Bondy can have the level below us.'

In your dreams—Rachel thought to herself. 'Don't you think the rent's a bit high?' she said instead. 'Do we really need an office in the city?'

Of course, he'd had his way, and now they were convening their first board meeting in those same rooms.

The directors comprised Malcolm, Rachel, and Sam. Sam wasn't a shareholder, but he received a generous salary. He also held fifteen per cent of Kooly Iron Pty Ltd, the new entity created to operate the iron ore mine. Malcolm and Rachel each owned a further fifteen per cent, with the balance held by KMC, the parent company. Malcolm assured Sam he would be 'on a winner' once Kooly Iron was fully operational. In the meantime, it was his responsibility to oversee its establishment and construction—and eventual operation.

This meeting was little more than a formality. They elected officers, assigned roles, and made general plans for the future. Malcolm would be based here, in Perth; Rachel would remain in Kalgoorlie, and Sam in Koolyanobbing. The frivolity that filled the air throughout this first meeting showed the collective optimism they shared. Each knew, however, that this new direction could signal impending failure as easily as success.

Speculators and corporate investors alike quickly bought up the issued shares. By the following June, when mining and crushing at the new mine began, the stock had almost doubled in value.

Malcolm and Rachel each held 30% of Kincaid Mining Corporation, giving them joint control of the company.

*   *   *

Over the next several years, KMC continued to prosper. Malcolm, ever the opportunist, maintained and strengthened his connections with Western Australia's political and corporate elite.

In 1987, the Labor Government of the time announced plans for a Gold Tax. Malcolm attended a meeting in the offices of a senior Cabinet member where he and several others pledged $250,000 each to a "fundraising group" to ensure the proposed plan was scrapped. In return for his donation, he received shares in a company created to offload a parcel of land to the WA Government at a massively inflated price. This became known as the 'PICL deal'; one of the more notorious affairs that in turn became a part of 'WA Inc', a major scandal of the time.

All of this he kept from Rachel. Managing the Two Brothers Mine was her domain, and hers alone. Managing Kincaid Mining Corporation, from the plush corporate offices in Perth, was Malcolm's.

Chapter 19

Sunday, June 11th, 1997

'SO, LACHLAN, how does it feel to be eighteen?' Malcolm asked.

'I'll tell you in two days, Uncle Mal,' the young man replied. 'My birthday's not until Tuesday.'

'OK, Smart-arse,' said Malcolm. Then he added with a smile, 'You've got pretty nice teeth for someone with such a lippy attitude. You must be fast on your feet.'

Lachie laughed. He and his Uncle Mal had a history of banter, and today would be no exception.

'And how's the posh boarding school treating you?' Malcolm asked. 'Seems they haven't turned you into a society snob just yet.' In times like these, Malcolm saw echoes of Jamie in his young 'nephew'.

'I hate it!' Lachie didn't mince words. 'Why Mum insisted on sending me down here, I don't know.'

'To try to turn you into a proper gentleman, Mate,' Malcolm replied. 'Special emphasis on *try*. Got to get that Kalgoorlie yobbo out of you somehow.'

'Good luck with that,' was Lachie's reply.

Malcolm had arranged Lachie's exeat from WA Boys Grammar School for his birthday party at Rachel's parents' home, despite his big day falling within the school term. A decent donation from Kincaid Mining Corporation had seen to that. The only concession was that it had to be on Sunday—and then, after morning church services.

Lachie missed the times when he'd spend his weekends on the Two Brothers mine site or out in the bush—camping, exploring, or four-wheel driving. Boarding school had its good points, but Lachlan Kincaid was destined for a different life to most of his schoolmates, and he knew it. Soon, he felt, he'd take his rightful and proper place within the company hierarchy, along with his mother and uncle. Until he graduated, however, he'd continue to live and study alongside the scions of Perth's elite, even though they would never accept him as an equal. Most of them cared little about anything more meaningful than who was screwing whom in their particular clique, or whether they were spending Christmas in Bali or Ibiza.

They mostly gave scant attention to their studies, being happy to coast through, knowing that their futures were already mapped out for them as long as they played the game and cultivated the right connections. If any looked like falling too far behind, the school arranged individual tutoring. The WABGS reputation had to be protected, after all.

Lachie found it difficult to blend in. He was—and always would be—a country boy at heart. He had one friend at the school, though. Jimmy Browne was, like himself, a Kalgoorlie boy.

On the first day in class, the master had asked each student to stand when he read out their name. 'James Archibald Browne,' he called, and invited the youngster to add any information he thought worth sharing.

James Archibald Browne stood and announced as proudly as he dared. 'Um, yeah, I was born in Kambalda, but I've lived in Kalgoorlie since I was six.' Then he added, as an afterthought, 'Actually, I prefer Jimmy, though,' and sat down.

'Brown, that's pretty fitting,' an anonymous voice from the back murmured, just loud enough to be heard. 'Bloody coon,' a second boy muttered. There was a general snigger that the master ignored.

Later, as they filed out for recess, one of the taller boys shouldered past Jimmy, muttering, 'Stand aside, Nigger Boy.'

Approaching the group, Lachie said in a loud voice, 'So, Jimmy, how're you finding life in the city?' He offered his hand. 'Lachlan Kincaid, Lachie to my mates. I've seen you around Kal a few times.'

They shook hands. 'My dad's name was James, but everyone called him Jamie.'

'My old man named me after James Brown, the singer,' Jimmy replied. 'I'm not all that keen on soul music myself, though.'

'Well, I reckon that's pretty cool!' Lachie replied.

Jimmy shrugged, and as the crowd cleared around them he asked, 'So how come you want to be seen with me? Your family owns that gold mine, don't they? I'd have thought you'd be busy mixing with the In-Crowd.'

'I pick my own friends,' Lachie said. 'I don't give a shit who your family are or what they do. I reckon you might just need a mate here, with this lot.' He gestured around. 'And seriously, you don't really want to try blending in with them, do you?'

Lachie and Jimmy quickly became firm pals. They came from similar backgrounds and found they had several mutual friends. A shared dislike of pretentious upstarts from privileged families also helped.

The big difference between them was that Jimmy was the school's token Aboriginal student. The WA Boys' Grammar School offered a scholarship each year to an 'Aboriginal student who shows above-average academic and social qualities' from a suitably remote area.

These scholarship recipients rarely went on to academic heights, though. This wasn't a reflection of their personal aptitude or motivation. It was simply that everyone, staff and students alike, assumed they'd achieve little and would eventually end up on the dole or in menial jobs at best. The school made little effort to help them fit in, and when they failed to do so, saw it as a vindication of their unsuitability. If they failed the year-end exams, which many did, they were sent home. As simple as that.

Having had primary school friends from Aboriginal families, Lachie had thought nothing of befriending Jimmy from the start. Discovering that it wasn't seen as "good form" only made him more determined to stand by his newest friend. There was the occasional fight, which Lachie and Jimmy always won, but eventually, the two were left to themselves. There were comments made, and in-jokes shared, but only outside of direct earshot.

* * *

'How's your mate—what's his name, Billy, isn't it?' Malcolm asked.

'Jimmy,' Lachie replied. 'And he's fine. We gang up on the posh crowd and make them do our homework for us.'

'Yeah, sure,' Malcolm said with a grin.

Lachie and his Uncle Mal had recently started communicating via email. Malcolm had gifted Lachie a computer when he started at WABGS and given the young lad his details. 'No need for your mother to know. She'll only worry that it might distract you from your studies,' he'd said.

Lachie hadn't told Malcolm about Jimmy's aboriginality. He was well aware of how his uncle felt about indigenous Australians. Mentioning Jimmy's heritage would have started a debate he didn't want or need right now. Lachie had no intention of turning his back on his friend when the time came for them to return to the Goldfields, though. In fact, he intended to do all he could to help Jimmy make a success of himself, even if it meant pressuring his mother and uncle to employ him themselves.

Jimmy Browne had astounded his tutors by coming near the top of his class consistently ever since starting at WABGS. At first, everyone assumed he was cheating—perhaps copying his friend's work—but as he outscored Lachie most of the time, the tutors had to admit his talent and dedication were real.

'Seriously, Uncle Mal, I can't wait to see the back of most of those stuck-up trendies,' Lachie said. 'And I can't wait until I can start working the mine with you and Mum.'

'Hmm, that's something I've been meaning to talk to you about, Lachie,' said Malcolm. 'I guess now's as good a time as any.' He looked around and gestured to the boy to follow him to a quieter corner of the garden.

The younger Kincaid eyed his uncle suspiciously as they walked, but waited for Malcolm to continue. 'Your Mum isn't too keen on that,' Malcolm began. 'As the company grows, there'll be less and less actual hands-on work for us to do. We have a decent workforce now, and our time's better spent in management. After all, if you have dogs, why do your own barking?'

'But where do I fit in then?' Lachie asked. 'You've always told me I'll inherit everything in the long run. How can I if I never learn how things work at ground level?'

That was what managers and supervisors were there for, Malcolm explained. If you hire the best managers available and concentrate on the top-level stuff, you'll be better able to see the big picture. Sure, as a mining company executive one had to be aware of how things worked, but Malcolm's, Rachel's and eventually Lachie's time was too valuable to spend on tasks that trained managers and overseers could do.

'There's one thing I'd like you to consider,' Malcolm added. 'You're a bit of a brainiac, and your grades are top-notch. Your Mum and I reckon you should go to university and study corporate law. We spend a small fortune on legal fees, and it'd be great to have our own legal department in the long run.

'I'm talking pretty long term, of course,' he continued. 'Lurie, Singh, and Partners might hire you as an intern once you get your degree. I'm sure I could persuade them to create a vacancy.' He gave a knowing wink. Oh yes, Lurie, Singh, and Partners would create an appropriate position for him all right. If they wanted to keep the company as a client, that was.

What Malcolm didn't tell Lachie about was the recent conversation in which Rachel had made it plain she wanted Lachie as far away from Malcolm's influences as possible. This included her son finding employment outside of the company. The law studies option had been Malcolm's suggestion. A compromise of sorts.

'Law?' Lachie stopped and took a backward step. 'Law? You think I'm smart enough for that?' He hadn't even considered any career course other than a degree from the WA School of Mines and working at the Two Brothers Mine.

'Mate, you can do it,' his uncle assured him enthusiastically. 'In fact, you can ace it!

'Mind you, it's your decision entirely. Corporate law wouldn't suit everyone. Least of all me.' he added with a chuckle.

'Just consider it, that's all. Give the idea some serious thought. I'm damn sure the school would support you. It'd be a feather in their cap to have a practising lawyer among their Old Boys. You can be a big part of how the corporation runs, and you'll have a profession you can fall back on if you ever decide you want out of the mining business.'

Lachie pondered his Uncle Mal's proposal, then fixed Malcolm with a determined look.

'Tell you what,' he said evenly, 'how about a little tit for tat—quid pro quo, in lawyer-speak? I'll agree to consider a legal career—providing that I can get accepted, that is.' He paused, his eyes not leaving Malcolm's, 'In return, I want you to finance Jimmy Browne to study at the WA School of Mines, then give him the job you would have given me. Don't worry, he'll make you proud. I can't think of anyone who'd make a better mine supervisor. He'll be loyal and hard-working too, and he won't mind starting at the bottom.'

And just like that, Lachie's and Jimmy's futures were decided. How Malcolm would react when he learned Jimmy's ethnicity, Lachie wasn't sure. What he was sure of was that he would hold Malcolm to his part of the agreement, no matter what.

* * *

Back at school the following day, Lachie shared the news with his friend.

'What?' Jimmy said. 'Me, at the School of Mines? Not gonna happen! Sorry, Lachie, I guess you mean well, but I'm not a charity case. It's bad enough here, with everyone looking down on me like I'm some leper.'

'Mate,' Lachlan stressed to his friend, 'it won't be a free ride. Uncle Mal'll push you hard. I'll be honest, he's not fond of blackfellas, any more than the crowd here is, but you've grown up with bigotry—you can weather it.

'He's agreed to sponsor you with your studies,' he continued. 'The rest you'll have to earn, which I know you will. Besides, what else are you going to do with yourself when we graduate this year—work in the local bottle shop?'

Then he added with a grin, 'And I can't think of a better way to stick it to the yuppies here, can you?'

Jimmy eventually agreed to accept the sponsorship on the condition that he repay the costs involved once he was working full time. His friend Lachie agreed, and so the die was cast.

Chapter 20

Wednesday, Dec 24, 1997

'C'MON, JIMMY,' Lachie called. 'We gotta get going.'

Jimmy Browne sprinted from his family's home in Wilson Street, Kalgoorlie, and climbed into Lachie's new Commodore V8, throwing his overnight bag onto the back seat. It was almost midday, and they'd need to waste little time if they were to make Perth before sundown.

'Pretty good graduation present, Lachie,' Jimmy said, admiring the interior of his friend's new vehicle. 'Bet she can really burn rubber, hey?'

'Yeah, she can move all right,' Lachie replied. 'I don't want to push her too hard though, the motor's still a bit tight.'

As they pulled out from the kerb, however, the young Kincaid couldn't resist doing a little tyre squeal, to the delight of Jimmy's younger brother and sister, standing on the verandah.

Aretha and Marvin Browne whooped as the Commodore sped away, leaving twin black streaks in its wake.

'You know she fancies you?' Jimmy said.

'Who?'

'Aretha, my sister. She thinks you're the duck's nuts.'

'What?' said Lachie. 'You must be kidding. How old is she—thirteen?'

'Actually, she'd just turned fourteen,' Jimmy said. 'She's had the hots for you for ages.'

'Well, she can forget it,' Lachie replied. After a pause, he added, 'She is rather cute, I'll admit, but I'm not into …'

'I'll tell her you said that.'

'Don't you bloody dare!' snapped Lachie. 'The last thing I need is a pubescent teenager mooning over me.'

Jimmy was chortling by now. 'I do reckon you'd make a good pair, though. Just sayin'.'

'Drop it Jimmy, ya black prick. You're so full of shit! No wonder you've got brown eyes.'

Lachlan Kincaid was the only person on Earth that Jimmy would have allowed to talk to him that way. Such banter between them was commonplace, though.

Looking to change the subject, Jimmy said, 'Hey, Lachie. Can we stop at the servo in Coolgardie for one o' those hot dogs with the chilli sauce?'

'Fuck you, you can go hungry,' his friend replied. He knew, though, that when they got there, he'd stop as requested.

Minutes later they were on the Great Eastern Highway, and as soon as they had cleared the built-up area he gunned the motor and they sped southwest toward Coolgardie.

Forty-five minutes later, they were parked outside the service station, demolishing two hot dogs each and sharing a two-litre Coke.

'So Lachie,' said Jimmy, licking chilli sauce from his fingers. 'Didn't you say your Mum's folks were Jewish? How come they celebrate Christmas—it's not part of their culture, is it?'

'I asked Saba the same thing last year,' said Lachie. 'I told him I reckoned he was having a quid each way.' He gave a chuckle. 'Actually, he says they can celebrate the spirit of Christmas, the goodwill and family friendship part, even if they don't believe in the religious bit.'

'It's good of 'em to invite me down, anyway,' Jimmy said. 'Are you sure I shouldn't have brought a present or something?'

'Nah,' his friend said, 'they're not much into the whole gift-giving thing. Saba says it's more about doing good deeds and stuff. You know, charitable acts and all that. They'll both be volunteering at the local soup kitchen tomorrow to serve up Chrissy dinner to down-and-outs.'

'I reckon they must've had a bit of trouble fitting in to Aussie life,' Jimmy said. 'Where did you say they came from, Germany? I read that the Krauts killed off most of the Jews during the war.'

'Well, the Nazis certainly tried,' Lachie said. 'Saba told me he and Savta were both lucky to get out alive. Savta was in a concentration camp for a while, but Saba's family got out of Germany just before the shit hit the fan. He was around ten or eleven, I think.

'They met over in the eastern states when Saba was working on the Snowy Mountains Scheme. Savta had just arrived in Australia, apparently.'

'Hey, we learned about that Snowy Mountains Scheme, didn't we?' It was more a statement than a question.

'Yeah,' Lachie went on. 'Saba immigrated at the end of the war. Skilled workers were in short supply and he got training through a Government scheme and became an engineer. They came over to the west when he got offered a job with Main Roads back in the 70s.' He paused momentarily, stuffing the last of his hot dog into his mouth.

'His name used to be Shimon Chen Rosen. He changed it ages ago to Simon Rose. I guess it helped him fit in.'

'Maybe I should change my name. How do you reckon Jimmy Beige, or Jimmy Tan, would sound?' his friend joked, and they both laughed.

'Well,' Lachie said, 'we'd best get a wriggle on if we want to be there before dark.' He fired the V8 into life and swung onto the highway. Once on the open road, they relaxed and settled in for the five-or-six-hour drive to the city.

The two chatted for some time, mostly small talk and boyish, off-colour jokes, before lapsing into silence. There was little on the radio to excite two 18-year-olds—and Lachie had forgotten to add his CD collection to the car's payload—so Jimmy soon drifted off to sleep.

It was almost six when he woke, just as Lachie was pulling up in the Rose family driveway.

*   *   *

Simon Rose had spent the last week of November working on the Christmas lights and decorations. This had become a tradition since his retirement—and on December 1st, when he proudly flicked the switch, everyone had Oohed and Aahed in admiration. The arrangement of figurines, tinsel, and assorted paraphernalia was impressive.

As Lachie brought his Commodore to a halt in the driveway, Jimmy's mouth gaped.

'Wow,' he exclaimed, 'they sure get into the Christmas spirit, Jews or not.'

'They certainly do, Saba especially,' Lachie replied.

'What's that big candle holder?' Jimmy wanted to know.

'It's for Hanukkah. That's a Jewish celebration that coincides with Christmas. I can explain it later, if you want.'

'It's OK, I'll take it on faith.' Jimmy chuckled at his own unintended pun.

Rachel emerged from the house as they exited the car, greeting each with a warm hug. 'How do you like our display?' she asked them, seeing Jimmy's expression.

'Awesome!' was the young man's response. 'You don't see that back in Kal, that's for sure.'

Rachel smiled proudly. This was the first time in years she had helped her father with his pet project. They had expanded the tableau, adding a rooftop Santa and sleigh, complete with kangaroos in the place of reindeer, a couple of snowmen, and various other decidedly non-Australian figures. The only traditional Christmas decoration missing was the Nativity Scene.

Rachel had given herself the last week of November off and travelled down from the Goldfields for just this purpose. Now, back from Kalgoorlie once more for the holiday break, she was again relishing the time she could spend with her parents.

'Well, come in, boys,' she said. 'Dinner's about ready. I'll show you to your room. We'll leave it to you to decide who gets the top bunk.'

'Are we going to have some of those lattes, Mum?' Lachie asked. Neither had eaten since Coolgardie and were both hungry.

'They're latkes, and yes, we will have them, so get to the bathroom and wash up.'

'A fried potato pancake,' Lachie explained, in answer to Jimmy's puzzled look. 'Sorta traditional, to do with Hanukkah. They're yummy, by the way.'

After dinner, everyone sat and talked—Simon and Marita didn't encourage TV at family gatherings. They gave the lads a quick lesson in playing dreidel, a gambling game based on a spinning top with Hebrew letters. Jimmy was especially lucky and finished the night with a decent pocketful of coins.

The boys retired early, Lachie telling everyone he felt especially tired from the long drive. In their room, the youngsters shared a hip flask of vodka, mixed with a glass of orange juice from the family refrigerator. They followed this with a joint of the finest Goldfields weed. After talking for some time, they both slept very, very well indeed.

Thursday, Dec 25th, 1997

'I really wish we could see you more often, Love,' Rachel's mother said over breakfast pancakes. 'We both miss you, and Lachlan too.'

'Actually, I've been meaning to bring something up with you, Mum,' Rachel replied. Marita Rose stopped with her coffee cup halfway to her lips and raised one eyebrow. 'Oh?'

'Now that he's graduated, we've talked Lachie into applying to study law at UWA.' Rachel paused. 'I really don't want him working with Malcolm, as you're well aware. Besides, it would be a great career move for him. If he's accepted, he'll study for a Bachelor of Law degree.'

'Sounds wonderful,' Marita answered. 'It'll be a lot of work—but he's a smart boy. To be honest, I'm not surprised you want to keep them apart. You know your father and I never liked Malcolm. When you went to Kalgoorlie with him, we worried ourselves crazy, but we couldn't say much.'

'I realise that Mum, but if I hadn't gone there in the first place, I'd never have met Jamie. I think some things are just meant to be.'

'Hmm ... so what is it you need to talk about?'

'If they accept Lachie, how would you two feel about him living here while he does his studies? You don't have to answer straight away. Talk it over with Dad and ...'

'There's no need to discuss it, Rachel. Of course, we'd both love to have him here. When will you find out if he's successful?'

'In January sometime. I wanted to bring up it with you before mentioning it to Lachie.'

Rachel glanced at the kitchen clock. 'Where are those two, anyway? It'll be lunchtime before they get up if we don't wake them.'

'They were awake and talking for quite a while last night,' Marita said. 'In fact, I'm sure I heard laughter at one stage. Give them another half hour or so, then I'll put some breakfast on for them.

'Jimmy seems like a nice boy. He's the one you'll be putting through the School of Mines, isn't he?'

'Yes,' Rachel replied. 'And yes again, he seems a decent type.'

'Has Malcolm met him?' Marita asked.

'No, not yet. They're catching up with him later today. Mal's at a friend's place somewhere down south—Lachie has the address.'

Marita smiled. 'That should be an interesting encounter. I'd love to be a fly on the wall.'

Chapter 21

THE SOUND OF TYRES CRUNCHING ON GRAVEL and the purr of the Commodore's V8 as it entered the driveway roused Malcolm from his afternoon nap. He hauled himself from the squatter's chair and stood as he watched Lachlan and his companion emerge from the vehicle. Shielding his eyes with one hand, he waved and called, 'About time, young fella. I thought you'd be here before lunch.'

'Savta insisted we have what she called a *decent meal* before leaving. You know how she is,' Lachie said with a shrug.

'Yeah. Well, I know how she is with some,' Mal replied. 'Whenever I visit, I'm lucky to get offered a cup of coffee.'

Malcolm studied the two visitors as they approached the house. The newcomer was taller than Lachie, with olive skin, a broad nose, and a mass of matted, curly hair that instantly betrayed his ethnicity. Malcolm bristled inwardly, but kept his composure as Lachie introduced them.

'Uncle Mal, this is my mate, Jimmy. The one I told you about.'

'Nice to meet you, Mr Kincaid,' Jimmy said as they shook hands. 'I've heard a lot about you from Lachie.'

Malcolm grunted in reply and turned to Lachlan. 'Can I have a private word, Lachie?' Addressing Jimmy, he said, patting his shoulder, 'Won't be a sec. Family business. OK?'

Jimmy shrugged. 'Sure. No problem.'

'You never told me he was a boong!' Malcolm hissed in a low voice once they were alone. 'You expect me to put him through the school—and then hire him as a supervisor?'

'I never thought to mention it,' Lachie lied. 'What difference does that make? He's smart, he's keen, and he'll be a valuable asset to the company. What more can you ask?'

He followed with, 'You're not thinking of backing out of our deal, are you, Uncle Mal?'

Malcolm glared. 'You set me up for this, didn't you, you little shit!'

'Sorry. No idea what you're talking about,' Lachie lied again. 'Jimmy's my best mate, and he deserves a chance, that's all.'

'And if I refuse?'

'You mean back out on our agreement?' Lachie said. 'I don't reckon you'd renege on a deal. Not my Uncle Mal.' He patted Malcolm's arm for effect, then added, 'No matter what my Mum or her family say, you made a pact, and I know you'll stick to it.'

Malcolm was outfoxed, and he knew it. It seemed Lachlan Kincaid was a chip off the old block, after all. He eyed the younger Kincaid for several seconds before replying, 'I'll keep my word. But I will tell you this: if your young coon friend turns up drunk, or I catch him with his hands in the till, he'll be out on his ear!'

'The same as for anyone else. I wouldn't expect any special treatment, and neither will he,' Lachie replied. 'As a matter of fact, he only agreed to accept your help on condition that he can repay all expenses out of his future salary. And he'll keep to his agreement too. He can be just as proud and stubborn as anybody.'

They were still staring each other out when Jimmy called, 'Should I take a take a walk? I can check out the garden for a bit, if you like.'

'No, all's good,' said Lachie. 'We're just talking about some guy from the mine.' Then, turning to Malcolm, he said, 'How about a couple of beers, Uncle Mal?'

'It'll be Coke for you two,' Malcolm replied. 'You're driving, and you're both barely legal, anyway.' He led the way inside and produced three cans of Coke from the fridge, which he plonked onto the table between them. After opening one for himself and taking a long swig, he turned to Lachie's friend. 'So, Jimmy, you're the one we're sponsoring through the SOM, hey? You better be worth it.' and raising his Coke he said, 'Here's to you, and your devious little mate.'

With that, he drained the can without it leaving his lips.

Later, as the three of them sat beneath a spreading Coral Tree at the back of the house, Malcolm turned to Lachie. 'I've been thinking of making you a Christmas gift, Lachie. How would you like to become a shareholder?'

'What's the catch, Uncle Mal? It's not like you to give anything away for free.'

'Can't a man offer his s—nephew a prezzie out of the goodness of his heart?' Malcolm protested. He quickly skewed the pronunciation to hide what was almost a crucial slip-up.

'Sure,' Lachie replied, 'but still, what's the catch?'

The catch was that Malcolm Kincaid was in a spot of bother with the taxation office. He needed to reduce his income without decreasing his assets. He considered trying to lie his way through the conversation, but remembered something he'd once heard many years ago—about weaving a tangled web. Perhaps it was something his mother had said? He didn't remember—but figured it might have been. The gist was that if you tell a lie, you'd better have a good memory and be prepared to maintain the story indefinitely!

He thought it best to come clean with Lachlan. The canny younger Kincaid would probably see through him, anyway, he reasoned.

He explained his predicament, but not before making it clear to Jimmy that this was a confidential discussion.

Diplomatically, Jimmy offered again to take a walk, but Malcolm brushed his offer aside. 'It's OK, mate. If you're going to be part of this company, you'll just as likely see and hear a few things you can't repeat. Anyway, if you spill your guts, I'll see that you end up at the bottom of a mine shaft somewhere out the back of Buggery.' He gave a smile and a wink that could have signalled that he was joking, but Jimmy couldn't be sure. He sat quietly as Malcolm explained the situation, adding that the company would be Lachie's eventually, and the income from the shares wouldn't affect his taxable income as a full-time student.

Malcolm received a generous salary from Kincaid Mining Corporation, and much of his earnings went straight into a trust, specifically set up to mitigate any taxation commitments. He didn't need the money, but he did need to keep his shareholding under his control.

'So the bottom line is that you'll own the shares—30% of the company, actually—but I'll retain control whenever it comes to a vote on anything,' Malcolm explained. 'And I don't see any need for your mother to hear about this, OK?'

Lachie considered the situation and agreed to the terms. What the hell, he knew little about the running of the corporation anyway, so he might as well go along. The dividends from the shares would certainly come in handy while he was at university full time, he reasoned.

Later, on the drive back to the Roses' house, Jimmy brought up Malcolm's comments.

'He was kidding about the mine shaft—wasn't he?'

'Yeah, don't worry about Uncle Mal. He's not as tough as he makes out,' Lachie reassured his friend. He had to admit to himself, though, that the way Malcolm had delivered the threat took him aback. Of course, he was joking. Obviously. Wasn't he?

'So, Jimmy,' Lachie said, changing the conversation, 'wanna head to the beach tomorrow? Maybe we can pick up a couple of surfie chicks. You never know your luck in a big city, so they say.'

Chapter 22

Monday, March 3rd, 1998

LACHIE'S FIRST FEW DAYS at the University of WA had flashed by in a blur. The orientation and settling in, and getting his head around the whole idea of studying at university, had rendered him almost oblivious to his fellow students. Perhaps that's why he hadn't noticed Bronte—yet Bronte had noticed him.

Seated in the library, poring over a heavy legal tome, Lachie was totally unaware of the slim redhead as she slid onto the seat beside him.

'Swotting already? You're keen, my boy.'

Lachie whirled with a start. He caught his breath at the sight of the young woman at his side. 'Oh, er, sorry, er, miles away,' he stammered.

'Bronte Sleeman.' She offered her hand. 'We're classmates, though I don't think you've noticed. And—I'm a bit offended.' She gave a little pout for good measure. Lachie had to suppress a smile at the way she pronounced her name. It came out as *'Brontay'*.

She flashed him a warm smile. Lachie opened his mouth to respond and closed it again. Swallowing hard, he managed a stilted 'hello' and 'good to meet you', or at least a decent semblance of such. Still holding her hand, he rose to his feet, pulling her with him.

'Brontay' Sleeman was possibly the most beautiful thing he had ever seen. Definitely the most gorgeous woman he had ever met.

Bronte stood slightly shorter than Lachie, even in high heels. Her fiery coiffure framed a delicate, high-cheekboned face complemented by deep blue-green eyes and full lips. He found himself imagining what it might be like to kiss those lips. His gaze wandered over her slim frame, and he contemplated what lay beneath her light cotton dress. Suddenly aware of how inappropriate these thoughts were, and sensing that somehow she might know what he was thinking, he hastily replied, 'Er, Lachlan Kincaid. Sorry, you caught me by surprise. I was just looking up a phrase our lecturer used today.'

'Well, pleased to meet you, Lachlan Kincaid,' she said warmly. He still held her hand in his, and they stood for several seconds, staring into each other's eyes. Bronte was the one to break the impasse. Gently removing her hand from his grip, she motioned to his chair, and they both resumed their seats.

'You really look like the proverbial fish out of water,' she observed. 'I'm guessing you're not from an academic background?'

'Not at all,' he replied. 'I'm Kalgoorlie born and bred. Aside from doing time at WA Boys' Grammar, that is.'

'Doing time—interesting turn of phrase,' Bronte mused. 'So what attracted you to law studies?'

Lachie delivered a brief history of his journey from Kalgoorlie lad to university student, including the deal with Malcolm. Bronte listened with interest, especially when he spoke of the times he missed most; the hours and days spent at the mine site or touring the Goldfields on the back of Malcolm's Harley. They often took metal detectors to scout for new potential gold veins. 'I wanted a bike of my own for a graduation present, but I ended up with a Commodore,' he said with a look of feigned disappointment. 'I'm guessing that was my Mum's idea.'

'So this mate of yours, Jimmy, is living your dream and you're living your family's dream. That's a familiar scenario,' Bronte said.

Bronte Sleeman was the product of two generations of legal tradition, she explained. Her parents and her grandfather were well-known and respected practitioners within the Western Australian legal community. Ian Sleeman senior gained admittance to the bar in 1954 at the relatively tender age of 23 and started his own company in 1958.

Eventually, Sleeman and Associates became a true family business when Ian junior joined as a solicitor in 1978, followed by his new wife, Claire, at the beginning of 1979. She had contributed little after that first year, however, as she fell pregnant with Bronte, who was born the following October. After that, Claire divided her time between motherhood and part-time law work.

'So,' she said, 'it seems we have much in common, despite our differences. I always dreamed of going into the fashion business, but coming from a family like mine, the die was cast before I was even born.'

'Any brothers or sisters?' Lachie asked.

'One younger brother,' Bronte replied. 'Harvey's at boarding school, too. Daddy's also expecting him to join the firm, eventually.'

They were getting annoyed looks from a few nearby library patrons, so the two adjourned outside to continue their conversation.

'So how come your brother didn't inherit the name Ian too?' Lachie asked after fetching a couple of takeaway coffees.

'There was another,' Bronte said after a pause. 'My brother Ian came a year after me, but he died from cot death at two months.'

Lachlan swallowed hard before answering. 'I'm sorry to hear that. You wouldn't have even got to know him. That's … sad.'

After a pause, he continued, 'I was about eighteen months old when my father died, so I don't really remember him, either. Sometimes I think I have memories, but I'm not sure if they're real or just what Mum's told me. She talked about him a lot while I was growing up.'

They had another class to attend before their day was complete, so Bronte and Lachie finished their coffees and headed off to the lecture hall.

Afterwards, they compared notes and Lachie bought fish and chips for them both, which they took back to Bronte's nearby unit. They were just clearing up when the doorbell rang.

Bronte opened the door to a trio of her friends. They entered noisily before seeing Lachie. 'Oh, sorry,' said one, a tallish, olive-skinned guy of around 22, with long, dark hair. 'Didn't expect you'd have company.'

'Everyone,' said Bronte, 'this is Lachlan. We're classmates at UWA. Lachlan's from Kalgoorlie. His family owns a gold mine—I mean, literally!'

She introduced them all around. Bruce, the dark-haired guy; Angela, his younger sister, and Greg, Angela's boyfriend.

It would be obvious to anyone that Bruce and Angela were siblings. The age differences aside, they could almost have been twins. Both sported similar long dark hair, pulled back in a ponytail—but that was just the beginning. Their olive skin hinted at Middle Eastern or Mediterranean background, while their prominent aquiline noses immediately reminded Lachie of Latin versions of Barbra Streisand. Both were tall and slim, Angela around the same height as Lachie, her brother a little taller. They each had that unmistakably arrogant bearing that comes from a combination of influence and affluence—a bearing he'd become used to seeing during his time at WABGS. Obviously well-connected, Lachie assumed.

Greg, on the other hand, reminded Lachie of himself, or at least how he assumed others saw him. Greg's hair was a tousled blond mess—there was no other way to put it. Where his companions were neat, manicured, and tidy, Greg was the epitome of casual. His clothes—which probably came from K Mart or Rivers, rather than some upmarket boutique—and even his shoes, spoke of a laid-back attitude Lachie hadn't seen for some time. How he came to be attached to someone like Angela was anyone's guess. Lachie liked him immediately.

Bruce opened a bottle of Bourbon and helped himself to a large bottle of Coke from the fridge. He poured drinks for all and returned to the kitchen, where he struck up a quiet conversation with Bronte.

Lachie was chatting with Greg and Angela, all the while keeping Bruce and Bronte in his line of sight. 'I'm not sure,' Lachie heard Bronte say, glancing in his direction. 'I've just met him.'

He excused himself and approached them. 'So, Bruce, what do you do with yourself?' he asked.

'Bruce is a musician,' Bronte spoke for him. 'He plays bass in a rock band.'

'Yeah, well, part-time, anyway. Greg's our drummer.' So that explained something, at least.

'From nine to five, I work at Bron's old man's firm. I graduated last year and I'm doing my internship.' He sized Lachie up, and looking him squarely in the eyes said, 'Do Kalgoorlie boys smoke pot?'

'I've been known to partake,' Lachlan answered. 'Why—are you holding?'

'Holding?' Bruce snorted. 'Man, that's a bit sixties, isn't it?'

Bronte suppressed a snigger, and Bruce continued, 'But to answer your question; yes, I do have a baggie with me. Care to share a joint or two with us?'

Bruce produced a plastic bag and papers and rolled a couple of fat doobies, which he then lit and passed around. Lachie had to admit that the last thing he ever expected to see was a lawyer smoking pot, and after a few rounds, he told them so. Everyone thought that was hysterical, but the smoke may have had something to do with the hilarity.

They sat around, chatting and drinking for an hour or two, and when everyone else was about to take their leave, Bronte discretely took Lachie's hand and whispered, 'Don't go. If you stay, I'll make you breakfast.' She gave him a gentle kiss, allowing her tongue to stroke his lips lightly, and added, 'And I'll make you very glad you did.'

After waving her guests off, Bronte turned to Lachie. 'You know,' she said, sidling up to him and running her hand across his buttocks, 'smoking weed always makes me extra frisky.' She put her free hand behind Lachie's neck and drew him toward her. He leaned in and placed his mouth on hers, wrapping his arms around her as he did so.

They kissed for several seconds, gently at first, then with more fervour. Bronte's tongue darted across his teeth, and when he opened them a little, it entered his mouth. Not sure what she expected of him, he tried clumsily to return the gesture. When they parted, she held him at arm's length and, gazing deep into his eyes, she said, 'Are you a virgin?'

Lachie blushed. Was it that obvious?

She was smiling now, a coquettish cat-that-ate-the-cream smile. 'Why, I believe you are!'

Lachie felt as if he would surely catch fire. He made to speak, but speech wouldn't come. She ran her hand up his leg, caressing his growing manhood. 'But I've got an idea that part of you knows what to do already.' Taking him gently by the wrist, she led him through to her bedroom.

Lachie followed, almost meekly. He had never known a woman who excited him the way Bronte did. Sure, he'd had girlfriends, but none to compare with Bronte Sleeman. His previous attempts at sexual activity had been limited to clumsy groping at the drive-in or a quick feel in the bushes after school, followed by urgent self-relief afterwards. Bronte was all woman and awakened in him feelings he didn't quite know how to handle.

Once inside her room, she began to undress him. Not sure what to do, Lachie reached for the straps of her dress, but she took his hands away. 'Easy, let me do it. You just relax and enjoy yourself.'

Bronte had his top off in seconds, and his remaining clothes down to his ankles in equally quick time. She guided him toward the bed and pushed him, so he fell backwards onto the mattress. She yanked his shoes and socks off in two quick movements, tossing them over her shoulders along with his jeans and underwear. Then, —in an instant, it seemed to Lachie—she shed her own clothing completely.

Bronte stood before him, arms akimbo and legs slightly apart, like a conquering Amazon. Lachie wondered what her next move might be, but he welcomed it, whatever it was.

Still smiling, she surveyed his nakedness before climbing onto the bed, straddling him. Her breasts glided across his body as she crawled up to where their faces met, and in a moment, she was kissing him deeply again, this time with more passion. She reached down and guided him into her. Lachie's breath caught at the first caress of her moistness. 'Easy,' she said, 'don't rush it.'

Lachie held out as long as he was able, which was about a minute. He let out a cry as he climaxed. Bronte thrust herself down onto him, as if trying to stem the flow, then pumped up and down fiercely. He closed his eyes for several seconds, relishing this first taste of genuine passion. When he reopened them, Bronte was staring at him with a self-satisfied smile. Almost a smirk. She still maintained her assault.

'Don't you go soft on me,' she whispered. 'Not yet.'

She was moaning now—softly, then more intensely. Lachie watched her face as she closed her eyes, relishing the moment. He wondered how much longer he could maintain his erection, but needn't have worried, as suddenly, Bronte reached her own climax. She let out a cry of pleasure before ceasing her thrusting and bearing down on him again, as if trying to consume him.

She collapsed across Lachie's body and lay, panting. *So this is what I've been missing out on*—Lachie thought. *No wonder everyone can't get enough of it.*

By the time the morning sun cast its first rays through Bronte's bedroom window six hours later, they had repeated the scenario twice—with some variations—and even managed to squeeze in a few hours of sleep.

Bronte made good on her promise of breakfast, though. She presented him with tinned mushrooms on toast and a poached egg, whispering in his ear as she set the tray before him: 'Eat up, my love. I've got a feeling you'll be needing all your stamina today.'

* * *

Over the next few weeks, they were rarely apart. Lachie took to spending most evenings at Bronte's apartment, although both returned to their respective family homes each weekend. Sometimes she'd invite friends to visit for a meal or drinks. These visits usually turned into a late-night smokefest. Bronte had a large glass hookah—a souvenir of a trip to the middle east—especially for such occasions. When this happened, Lachie would make his excuses and disappear for a few hours or say he needed to study. Bronte's clique reminded him too much of the boarding school crowd he was so glad to be free of.

After the group had departed one night, Bronte confronted him.

'Do you have an issue with my friends?' she asked, her voice tinged with indignance. 'They all reckon you think you're better than us. If that's true, we may have a problem.'

He gathered his thoughts, searching for the right words. 'No, nothing like that,' he said. 'I really need to study more than you, apparently. Look, I have to admit, I'm struggling a bit, and the dope doesn't help. I don't want to smoke that shit so much anymore, and if I stay out there, they'll expect me to join in.'

That last part was totally true. Lachie had been in the habit of smoking the odd joint for a couple of years now, but the novelty had worn off. He no longer enjoyed being around when others were getting off their faces. Besides, the visits had become more and more frequent and he had to admit—though he'd never say it to Bronte—he thought her friends were, for the most part, a pretty superficial lot.

'Well, maybe when the crowd is coming over, you ought to stay at your place,' she said, adding, 'Listen Lachlan, I love you, and I want you here. These are my friends, though. It makes it tough for me when they assume you're snubbing them.'

'I'm not snubbing them.' he declared. But he was, wasn't he? Could he—should he—keep protesting his innocence?

They stood face to face for a minute, before Bronte said, 'Let's talk this out in the morning. I'm ready for bed.' She may have been ready for bed, but she wasn't quite ready for sleep. One thing Lachie had learned was that marijuana always made Bronte incredibly horny. She stripped off and climbed into the bed, and he followed. Oh well, he thought, every cloud, and all that …

Eventually, they arrived at a compromise. Bronte informed her friends she would only get high on Fridays or weekends. No, she insisted, not because of Lachlan, but to keep her own head clearer for study. Lachie, in turn, would spend Friday nights, and each weekend, at the Rose family home in Claremont. This arrangement soon became the new norm for them both. They still shared the occasional midweek joint, but not to the extent they had when Bruce and the crew visited.

*   *   *

It was a few days into April. Marita and Lachie were enjoying a morning cuppa in the back garden when she thought it was time to raise the subject of her grandson's repeated absence. 'So Lachlan, when are we going to meet the girl who's been monopolising your life lately? I presume it's a girl—you're not going over to the Dark Side, are you?' she added with a laugh.

Lachie almost choked on his coffee. 'No, Savta,' he said after regaining his composure, 'I'm not turning.' He paused, still chuckling. 'You know, sometimes you come out with some really inappropriate stuff for a grandparent.'

'I haven't lived my life in a nunnery,' she said with a smile. 'Anyway, I thought you young folk were unshockable.

'So who is she, and why have you been keeping her from us? Come on, I want to know all the lurid details.'

Lachie gave her as much of the "lurid details" as he dared, which wasn't much more than a summary of how they met and what Bronte's background was. This was his Savta, after all. There's only so much a young bloke can share with his grandmother.

'Well,' Marita said, 'it's Easter next weekend, and your mother's coming to visit. You'll be on a break, so how about we invite her over for dinner on Saturday?' She added with a conspiratorial wink, 'I'll even let her sleep over.'

The Roses didn't celebrate Easter, of course, but Marita thought they should take advantage of the holiday break to get to meet whom she presumed to be Lachlan's first real love. How long it would last, who knew, but Marita figured it couldn't hurt to meet the girl who seemed to have his heart—for now, at least.

Chapter 23

Easter Saturday, April 11th, 1998

IT WAS JUST AFTER 2:00 PM when Lachie's Commodore pulled smoothly into the Rose family driveway. Bronte wanted to drive them there in her BMW, but Lachie had persuaded her to slum it for the weekend. He needed her to make a good impression, and that didn't mean coming across like a spoilt socialite—even though, he had to admit; it was pretty close to the truth.

Lachie had hoped to be there before lunch. Bronte, however, had taken her usual two hours to choose the appropriate clothes and apply her makeup, despite his insisting that it would be a low-key affair.

'It's only a get-to-know-you thing,' he'd stressed, 'not a Royal Gala Performance. And forget about it being Easter; they're Jewish, remember, so it's just another weekend to them.'

Bronte hadn't said so, but she was grateful Lachlan himself had not embraced the Jewish faith. She'd omitted confiding that part of him to her family and made a mental note to corner Lachlan and make sure he didn't mention it when they met him. They'd find out eventually, she reasoned, but that was a bridge they could cross at a later date.

Bronte's folks didn't subscribe to any religious bent and cared little about Easter except that it meant four days off work. They were spending the time on their yacht and expected Bronte and her latest infatuation for lunch on Sunday.

Rachel opened the door as Lachie raised his hand to knock. 'So good to see you, Lachie,' she said, throwing her arms around him. 'I hate us being so far apart.'

Turning to Bronte, she ignored the visitor's offered handshake, opting instead for a warm hug—which caught Bronte completely off guard.

'And great to meet you at last, Bronte,' she said. 'Lachie's been bashing our ears about this gorgeous girl he's met. Sometimes I can't get him to shut up about you!'

'Mum!' Lachie said, blushing with embarrassment. 'I have not! Do you have to?'

Rachel laughed, enjoying his discomfort. 'Come through,' she said. 'I'll introduce you to Lachie's grandparents.'

She led them through the house to where the family was gathered in the backyard and made the introductions.

Besides the immediate family, Marita had also invited a workmate of Simon's. Graham McKinley was a widower in his late forties with two teenage sons and had recently arrived from New Zealand. Marita still entertained hopes Rachel might find someone new to share her life, and couldn't resist the chance for a little matchmaking. Graham, oblivious to Marita's ulterior motives, had readily accepted the invitation, along with his boys.

Once the formalities were out of the way, Marita excused herself and disappeared indoors. 'So, Bronte,' Simon said. 'Lachie tells me your folks are something of a legal institution. Do you have a family practice then?'

'Sleeman and Associates,' Bronte replied. 'Mummy and Daddy both work as solicitors. Mummy is only part-time, though. Grandpa is a barrister, though he keeps saying he wants to retire.'

'Nothing like keeping it in the family, I guess,' Rachel offered.

'That's what Daddy says. My younger brother, Harvey, will join too when he graduates. I think Grandpa wants me to become a barrister like him. Perhaps that's why he hasn't retired yet.'

'Is anyone hungry?' called Marita, as she emerged from the house bearing platters of food. 'We skipped lunch, so I've fixed us all a snack.'

She placed the trays on a large table under the patio, along with a coffeepot and beakers. 'Come on, all,' she said cheerily. 'Let's not be shy.'

As they all moved to the table to view Marita's offerings, Rachel overheard Bronte whispering to Lachlan, 'What's that?' pointing to a small plate of savouries.

'Smoked oysters,' Lachie replied. 'They're Mum's favourites. Apparently, she had cravings for them when she was carrying me, and still ...'

'You mean, like, from a can?' Bronte screwed her face into a grimace. 'Eew, perhaps I'll try a little of that pâté. Be a dear and get me some, will you?'

Rachel met Graham McKinley's eyes across the table. He'd obviously also overheard. He raised his eyebrows as they shared an amused smile.

Lachie was too busy waiting on Bronte to notice. He passed her a plate of assorted treats and they moved to a table under a shady tree, where they sat sipping their coffees.

'I can't wait for you to meet Daddy tomorrow.' Bronte oozed, adding, 'And I can't believe you've never been sailing!' She gave his thigh an exaggerated slap.

Lachie chuckled. 'Kal's a bit far from the ocean, Bron. My sporting interests are confined to motorbikes, 'roo shooting, and the odd game of footy.'

She frowned. 'I wish you wouldn't call me that. My name is Bronte, not Bron. And you, my love, are Lachlan, not Lachie, as your family insists on calling you.' She smiled and gave him a playful shove. 'I'll civilise you yet, my boy.'

They looked up as Rachel and Graham approached, flanked by his two sons.

Rachel had shared a brief conversation with Graham earlier in the day, when everyone was awaiting Lachie and his guest. Later, while Rachel was helping Marita set the table, she'd noticed his gaze following her. Rachel was well aware of her mother's matchmaking instinct; and that this was the real reason he'd been invited. She also knew that if she didn't want another grilling from Marita, she would at least have to spend some time getting to know him before she snubbed his advances.

Not that Graham wouldn't have made an excellent catch, she admitted. He was blessed with rugged good looks and a rather pleasant nature.

Graham and his boys had been standing near the swimming pool, and as Rachel approached, he flashed her a welcoming smile. 'Did you meet Michael and Jason? They just arrived. Michael insisted they come in his car.

'I think that's so they'll be able to skip out early,' he added in a fake whisper, cupping a hand to the side of his mouth.

Michael, the older of the two and presumably the driver, gave a sheepish grin.

'I'm sure nobody will be offended if you've got somewhere else to be,' Rachel said. 'Have you had something to eat, though?'

They nodded. Yes, thank you. They had eaten. Rachel wondered whether it was politeness or shyness; they seemed to have little to say.

'The sun has a bite today,' Rachel said. 'Shall we grab some shade? There's room over where Lachie and Bron are sitting.'

After Lachlan and Graham rearranged the chairs, there was just enough space around the table for the group of six. Rachel found herself seated next to Graham, Lachie noticed. He watched as they chatted amiably. Maybe Graham just might be the one to break his mother's self-imposed solitude, he thought. She'd had a limited social life for as long as Lachie could remember and certainly deserved some happiness. He hoped she might find something with Graham, even if it was only friendship.

By the end of the afternoon, Graham had convinced Rachel to accompany him and his sons for a picnic the following day. The shared glance, and the expression on the boys' faces, suggested they would probably find an excuse to beg off, however.

Chapter 24

LACHIE AND BRONTE departed a little after breakfast the following day. They picked up her brother Harvey from East Perth on the way to Fremantle, where the Sleemans moored their yacht. His parents believed he was staying with a schoolmate and his family. Bronte, however, had confided to Lachie that he was spending the time with his newest girlfriend at her flat.

Harvey was waiting outside when they arrived, his overnight bag packed. Lachie pulled the release catch as he stopped at the kerb, and Harvey tossed his bag into the trunk.

'Morning, Ranga.' Lachie called as Harvey climbed into the rear seat. He noticed Bronte's expression of distaste, but for once she made no comment and Lachie didn't acknowledge his infraction.

Harvey had inherited the same bright red hair as his sister, hence his unfortunate nickname. Other than that, and his eye colouring, he bore little resemblance to Bronte. He was a good deal shorter, and fatter, with a face covered in freckles. Lachie often thought of just how grateful Bronte must have been that she missed out on that particular feature!

What Harvey lacked in suave looks, however, he made up for in spades with his exuberant personality and all-around good nature. He and Lachie had hit it off right from the start, and despite their age difference, they became firm friends. Lachie still smiled when he recalled their first meeting:

Bronte: 'Lachlan, I'd like you to meet my brother Harvey.'

Lachie: 'G'day Ranga, nice to meet ya,'

Harvey: 'Ranga? No, that was my nickname in primary school.'

'I'm older now; people just call me Harvey, or Harve.'

Lachie: 'Best of luck with that, Ranga,' winking as Bronte rolled her eyes with disgust.

'We've got some time to spare,' Lachie said. 'Wanna stop off in High Street for a cappuccino on the way?'

'Does the Pope wear a funny hat?' Ranga replied with a cheery grin.

An hour later, the three of them were putting away the last of the carrot cakes Bronte had ordered along with their morning caffeine fix. Rising to her feet, she said, 'Best we be on our way. I told them we'd be there well before lunch. I think Daddy wants to go for a sail before we eat. Maybe to Rottnest Island.'

'Rotto?' said Harvey. 'You better keep Dad away from the champagne and whisky, in that case. Otherwise, he'll never make it out of the harbour!'

Bronte sniffed and gave him an irritated look before leading the way back to Lachie's Commodore.

The Fluctus Saltator

They walked along the marina boardwalk, carrying a bag between them containing their bathers and towels. Bronte had insisted, just in case.

Lachie and Harvey chatted aimlessly until Bronte spoke. 'This is the one,' she said, indicating a sleek white-hulled boat with dark blue trim.

Moored before them lay a 12-metre Bermuda-rigged sailboat that had been Ian Sleeman's pride and joy since he purchased her some four years earlier. The boomed mainsail and single headsail provided enough surface area to satisfy his moderate need for speed, yet enabled him to sail her virtually unaided when he chose to. A blue and white striped spinnaker lay hidden in the forward storage locker—for those occasions when he felt more adventurous, usually when he sailed with experienced hands to assist him.

All this detail Lachie was oblivious to, but he was still suitably impressed. His eyes widened as he surveyed the scene, admiring the sleek lines and gleaming brass fittings. At the stern was a plaque emblazoned with *Fluctus Saltator* in dark blue Copperplate script with a gold shadow.

They stopped briefly as Lachie studied the name. 'It's Latin,' Bronte said. 'It means Wave Dancer, the name Daddy first chose. He found out there was already a local boat called *Wave Dancer*—so he changed it to the Latin equivalent.'

'Clever.' Lachie mused.

At that moment, two figures appeared from below. 'Daddy! Mummy!' called Bronte, waving excitedly, 'Happy Easter!'

'Come aboard.' Bronte's father gestured to them. 'We're just about to open a bottle of champers.'

Ian Sleeman was a surprisingly short man, at least compared to the image Lachlan had conjured in his mind. He looked to be in his mid-forties, yet was already showing significant greying at his temples and in his prominent sideburns. His physique had probably once been impressive, but now middle-age spread had begun taking its toll.

He wore loose navy blue shorts, almost reaching his knees, and a collarless T-shirt with broad horizontal stripes that only exaggerated his paunch. On his feet were canvas plimsolls, sans socks; the tradition within the sailing fraternity. The only thing missing that would have completed the cliché was a Skipper's cap to cover his balding pate. In fact, Lachie had a brief image of Alan Hale Jr. as The Skipper in Gilligan's Island, and had to suppress a laugh.

By contrast, Claire Sleeman was the epitome of fashion and elegance. She was noticeably taller than her husband, slim and well-dressed, with skin reminiscent of fresh cream. Her high cheekbones and ginger hair left no doubt which side of the family Bronte inherited her appearance from. She wore large, heavy-rimmed sunglasses, but Lachie was certain those same blue-green eyes lingered behind them. Her floral patio dress, with its matching sunhat, would have cost an average worker's weekly wage in some trendy Nedlands boutique, he assumed. The dress, along with her coiffured hairstyle and diamond eardrops, looked totally out-of-place on a sailboat. How she would manage if they met with a good wind would be anyone's guess.

Once on board, and with the first bottle of champagne opened and introductions made, Lachie and Bronte settled onto a pair of deck chairs in a shady spot near the stern.

'Well, Lachlan,' Ian Sleeman said, 'Bronte tells me this is your first taste of the sailing life? I hope you're not prone to seasickness.'

'I guess we'll find out soon enough,' Lachie laughed. 'Are we going to sea, then?'

'Just a short spin, probably for an hour or two. Enough to test your sea legs,' Ian replied. 'And we'll see how you perform as a deckhand.'

Ian gave Lachie a crash course on the terminology and mechanics of sailing and then decided that they'd all have lunch first and hit the water afterwards.

Lunch with the Sleemans was a much grander affair than Lachie was used to. There was ham, turkey, assorted cheeses and pickles on toothpicks, complete with bright cellophane bows on each, and even caviar and smoked salmon. All this, accompanied by dainty triangles of crisp bread and a mixed salad containing cherry tomatoes, olives, walnuts, and various other items he'd never before seen together on the same platter. There was even a mouldy cheese that everyone seemed to think was extra special, though Lachie couldn't bring himself to try it.

As Bronte leaned over to refill his wine glass, he placed his hand over the rim and shook his head. 'No more for me. Not if I'm expected to help drive this thing. Besides, it might just be so much more to chuck over the side later.'

Lachie needn't have worried. As it turned out, it was as if he were born for the ocean. Once out of the harbour and under full sail, the *Fluctus Saltator* lived up to her name admirably. Lachie revelled in the surging sway of the yacht as it sped through the waves, sending salt spray high into the sunlight where it burst forth in a never-ending rainbow, first on one side, and then on the other. Ian couldn't suppress his own smile, watching Lachie beaming with delight as they raced ahead of the breeze and across the deep blue water of Gage Roads.

Most of the time, there wasn't a lot required of Lachie and Harvey, except for minor trim adjustments. When Ian needed to bring the boat about, the two would lean their weight out over the side as counterbalance, holding onto the railing or rigging. Lachie relished the feel and taste of the misty spray. He knew he'd be sunburnt by evening, despite the lotion Bronte had insisted he apply, but he didn't care.

When Ian called 'Luff!', the pair would duck as the mainsail swung across to the opposite side. Then they'd adjust the trim while their skipper tacked the boat to catch the wind from the other direction. This accomplished, the yacht would then speed off in the newly designated heading, urged onward by the Fremantle Doctor; the local sea breeze.

Despite his comical appearance, Ian Sleeman was a skilled sailor. He was also an excellent teacher. Lachie learned how Ian had narrowly missed out on a place aboard Australia II when she defended her America's Cup trophy a few years earlier and counted many celebrated yachties among his friends. He had also been a crew member on a Sydney to Hobart Race entrant in 1984.

All too soon, Lachie's introduction to sailing was over. By late afternoon, the *Fluctus Saltator* was securely back at her moorings and the young apprentice sailor and his teacher were saluting their success with a glass each of single malt whisky. Ian informed Harvey his choice of drinks was limited to lemon squash; lemon, lime, and bitters, or water. 'You're still underage,' his father reminded him. 'And anyway, you'll be fetching dinner later. Nobody gets behind the wheel of my Beamer with a skinful, you know that.'

He turned to Lachie, 'Any time you want to come out for a sail, you'll be more than welcome, Lachie. For a self-confessed bushie, you did well today.' He raised his glass in a mock salute, and Lachie responded.

'It's Lachlan, Daddy.' Bronte chimed in, 'You know Mummy and I hate it when you shorten names like that.'

Ian gave her a dismissive wave. 'Women!' he said with a laugh. 'I wonder if you realise what you're getting yourself into, Lachie my boy.' He placed special emphasis on *Lachie* for Bronte's benefit and chuckled at her disgusted look. 'I meant what I said, though. Any weekend you want to come out on the *Saltator*, you just let me know.'

'Thanks, Mr Sleeman. I reckon I'd like that.'

'Mr Sleeman is my Dad,' Ian said curtly. 'You call me Ian. Call me Ian and we'll get along fine. How's your drink, by the way, ready for a refill?'

By seven o'clock everyone was hungry, so Ian sent Harvey out to a local Chinese restaurant, the Hai Palace, for takeaways. 'Best Chinese tucker for miles,' Ian informed his young apprentice yachtie. After a short while, the food arrived, and Claire laid it on a trestle table at the stern. Claire and Bronte picked at their meals with little enthusiasm. Chinese food, apparently, was not their preferred fare.

That night marked one of only a few times Lachie and Bronte had spent the night together without making love. Actually, together is a relative term, as the cabin they shared had single bunks. Bronte made much of stressing how tired she was from their day on the water. Would he mind? Of course he wouldn't, he assured her.

Also, for the first time that Lachie remembered, she retired without the usual toke, and Lachlan thought perhaps this accounted for her lack of libido. That, or maybe the proximity of her parents, might have had something to do with it, he reasoned.

Harvey borrowed Ian's BMW and left, supposedly to spend the evening at his school friend's place, as the boat only had two cabins. Ian reminded him firmly of the 'no alcohol' rule before he left, but Lachie and Bronte guessed that all bets would be off once he was out of sight.

* * *

The rest of the weekend went by in a blur for Lachie. Everyone was up fairly early Monday morning, and as soon as Harvey arrived, they made ready and sailed across to Rottnest Island. Once there, they held an onboard barbecue, and later, Harvey gave Lachie a quick introduction to snorkelling in the sheltered water of Little Salmon Bay.

Lachie was hooked immediately. Even in the shallow water, the abundance of marine life was breathtaking. He marvelled as a school of yellow and black Damselfish drifted by, one or two even swimming so close as to peer at him through his face mask. They disappeared in an instant when a large Wrasse—as long as Lachie's arm and resplendent in bright pink with blue and yellow lines across its body—appeared and then vanished effortlessly into the distance. All this against a background of limestone outcrops, corals, and swaying seagrass.

'That's gotta be the best thing ever,' he beamed, as he surfaced and began removing his fins before climbing back on board. 'Better than sex!'

He saw Claire Sleeman's eyes flash slightly at this remark.

'Not that I'd know, of course,' he quickly added, glancing in her direction.

'Nice recovery,' Ian Sleeman murmured as he grabbed Lachie's arm and heaved him aboard. Bronte giggled to herself, turning her face away.

'I will definitely be learning to dive,' Lachie said enthusiastically. 'Hey Ranga, whaddya say we learn SCUBA diving, you and me. You should too, Bron. We can all do it together.'

'Bronte,' she reminded him, for probably the fifth time that day. 'And no, I don't think it's really my sort of activity. I get nervous putting my head underwater in the Jacuzzi!'

'She'd be too scared of ruining her coiffure,' Harvey cut in. 'And her mascara might wash off,' he added with a laugh.

'Funny boy,' Bronte said, with the most indignant look she could manage. 'And I suppose you're the epitome of adventure, are you?'

There was a round of good-natured banter, which Claire Sleeman broke by opening a fresh bottle of Champagne. 'Well, here's to Aquaman,' she said, raising her glass in Lachie's direction.

All too soon, they headed back to Fremantle. After a light supper, Lachie, Harvey, and Bronte left, with Harvey in the front seat this time, and Bronte in the rear. Harvey and Lachie chatted all the way to East Perth and by the time they dropped Harvey at his girlfriend's place, he and Lachie had resolved to sign up together for SCUBA classes as soon as they were able.

Bronte couldn't wait to get home, so she could have a joint and go to bed.

Chapter 25

Saturday, April 25th, 1998

ANZAC DAY WAS NOT ONE of Malcolm's favourite days. His memories of what is arguably Australia's most revered public holiday mostly concerned his father getting totally pie-eyed, staggering home in the early hours sporting a cut lip and black eye or other souvenirs of a barroom fight, and taking his bad temper out on his hapless family.

For that reason, Malcolm usually made himself scarce on that one day of the year. This often meant a camping and fossicking trip as far away from civilisation as possible. As he loaded his swag onto his motorcycle, considering just what direction to take, his phone rang.

'Malcolm, how you doin', Bro?' The voice seemed familiar, yet it took several seconds before he put a face to it.

'Moose!' he said once the penny dropped. 'Long time no see. What's up?'

After the Hand of God affair, Malcolm had taken to socialising with the Vulcans Motorcycle Club at their Fremantle headquarters. Although not one of the 'Big Four' (or five) outlaw bikie gangs, they were loosely affiliated with the Gypsy Jokers, who were definite contenders for inclusion.

Malcolm once considered joining the Vulcans, before deciding that his position with KMC precluded it. Affiliations with bikie clubs, outlaws or otherwise, weren't ideal for a senior executive of one of the state's major mining companies. Once the club realised he had no plans to join, they'd informed him he was no longer welcome at the clubrooms. He'd kept in contact with Moose for a while, but they hadn't spoken for several years.

'I got a spot of bother, Mal,' Moose said. 'I don't wanna talk about it on the phone; can we meet somewhere?'

Malcolm thought for a moment. Moose wasn't exactly the sharpest knife in the block, but his hesitancy suggested he might think someone had bugged his phone. Malcolm's old paranoia stirred.

'I'll text you an address. Delete it and meet me there in two hours.'

The address in question was a tavern on the Great Northern Highway, close to where Malcolm was living. He knew it well, though not so well that anyone would know him, he thought. Surrounded by bush, and with a clear view of the highway in both directions, it seemed the safest option. Within fifty minutes, he was seated on the front verandah with a beer, surveying the access road and waiting for Moose's arrival. There were a few patrons—mostly regulars, he guessed, as one or two looked familiar—but thankfully, he recognised none of the staff on duty.

At ten before the hour, he heard the unmistakable throb of a Harley V-Twin, and Moose's cycle cruised into the parking lot. Malcolm was pleased to see he was not wearing colours—that would likely have attracted unwanted attention. Malcolm had opted for denims and an open-front sports shirt. His leather jacket lay out of sight under the chair. Moose entered the bar and looked around, then walked over and sat opposite him.

Malcolm ordered them two more beers and, raising his glass, said, 'Here's to old times and absent colleagues.'

They both drank deeply before Moose leaned conspiratorially toward him. 'I need your help, Bro. The cops may be onto me.'

Henare (Henry) Parata—Moose, to his friends—wasn't one to stay out of trouble for long. In fact, it was a minor miracle he'd avoided running afoul of the law for as long as he had. Moose and another club member had been operating a vehicle rebirthing racket for a few years and had been doing well out of it until they got careless. Police had swooped on a rural property they used as a chop shop and taken both into custody.

'One o' the pigs recognised me,' Moose told Malcolm. 'He'd been on the crew looking into the mine break-in back in '81.

'Next thing, he's leanin' on me and says he can get me immunity from the rebirthing rap and everything else if I cough to the mine job an' name some names. Then he starts talking about witness protection.'

Malcolm's face clouded. 'Did you make a statement?'

'Fuck, no!' Moose blurted. 'I stonewalled the hell outa them. I knew they couldn't hold me forever. I'm out on bail, but now the guys at the club think I'm gonna roll over. I'd never do that! You know I wouldn't. You gotta help me!'

His voice edged up a notch, and Malcolm raised a hand to warn him. 'Shh, steady mate.' He glanced around the room. 'Keep it down to a dull roar, OK?

'What do you want from me?' Malcolm had an idea where the conversation was heading; Moose needed some private witness protection. They both knew the Vulcans would never let him testify—not if it meant informing on Robbo, or anyone else. And even if he didn't, his time behind bars for the rebirthing rap might be short-lived. Loose ends were a luxury the club could ill afford, and once doubts had been raised …

Moose was fast becoming a liability Malcolm couldn't afford, either.

'You have money, connections,' Moose was saying. 'You can get me out of the country. Somewhere there's no extradition treaty. South America, I don't care where. Just help me disappear!'

Malcolm studied his co-conspirator intently. Yes—he had the money, and possibly the connections; he could help make someone vanish if he wanted to. 'Go home and sit tight,' he said. 'I reckon I can sort things out. Don't go near the clubhouse. Don't contact anyone from the Vulcans at all. Don't speak to your lawyer, even if he calls you. Wait for my phone call.'

Moose nodded. 'Thanks, Bro, I knew I could count on you.'

The big Maori left, and Malcolm sat quietly, considering the options. After ten minutes and another beer, he had the plan down pat. He just needed to make a few calls and Henry Parata would disappear—never to be seen or heard from again. And then Malcolm could relax once more.

* * *

On the Monday after their conversation in the tavern, Malcolm texted Moose to arrange another meeting. This time, the location was a busy coffee shop in Midland, a northeastern suburb.

'Did you delete the text?' he said as the Maori slid onto the seat opposite.

'Sure thing, Bro,' Moose replied. 'Like you said, can't be too careful, 'ey?'

'OK, here's the plan. We leave on Friday. I've hired a four-wheel-drive camper and we're cutting across the centre, through the Great Victoria Desert via Leonora and Warburton. That way, there'll be no chance of anyone recognising either of us.'

Moose was nodding. Malcolm wasn't sure if he had ever heard of the places he had mentioned. 'Good thinkin', I'm on bail and s'posed to report every few days. We don't wanna be picked up at the border, 'ey?'

'I've arranged things in the east,' Malcolm said. 'You'll be out of the country before you know it. The people who're organising things over there are expecting us by the end of the month. We can't be sure how long the trip will take, but a couple of weeks should be plenty.

'There'll be a passport waiting for you, and a one-way ticket to Ecuador,' he added. 'What you do from there is up to you.'

Moose seemed to like the sound of that. He nodded again, smiling this time. 'I've arranged to get rid of my Harley, so I'll have a bit of spendin' money.'

'OK,' Malcolm answered. 'Have you closed all your bank accounts?'

Moose nodded. 'Good,' Malcolm said. 'No bank accounts, no credit cards. Cash only from here on. We need to make sure there's no paper trail.'

Moose raised his glass. 'Here's to Ecuador,' he said. 'I knew you wouldn't let me down, Bro.'

Chapter 26

Lachie's 19th Birthday

IT WAS THE WINTER BREAK, and Lachie had opted to stay in Perth, rather than return to Kalgoorlie. He and Bronte had moved from her small flat in Nedlands to a unit in the southwestern suburb of Cottesloe. They were within easy walking distance of the ocean, and Lachie went for a run along the sand most mornings. Sometimes, if it was an especially nice day, Bronte accompanied him to the beach and acted as his timekeeper. Mostly, though, she stayed home. Today was an especially nice day, she'd decided.

'You push yourself too hard, my boy,' she said as he struggled to regain his breath. 'All this puffing and panting—for what?'

'I need to increase my lung function,' he managed between breaths. 'Since Ranga and I have been diving, I've realised how unfit I am.'

Bronte shook her head. 'Well, I think you're both crazy.'

Lachie and Ranga had made good on their mutual promise. They were now both qualified PADI divers, and often spent Sunday afternoons on, or under, the water. They'd joined a local SCUBA diving club, which owned its own boat and arranged regular dive trips to various offshore reefs.

'I don't hear you complaining when I come home with a rock lobster or two,' Lachlan said as he pulled on his track pants.

'That's different—you're doing your bit as a hunter/gatherer. It's part of your job description.' They both laughed.

'Anyway, we'd best be going. You don't want to be late for your party.'

Simon and Marita Rose had arranged a family gathering for Lachlan's 19th birthday. Even Malcolm had announced he'd be putting in an appearance, but stressed that he couldn't stay long. Apparently, there was a business meeting he needed to attend— involving some prominent high fliers, or so he'd hinted. Nobody seemed too disappointed about that.

Malcolm had become embroiled in several shady deals over the past decade; one, in particular, had cost him dearly to the benefit of a well-known entrepreneur. Today's get-together, he assured Rachel and Lachie, was to organise another deal designed to reimburse his earlier losses. They both suspected he was being set up for a fall once more, but Malcolm, as usual, knew best.

*　*　*

Lachie and Bronte arrived at the Roses' house around midday. She had insisted on stopping off at Bruce's flat on the way and picking up a small bag of marijuana that Bruce announced he was giving as a birthday gift. 'You may be in for a special treat tonight,' she'd whispered in Lachlan's ear when Bruce left the room.

Rachel arrived about a half-hour later, along with Graham McKinley.

'Hello all,' Rachel said, hugging everyone in turn. She seemed relieved that Malcolm hadn't turned up yet. A hug for him would be a bridge too far, she thought.

'Graham,' Lachie said, shaking the older man's hand as Rachel headed for the kitchen. 'I remember you from last Easter. Are you and Mum ...?'

'Just friends,' Graham cut in. 'Nothing serious. No need to worry.'

'I wouldn't be worried, mate. Unless you gave me reason to,' Lachie answered with a smile. 'If Mum reckons you're worth spending time with, that's all good with me. Us Kincaids are an easy-going lot, in case you hadn't noticed.'

'Sorry, I guess I'm apprehensive about what Rach's family might think. I'm only widowed a couple of years myself. Still not sure if I'm ready to move on yet. Your Mum's been great company, though.'

'Well, she thinks enough of you to invite you here. That says a lot,' Lachie said. 'Anyway, how about a beer?'

'Sure, thanks. I guess one or two won't hurt. A light one, if you've got it. I'll be driving home later, so I'd better go easy.'

'If I know Savta, you'll be spending the night,' Lachie answered, smiling.

'Well, if I do, it'll be on the couch,' Graham responded. 'We're not ... you know ...'

'Sure, mate, whatever you say,' Lachie replied, patting Graham's arm. 'I'll get you that beer.'

As Lachie rummaged through the Esky, looking for a light beer for Graham, Rachel approached him from behind, flinging her arms around him.

'It's so nice to catch up, Lachie. Happy Birthday, by the way.'

'Thanks, Mum.' They exchanged another hug. 'How's Jimmy settling in at the mine? I hardly hear from him these days.'

'He's doing great. He still spends a lot of his time at the School of Mines, and the rest learning the ropes on the mine site. His studies are going really well. Even Malcolm has to admit he'll be an asset to the company, long-term.'

'Wow! Coming from Uncle Mal, that's something!

'He came to visit us at the Cottesloe unit a while back, but he and Bron didn't hit it off. She's not fond of darkies, and she didn't hide the fact.'

'How are you and Bronte getting along? I mean, really?' There was concern in Rachel's voice.

Lachie mulled the question over. 'OK, I guess. We're still getting used to each other. Bron's had a totally different upbringing to me. Still, it'd be pretty boring if we were all the same, wouldn't it?'

Rachel nodded in agreement. 'I suppose so.'

Lachie would have been the first to admit how smitten he was with his beautiful Bronte, despite their differences. She doted on him, and he on her. The sex wasn't bad either.

The rest of the day and evening went well enough. Malcolm arrived just before 2 pm, accompanied by what everyone assumed to be his latest flame, and presented Lachie with his birthday gift. Lachie opened the parcel carefully. Inside was something he had before today only seen mounted behind glass on the wall of Malcolm's office. His eyes widened as he examined the prized gift.

The *skean dhu* had belonged to his grandfather. That much, he knew. He'd admired it often enough in the past, though he'd never held it. It measured about eight inches—or twenty centimetres—with a double-sided blade that accounted for half that length. The scabbard, fashioned from hard black ebony and trimmed with fine silver, gleamed as he turned it in his hands. The handle comprised a single piece of what appeared to be deer horn and was yellowed with age. On the blade, near the hilt, was a small hand-carved crest featuring a three-turreted castle with an arm protruding and holding a sword aloft. There was writing, but he couldn't read the words.

'It's Gaelic,' Malcolm said, seeing Lachie peering at the inscription. 'It translates as 'This, I'll Defend'. That's the clan motto.'

Lachie turned the knife in his hands, sheathing and unsheathing it in wonderment. 'I can't believe this, Uncle Mal.' he said almost reverently. 'You've never let anyone touch this before.'

'I had planned to give it to you on your twenty-first,' Malcolm said. 'But I reckon you're old enough now to appreciate its value, and what it means to the family. That knife is a hundred years old, maybe more. It's the only thing left of what my Dad brought with him from Scotland.' Then he added, with a chuckle, 'There was a tartan, but the moths got it.'

Lachie noticed a small piece—about three millimetres long—missing from the point of the blade. He ran his fingertip over the broken edge. 'That's from the Battle of Culloden,' Malcolm said.

'Yeah, right,' said Lachie. 'I thought you said it was about a hundred years old? The Battle of Culloden was way back in the mid-1700s, wasn't it?'

Malcolm shrugged. 'Well, I'm sure it was from a heroic battle, anyway.'

Lachie proudly showed everyone his amazing gift. 'I promise I'll look after this,' he said to Malcolm. 'I'll mount it in pride of place. I know just the spot.'

'I'll send the display case down to you,' Malcolm said. 'We don't want just any sassenach laying their hands on it.'

Lachie was still admiring the knife when Bronte addressed Malcolm. 'I can see we'll never be introduced if we wait for Lachlan. I'm Bronte, Bronte Sleeman.'

She offered her hand, which Malcolm took with a smile. 'Good to meet you,' he said. 'Your father's Ian, isn't he? I met him once. I believe his firm does a bit of work for Bond Corp.'

Lachie fetched a round of drinks while Bronte chatted with Malcolm and his guest.

Rachel was maintaining a decent distance between herself and Malcolm, preferring to socialise with Graham or her parents. 'Bron appears to be getting along with Malcolm,' she observed as Lachie passed.

'Yeah, seems so,' Lachie replied, glancing back. 'Uncle Mal sure looks different without his beard, doesn't he?'

Rachel looked to where Malcolm and Bronte were talking animatedly. Yes, he looked different, that was certain. Malcolm had done away with his full beard some time ago—reverting to his earlier look with the neat moustache—but lacking the sideburns. In fact, Malcolm appeared almost the same, albeit older, as when Rachel had first met him. Her mind drifted back to those early days. She had fallen quickly and heavily for the suave Malcolm Kincaid, agreeing to accompany him to Kalgoorlie within months of meeting him. But that was before he had let his guard down. Before he showed his true domineering and sometimes violent nature. No matter how much he reminded her of good times, he reminded her of bad times even more.

And what was it with his current choice of girlfriends? Every time Rachel saw a new woman on Malcolm's arm, she seemed younger than the last. How old was this one, she thought, fifteen? OK, that was an exaggeration, but Malcolm was close to fifty now—his latest 'significant other' looked no more than twenty. Rachel tried to recall her name, Portia, was it? She wasn't sure. Not that it mattered. They never lasted long. Girls these days were less naïve and more assertive than in her day. They soon saw through a man like Malcolm Kincaid, no matter how much money he splashed around.

How could two brothers, even half-brothers, turn out so differently? They'd obviously shared the same upbringing. And Jamie, sweet Jamie; oh how she missed him—even after all these years. She found herself once again wishing it had been Malcolm, and not

Jamie, who had died that fateful November night. How much different would their lives have been? She could only guess.

Rachel was suddenly aware of tears welling. She quickly tore herself away from her reverie, mentally admonishing herself for having such uncharitable thoughts. She pulled a tissue from her purse and dabbed at her eyes. *Look up*—she told herself—*look up.*

She rolled her eyes upwards as if trying to examine her own eyebrows, at the same time forcing her tongue against the roof of her mouth. It was a ploy she sometimes used whenever she sensed she was about to cry—something she'd heard, or read somewhere. Over the years since Jamie's death, Rachel had found it useful many times, and it looked like she may well be resorting to it for some time yet.

She glanced across at Graham McKinley. He and Lachie were deep in conversation about clan tartans and family crests. Graham, it seemed, had revealed himself to be a genealogy buff of sorts.

Graham often wept for his late wife, she knew. They hadn't discussed it, but she recognised the wistful expression whenever he mentioned her. She could do a lot worse, she reasoned. He'd made no advances, but Rachel sensed it may come one day soon. Sometimes, shared grief can bind people as tightly as love. And sometimes love can grow without us even being aware of its presence. She liked Graham, liked him a lot, and that was a start, at least.

After an hour or so, Malcolm and his guest left and Rachel's mood lifted markedly. Graham McKinley and Simon Rose found they shared a love of chess and played several games at the outdoor table while Lachie, Rachel, and Bronte swam or sat by the pool. At around five o'clock, Marita called her husband away to man the barbecue. Bronte managed to get through the party and evening meal without offending anyone and even joined the family in a game of canasta at the dining table.

By nine o'clock, though, she insisted she was tired and she and Lachie made their excuses and retired to their room. Once out of sight and earshot, she rolled a joint, took a long toke, and offered it to Lachie. He shrugged and accepted it, inhaling deeply as he watched her slip her dress to the floor. It was his birthday, after all, and they were on holiday from uni. They passed the doobie between them as they slowly undressed, one article at a time.

When she was down to her panties, she stopped and gave him an enticing smile. 'Do you know what a Brazilian is?'

'Someone from Rio, I guess.'

'Not necessarily,' Bronte said, and slipped her panties to the floor, picking them up between her toes and flinging them in his direction.

Lachie stood with his mouth ajar, the last of the joint burning away between his fingertips. 'Wow!' was all he could manage.

'Happy Birthday.' She allowed his gaze to take in all of her full and now complete nakedness, relishing his obvious arousal. Then she asked, 'Would you like to kiss it?'

'If I do, will it kiss me back?'

'Maybe. You'll just have to find out.' Bronte slipped beneath the top sheet, temporarily removing her depilated body from his gaze.

Lachie sucked in the last bit of smoke, burning his fingertips as he did so, but not caring. He dropped the butt into the ashtray and bounded across the room and onto the bed.

He pulled back the sheet, and leaning over her on his knees and one elbow, he kissed her deeply, caressing her entire body with his free hand. He allowed his fingers to linger on Bronte's newly bare mons pubis, and labia, before moving on. The more slowly he aroused her, the better, and yes, he decided, he did want to kiss it. He wanted very much to kiss it.

Lachie turned his attention first to Bronte's earlobes, nibbling them gently the way she liked—then to her by now very erect nipples—before slowly working his way down her body. He paused for a minute at her navel, then eventually reached his intended target. He traced his tongue around the outline of her vagina and wondered why he had not done this before.

Bronte began making soft moaning sounds and opened herself to allow him full access to her most intimate parts. He probed with his tongue and found her clitoris; that tiny, secret thing he hadn't even known existed just three months ago. She spread herself wider, raising her hips as she did so. Her arousal was obvious now. Lachie turned himself until he was looking straight between her legs at her inverted V-shape. *Will you kiss me back*—he wondered.

'We'll need to be quiet Bron, er, Bronte. These walls are paper thin,' he whispered.

'I can be quiet, big boy,' she replied. 'But can you?'

With that, she moved herself quickly to reach his penis, taking his manhood with one hand and guiding it to her lips. Lachie sucked in his breath as he felt her take him into her mouth. His probing tongue stopped briefly as he savoured this new experience. Moving slightly once more, he shifted to take his body weight on his knees, allowing her to do as she wished without hindrance.

How often had she done this before? She definitely seemed to know what she was doing! She first sucked gently, rolling her tongue around in swirling circles, tickling the tip on his urethra and causing him to cry out as if in pain, before drawing him completely into her, then moving backwards and repeating the process.

Lachie was now feeling the ache and knew his climax was near. He turned his attention again to her clitoris, caressing it with his tongue as he inserted his index finger into her as far as he could and moved it inside her. Bronte was past the point of no return now, but didn't break her rhythm. She moaned and bucked in ecstasy, along with Lachie—yet neither of them stopped their efforts for what seemed an eternity, and surely was at least several minutes. Lachie wasn't even sure if they each came once, twice, or more. It seemed to go on and on forever. His head spun. Bruce's birthday gift had certainly done its job.

Finally, they both relaxed and lay panting. 'Happy Birthday, Lover Boy,' she murmured. Lachie was silent for several seconds. 'Where did you learn ...' he began, then decided he didn't want to know.

* * *

The following day, Lachie and Bronte left early, without staying for breakfast. Bronte had spent the first several minutes of the day hunched over the toilet and opted for nothing more substantial than a cup of coffee. Assuming it was somehow connected to the previous night's activities, Lachie had been sympathetic but said little. Now they were alone, she broached the subject that had been on her mind for some time.

'Lachlan, I've missed my period, and this month's is late. I think I may be pregnant.' She waited while the news sank in. 'My parents will be absolutely furious! What are we going to do?'

'How did ...?' he began.

'You're not really asking how it happened, are you?' she said. 'For fuck's sake Lachlan, don't go all stupid on me now.'

'Have you used one of those over-the-counter test kits?'

'Yes. Negative. But I've heard they aren't all that reliable in the first month or two.'

After several agonisingly long seconds, during which he swallowed numerous times, Lachie said, 'Well, we have to know for sure. No point worrying if it's a false alarm. You, my love, need to visit a doctor, and pronto!'

She looked across, trying to read his thoughts. He glanced her way, saying, 'We'll be fine, Bron. If you are, we can decide what to do together. If not ... well, let's not get ourselves in a twist over it right now, anyway.'

Bronte was relieved to see that Lachlan saw it as a shared problem. She hadn't allowed herself to consider how she might react if he walked away. Their relationship was still young, she realised. Yes, she had been taking the pill, she explained, but she often forgot it when she was stoned. In retrospect, maybe she should have taken it in the mornings, not evenings. It was too late for second thoughts now, though.

Lachlan and Harvey were to meet up for a shore dive mid-morning. He offered to cancel, but Bronte insisted he keep with the arrangements. 'Harvey looks forward to your little diving trips, and so do you. As you said, there's nothing we can do about it today.'

The rest of the drive to their apartment passed without conversation—each engrossed in their own thoughts.

Chapter 27

BRONTE HUNG UP THE PHONE. She turned to Lachlan, her eyes brimming with tears.

'It's positive,' she said. 'I'm pregnant, Lachlan. I'm pregnant!' Tears flowed down her cheeks.

He held her close as she sobbed softly. 'I'll have to terminate,' she said. 'We can't be parents, not the way we live.'

Lachie had agonised over how he'd react to this news. He had expected Bronte's initial reaction, though she'd refused any discussion up to now. 'I'm not sure I can go along with that,' he said. 'It's a person, Bron. It doesn't matter how little it is—a life is a life. I can't help it, but that's how I feel. Imagine if our parents had decided they weren't ready when we were conceived—we wouldn't even exist today.'

Bronte examined his eyes for several seconds, as though assessing his commitment.

'That's fine for you,' she said eventually. 'You aren't the one who has to carry it. You won't have to choose between a career and a baby. Can you imagine me wheeling a pram around the university? Can you even begin to imagine what my parents are going to say?' With that, she lost control and burst into tears once more. 'I can't talk about it for now. I can't ...'

Lachlan took her into his arms again and gripped her sobbing frame. It was fully two minutes before she regained control.

'Bronte,' Lachie whispered. 'Whatever you decide, I'll support you. It has to be your choice. I just wanted you to understand how I felt—how I *feel*.'

He waited for a reply. When there was none, he continued, 'I've always thought that life is precious. I'm not religious—it's nothing to do with that. I do believe in fate though, and that all things happen for a reason.'

He paused for a moment, surprised at his own introspection.

'But the ultimate choice has to be yours. Just know that I'm with you, and we don't have to decide right now.'

Bronte held on, not speaking. Despite her otherwise shallow and self-serving nature, Lachlan's frank speech touched her heart, and somewhere, deep within herself, she nurtured similar thoughts. There was indeed a tiny person inside her, and she sensed she had to protect it.

'All right, Lachlan Kincaid,' she said, stepping away and wiping her eyes. 'That was a touching speech. We'll see whether you change your mind a few days from now. I don't want to talk about it until we've both had time to consider it fully.' She turned and walked out onto the patio, where she stood for several minutes, regaining her composure.

*   *   *

Six days later, Lachlan once again raised the subject.

'Bron, you're well aware I've been finding law studies difficult. My heart just isn't in it. I'm not cut out to be a lawyer, and I reckon we both know it. You, on the other hand, seem to relish it.'

Bronte sensed where he was going, but decided not to break his train of thought. 'I guess what I'm saying is that I'd be happy—well, maybe relieved, if I'm honest—to give up full-time study and become a stay-at-home Dad. You keep up your studies and I'll do business law part-time, as a minor subject. It's what I'd originally wanted, anyway. I can also enrol with the School of Mines as a distance student. Again, that's what I really wanted to do from the start.'

'You'd do that? I thought you were just as keen on a legal career as I am.' She knew he wasn't as academically gifted as herself, but she never imagined she'd hear him say he wanted to give it away.

'Not really,' Lachie replied. 'I always wanted to be a part of Kincaid Mining and studying law was just another way for me to do that.'

After a moment, he said, 'What about us getting married? Surely you've considered the idea, even if neither of us has mentioned it.'

'I can't say it hasn't crossed my mind. I don't want you to feel trapped, or pressured, though.' She swallowed hard. 'This is not the way it's supposed to be! We're supposed to plan these things! I always wanted a long engagement, a party, all the trimmings. There'll be no time for any of that.'

'I love you, Bron,' Lachie said with conviction. 'I love you, and I'd love to be your husband if you'll have me. To hell with all the trimmings!'

She fell into his embrace, flinging her arms around him and nuzzling into his neck. 'Of course I'll have you! I wish it could have been different, that's all.'

They held each other tightly for fully two minutes before Lachie spoke. 'OK, so that's settled. Now, there's the next obstacle—telling your folks.'

*   *   *

There were a few days left before the second semester began, so Bronte rang her parents and organised a dinner invitation. She avoided giving any reason for the visit. She didn't want to go into it over the phone and certainly didn't want to start any speculation on their part.

They waited until the meal was complete and Ian, Lachie, and Claire were enjoying an after-dinner port. Bronte had declined and was sipping mineral water.

Ian's 'Lawyers' Radar' had been working overtime ever since they arrived, and he couldn't contain himself any longer.

'So what's the real reason for the visit?' he asked, looking first at Bronte and then at Lachie. 'I can see there's something you're itching to say. May as well spit it out.'

'I'm pregnant,' Bronte said flatly. No point in standing on ceremony, she decided.

Claire's hand froze, her wine glass halfway to her lips. Obviously, she hadn't picked up the vibe as Ian had. 'What?' she spat. 'You're what?'

'Pregnant, Mummy,' Bronte said, turning to face her mother. 'You know, like you were when you and Daddy got married.' There was a palpable pause. Claire's face turned pale, then crimson, reminding Lachie of a cartoon sequence.

'Yes, I've known for ages,' Bronte continued. 'I found your Marriage Certificate when I was looking for the paperwork to get my driving licence three years ago,'

After several more seconds of silence, Lachie spoke. 'We're getting married, with your approval, of course.' He turned to Ian as he said the last part. 'I'm guessing this isn't what you had in mind for your daughter. It's definitely not what we'd planned.' He took Bronte's hand. 'We've talked it over and made a few decisions. We just hope you'll be OK with it all.'

Once Claire had regained her composure and Ian had swallowed the rest of his port and poured another, Lachie and Bronte detailed the plans they had framed. Ian listened quietly, glancing occasionally at his wife, who for once seemed lost for words.

The discussion continued for some time until the young couple convinced the Sleemans that they were fully aware of the decisions they were committing to.

'Well, I suppose we'd best start making arrangements,' Ian announced. 'Nothing can happen inside of a month at least, but aside from that—unless you want your wedding photos to be waist up only—we'd better get a wriggle on.'

Lachie turned to his bride-to-be and said, 'Next, it's my Mum and her family. Ready to do this all over again, Bron?'

'Bronte' she reminded him—again.

* * *

The following day they repeated almost the same sequence with Rachel and the Roses—except for Bronte's revelation about her parents.

Rachel expressed the same reservations about Lachie's future, though she had slightly different reasons for concern. The thought of having Bronte as a daughter-in-law she found distasteful, to put it mildly. She had always hoped the relationship would die a natural death; that sooner or later—sooner, if she were honest—there would come the inevitable clash of opinions or ideals, and they would part. Lachie would soon get over her and move on, while Bronte would find a more suitable partner within her own social clique. Her 'bit of rough', as Rachel assumed she saw Lachie, would become nothing more than another small adventure in her cosseted life.

Rachel hadn't confided these feelings to Lachie, of course. Now, it seemed, she'd have to keep her sentiments to herself or risk alienating her son. Lachie and Bronte were worlds apart in almost every way, but Lachie was, to put it in the bluntest of terms, pussy-struck. He remained smitten by his beautiful fiery-headed siren, and that was that. What Bronte did to keep him that way, Rachel didn't allow herself to contemplate.

Also, a big part of Rachel's motivation in encouraging her son to study law was to limit Malcolm's input in his life. The last thing she'd want would be for Lachie to end up anything like Malcolm Kincaid. The less contact they had, she reasoned, the less chance of Malcolm having any negative influence on him. If Lachie gave up his legal studies in favour of a more hands-on approach within KMC, he would, by necessity, have more contact with Malcolm.

Lachie was a grown man now though and seemed to have formed his own opinions about his 'uncle', so that particular concern held less importance. Rachel's biggest worry was about his future. He would be throwing away a legal career to allow his wife to follow hers. By his own admission, he lacked the motivation to study for a law degree any longer. Would he be able to maintain the self-discipline required for his Plan B with a child under his care?

She expressed these and other doubts to Lachie, but he reminded her of how well she'd coped—and raised him—on her own. There was no way for her to argue with that. Besides, Marita pointed out, all the support he could want was only a suburb away at the Roses' house. In the end, they all agreed on a wedding sometime in July or August.

Chapter 28

Saturday, Aug 1, 1998

THE WEDDING DAY went well, though there had been a few minor dramas in the lead-up. Bronte proved unwilling to accept any form of compromise, despite the short timeframe. She bickered and squabbled with everyone concerned, but eventually accepted that many of her aspirations were unrealistic.

There were five bridesmaids, two flower children, and an acre of flowers and pink and white ribbons. Lachie press-ganged a couple of casual acquaintances to step up as bridegrooms, to make up the numbers. Much to Rachel's distaste, these included Malcolm. Jimmy Browne was Lachie's Best Man while Harvey stepped up as Chief Groomsman.

They held the reception in the palatial gardens of one of Sleeman and Associates' corporate clients, overlooking the Swan River.

After the speeches and other formalities, Jimmy, Lachie, and Malcolm found themselves together, away from the throng. 'Well, Lachie,' Malcolm said, 'I guess you can say goodbye to your sex life now, hey?'

Lachlan gave a quizzical look, to which Malcolm replied, 'You know what they say: No food known to Man destroys a woman's sex drive like wedding cake. Add that to giving birth and I reckon you'll become a regular at the knocking shops in no time.'

He laughed heartily at his own humour, before draining his whisky and stumbling off to revisit the bar.

'How're you getting along with him?' Lachie asked once Malcolm was out of earshot.

'I hardly see him these days,' Jimmy replied. 'He spends all his time in Head Office or back-slapping with the WA Inc mob. Which—between you and me—is the way I prefer it.'

They shared a laugh, before Jimmy asked, 'Where's the honeymoon?'

'Cook Islands. Bron's Dad knows someone, who knows someone, who owns a resort on Aitutaki.'

'Atu-whati?'

'Aitutaki. It's an atoll north of Rarotonga, in the Southern Cooks. Reported to be a genuine tropical paradise.'

'You taking your SCUBA gear?'

'Nah, too costly. I hear you can hire it there, though.'

'Well, if Mal's right, you might be needing it.' Jimmy guffawed, and Lachie joined in.

'Aretha's broken-hearted, you know,' Jimmy said, nudging Lachie's arm. 'She was sure you and Bron would break up before long.' Lachie dismissed his friend's comment with a wave.

Changing the subject, Jimmy asked. 'What about your studies? I reckon your Mum must be pissed off that you're giving that away?'

'I'm doing Business Law as a minor, and taking a course at the School of Mines, as a distance student. Not sure what subject yet. I'm still looking at options.'

'OK, so we'll maybe see you in Kal again one day?'

'That's unlikely. Bron still has her studies and her career with the firm.'

'You make it sound like the Mafia!' Jimmy laughed. Again, Lachie joined in.

'Let's head back to the bar,' he said. 'I need a refill.'

Chapter 29

'I REALLY DON'T HAVE TO GO,' Lachie was telling Bronte. 'Ranga and I can dive any time. I'm not keen on leaving you home on your own right now.'

'Don't be stupid,' she replied. 'The baby isn't due for two weeks, you know that, and I want to finish setting up the nursery—without you in the way!' She gave his chest a playful push to emphasise the point. 'You said you're not going out on the boat this week, and you'll have your mobile phone with you, so stop worrying will you? Just go!'

Lachie and Harvey had been diving regularly over the summer break, mostly from the dive club's boat. This week, they'd agreed to do a shore dive from Cape Peron, west of Rockingham. Lachie wasn't comfortable being on the boat in case 'The Call' came while they were offshore.

There was a little-known reef north of Bird Island, where there were always a few rock lobsters to be found. It was a bit of a swim, but both were young and fit, especially since Lachie had given up smoking pot completely now. With some coaxing, Bronte had also agreed to give up marijuana and alcohol—at least for the immediate future.

They'd assembled a large inner tube with a net drooping about a metre down from the middle, where they stowed their catch, and which they towed behind them. A light anchor and a blue and white 'diver below' flag completed the setup.

Andy Peters and his wife Jean ran the kiosk near the boat ramp. The boys had become friendly with them and usually left their belongings at the shop when they dived in the area. Andy and Jean could always count on a large order of fish and chips when the lads returned, and often a cray or two as a bonus.

It had become a favourite spot for them lately. Few people knew of the location, and the shallowness of the reef meant they could dive for much longer without decompressing.

The two were about fifty metres from the beach, on the return journey, when they heard a yell.

They looked to see Andy approaching the shore at a trot; or at least, what counted as a trot for someone of Andy's build. He was a little over a hundred and sixty centimetres in height, with a paunch that bobbed up and down even when he walked and which now looked like a jelly on a plate. His face was flushed, and he wheezed audibly.

'Here comes The Face That Lunched a Thousand Chips,' Lachie chuckled. 'Wonder what he wants.'

'Lachie!' Andy puffed. 'Just got a call from the hospital. Your wife is in labour!'

'What!' exclaimed Lachie and Harvey in unison. Lachie continued, 'She isn't due for at least two weeks!'

'Well, nobody thought to tell the baby that. You better get out of your dive gear and get moving. The nurse who rang wouldn't tell me anything, but she sounded a bit worried. Just as well you left your phone with me. I nearly didn't answer it.'

The lads quickly dumped their diving gear on the floor of the shop. 'Don't bother putting it away,' Andy said. 'We'll take care of all that. You get going!'

Within minutes, they were in Lachie's Commodore and speeding off toward the hospital. 'What's happening?' Lachie demanded when they finally stood before the doctor. 'Is Bronte OK? What about the baby?'

'Bronte had a fall,' the doctor said, with practised calm. 'I'm afraid her water's broken, and the baby is on its way. I don't think things are all that bad, but she insisted we let you know straight away.'

'Can we see her?' asked Harvey.

'Give me a minute,' the doctor replied. 'I'll check that she's settled and stable. Then you, Lachlan, can see her briefly.' He glanced at Harvey. 'I'm sorry, but it's only one at a time.'

'No problem,' said Harvey. He looked at Lachie. 'I'll wait here. Go see her and give her my best.'

After what seemed ages, Lachie returned, looking troubled.

'Well?' demanded Harvey. 'What's happening?'

'She was hanging drapes, for fuck's sake. How many times have I tried to tell her not to do stuff like that? Bloody obstinate woman.'

'Is she going to be OK?' Harvey's voice shook with emotion. 'And how about the baby?'

'They say she should be OK, but the baby's breech, and not waiting for anyone, so they have to do a caesarian, She had a terrible reaction last time they gave her anaesthetic, but the doctor said they have little choice.' He held his hands over his face, elbows on his knees. 'I'm worried, Ranga. She didn't seem well at all. They're taking her down now. We just have to wait. It's all we can do.'

Lachie felt as if he were in a badly written movie—like he was a parody of the expectant father. He paced, he read, he drank coffee after coffee; he paced some more. He would have smoked a whole packet of cigarettes had he, in fact, been a smoker.

Harvey sat quietly. He wasn't one for worrying much about anything as a rule, and usually let things wash over him. For probably the first time since Lachie and he had met, Harvey couldn't manage even the faintest trace of a smile.

How long had Bronte been in surgery? One thing Lachie felt sure of: it seemed like forever. Eventually, the Registrar appeared in the doorway. One look told them all they needed to know. Pale-faced, Lachie sank into the nearest chair. 'Please say she's all right.'

'There were complications. I'm afraid we had to perform an emergency hysterectomy.' He allowed the news to sink in, then continued, 'I'm so sorry guys, she will not be having any more children. The baby, a boy ...'

'Ian,' said Harvey. 'Ian. If it's a boy, his name is Ian, after our Dad.' He glanced at Lachie, who gave a slight nod of approval.

'Yeah,' Lachie said. 'Bron always said she wanted that.'

Tears welled in his eyes. 'Are ... are they both OK?'

'The child is well, but ...'

'Ian'. Harvey interrupted.

'Yes, Ian.' The doctor cleared his throat and continued. 'He will need to spend some time in a humidicrib, but he'll be fine in a few days. Bronte should be OK. There was some blood loss, but probably no long-term damage.'

'Probably?' it was Lachlan this time.

'She's receiving a transfusion as we speak. Severe blood loss can be a problem, but I'm confident we have everything under control.'

The two friends exchanged concerned looks. It was Lachie again, who spoke first.

Looking at his brother-in-law, he said, 'We'll take turns at waiting with her. If that's all right?' he added, turning to the medico.

'There's really not much you can do,' the doctor said. 'I'd recommend that you go home and get the best night's sleep you can and be here bright-eyed and bushy-tailed in the morning. I think she'll be needing all the support you can give her, under the circumstances.'

They watched Bronte through an observation window for several minutes before leaving. She was obviously sedated. A plethora of tubes and wires connected her to various monitors, and a transfusion bag hung over her. Lights blinked, and the machines beeped, emphasising to Lachie the severity of her situation.

Harvey opted to sleep on the couch in their Cottesloe unit; Lachie agreeing to return him home in the morning. Lachie slept fitfully. He tossed and turned and every dream ended with the same image of Bronte as he had last seen her—surrounded by the trappings of modern medicine, yet so seemingly vulnerable.

When Lachie arrived the next morning, Bronte had just been moved to a private room and was feeding her new infant, assisted by nursing staff. Lachie was relieved to see they had removed the tubes and only her vital signs were being monitored.

She managed a faint smile as he entered, before turning her attention back to the baby. 'Look,' she whispered. 'It's your Daddy.'

The smile, though weak, seemed genuine. Lachie could see, however, that Bronte was still not well. He maintained a distance until she had suckled her new son, then sat beside her, cradling her hand in his.

'Did they tell you all the details?' Bronte asked. Without waiting for his response, she continued. 'I'm so sorry, Lachlan. I so wanted a large family. I know you did too.'

'We have a son. And you're OK. We can't ask much more than that.'

He placed his arms around his distraught wife, holding her close as she sobbed softly. The nurse scooped up the new young Kincaid, who was now sleeping in blissful ignorance of the sad scene being played out so close by.

'I'll take him back to the nursery. If you need anything, just buzz.'

After a short while, Bronte's tears ceased, and she drifted into sleep. It seemed the sedatives they had given her were still having an effect.

Lachie disentangled himself and settled into a nearby chair, where he watched her sleeping for several minutes before tiptoeing out to fetch himself a coffee from the canteen.

As he passed the nurses' station, a receptionist gestured to him. 'There's some paperwork we need filled out,' she said. 'Mrs Kincaid won't be up to it for a bit. Can you take care of it?'

'No problem,' Lachie replied. 'I'm off to grab a coffee. I'll be back as soon as I've got my caffeine fix.'

Fifteen minutes later, as he sat in the ward filling in the birth details, Bronte woke briefly.

'Bron,' Lachie said. 'We haven't talked about a middle name. Have you thought of anything?'

'Ian Wesley,' she murmured. 'My Dad's two names. Unless you want to add your father's name as well.'

'OK,' Lachie said, after a moment's thought. 'Iain Wesley James Kincaid it is.' Then he added, 'Actually, my grandfather had a brother called Iain; it's a family name twice over.'

And he promptly entered those details precisely. Lachie had never actually seen the name Ian spelled out, so he assumed the Scottish variant Iain was the only correct spelling.

'Iain Wesley James Kincaid,' he mused aloud. 'Has a nice ring to it, don't you reckon?' He looked across to Bronte, but she was already asleep once more.

It would be several days before Bronte discovered the anomaly.

Sunday, January 17, 1999

Two days after Bronte arrived home from the hospital, Ian and Claire Sleeman came for their first formal meeting with their grandchild. Bronte had purposely and steadfastly refused to tell them his chosen name.

After welcoming them in, and opening a bottle of champagne bought especially for the occasion, Lachie ushered them into the small spare room, which was now the nursery.

'Sorry, but he's still asleep,' he whispered. 'We thought he'd be stirring by this time, but Bron couldn't bring herself to wake him.'

They gazed at the sleeping infant for a few moments before Claire whispered. 'So what is his name, then? And why all the secrecy?'

Lachie handed them a large manilla envelope. 'Have a look for yourselves,' he said, beaming.

Ian Sleeman opened the envelope with exaggerated slowness, prolonging the tension and infuriating Claire more and more as he did. Eventually, they both read the enclosed birth certificate with puzzled expressions. It was Ian who first spoke.

'Is this a mistake? I mean, I'm flattered and all that, but why the strange spelling?'

Bronte snatched the certificate from him and read, for the first time, the names written. Her mouth fell open. She turned to Lachlan, whose expression hadn't changed from the look of expectancy he had when he handed the form to her father.

'What the hell is this?' she spat. 'We talked about his names several times. I even let you add your father's name. What's this?' she stabbed the offending item with her index finger. 'Since when do you spell Ian like this?'

Lachie took the document and read aloud: 'Iain Wesley James Kincaid. What's wrong with that?'

'Ian is I-A-N!' she almost screamed. 'Where did you get the extra 'I' from? Were you drunk?'

'But … that's how my Great Uncle spelled his name. That's the only way, isn't it?'

'It's OK.' Ian cut in. 'Really, Bronte, don't make a fuss over it. His name is Ian, however it's spelled. I appreciate the gesture, and I thank you both.' He shifted his gaze to include Lachie as he spoke.

'You fucking idiot!' Bronte hissed at Lachlan. 'I can't rely on you to do anything right, can I.'

Lachlan stood open-mouthed, caught totally off guard by her onslaught. She had been moody since the birth, but this ...?

'Bron,' her father spoke, 'there's no need for ...'

'Like fucking hell there's not!' Bronte was really steaming now. 'I've been carrying this loser for ages. Did you know he's planning to drop out of law studies altogether? Apparently, it's all just too hard for Mister Lachlan Kincaid! Oh, didn't we tell you that part? He wants to be Mister Mom while I study and then earn the money. What sort of man does that sound like to you?'

She directed her attention to her hapless husband, while Ian and Claire watched, stunned. 'Do you really think your precious Uncle Malcolm is going to carry you forever?'

'Bron,' Lachie stammered, 'this isn't the time or place for this conversation. That's something we've only talked about, and I said I'll continue for now. In any case, I'll be part of Kincaid Mining in the long term. Uncle Mal says ...'

'Uncle Mal,' Bronte sneered. 'You want to hear about your Uncle Mal? The first time I met him, he tried it on with me. He's an arsehole and a loser!'

The baby Iain was now well and truly awake and screaming his protest at the disturbance. Bronte scooped him into her arms and held him close, simultaneously cooing in his ear while shooting daggers at Lachlan.

'Perhaps we should go,' Ian Sleeman offered. 'Thanks for the invitation, both of you.' Then he added, 'I really think you have some serious talking to do.'

'You may as well take him with you,' Bronte said. 'I don't want to see his face right now.'

Lachie grabbed his coat and keys and started for the door. 'I'll be spending the night at Ranga's place,' he said over his shoulder.

At the threshold, he turned and added, 'Bron, I know you're not well, and I appreciate that you're pissed off. When you feel ready to talk this over, call me.'

With that, he left. He was in his car and out of the driveway before Ian and Claire were clear of the front porch.

* * *

Bronte rang a little before midday the following day. Lachie had barely slept, and he lay on the lounge in front of the TV, idly flicking from one channel to another. 'Yeah?' he said.

Lack of sleep and brooding about Bronte's outburst had left him in a dark mood. There was also the revelation about Malcolm making a pass at her. Could that be true? Maybe she'd made it up for extra effect?

After several seconds of silence, Bronte spoke. 'Come home, Lachlan. I'm sorry I overreacted. Please come home and let's put last night behind us.'

He waited for a moment before replying. He knew how difficult it would have been for Bronte to say those words. In fact, it was possibly the first time he'd actually heard her apologise for anything. Of course, he'd come home. Of course, he'd forgive her. Yes, he was aware of how much she wanted to please and surprise her father. He stopped short of agreeing he should have checked the spelling with her, though. That would have been a little too much back-pedalling.

On the drive back to Cottesloe, Lachie replayed the incident in his mind. All the things he planned to say to her—everything he'd mentally rehearsed—were now evaporating. What was the point, anyway? Lachie just wanted to hold her in his arms and forget the previous night's drama altogether. And he wanted to hold his son—the newest Kincaid, and the eventual heir to the throne of Kincaid Mining Corporation.

Chapter 30

Tuesday, April 6, 1999

MALCOLM SWALLOWED the last of his beer and ordered another, and a malt whisky chaser. 'In fact, make that a double,' he told the barmaid.

Malcolm had arrived in Kalgoorlie a little over an hour ago—having ridden up from Perth on his newest acquisition, a Harley Davidson Fat Boy—and now sat firmly ensconced at the bar of the Lucky Miner. He'd picked up this new toy the previous day and set off just before dawn on his new ride's maiden trip. He told himself it was to run the machine in, but there was also an ulterior motive.

His plan was to ride straight to the Two Brothers mine and take care of business as only he could. On arriving in town, though, he succumbed to the desire for a decent drink and detoured to the tavern.

The decor was changed, and the venue didn't seem as welcoming as it once had. Although several years had elapsed since he'd last visited, he somehow expected to see familiar faces and hear familiar sounds. Instead, the room was empty except for a couple of middle-aged suit-clad businessmen in a secluded booth, and a group of twenty-somethings chattering noisily and sharing videos on their phones. Gone were the dance floor and stage, replaced by a buffet bar and a CD jukebox; the latter assaulting his ears with some hip-hop crap that somehow seemed to match the gaudy colour scheme.

At least, Malcolm grudgingly admitted to himself, that fag Jerome had kept the place looking good when he was in charge. The beer was still excellent, however. The Scotch was even better.

He finished the whisky in quick time and ordered a refill. Oh, yes. There was business to take care of, and he was just the man to do it. For now, though, he would enjoy one more drink before firing up his new machine and heading north.

As he reached the mine entrance, Malcolm throttled down and pulled to a halt opposite the white quartz megalith. The bold red lettering was still there, if faded somewhat.

Scars and gouges, along with the last traces of grey paint and black rubber, bore silent testimony to the horror that had occurred there so long ago. Time marches on, but memories can remain—burned into the consciousness as if by an infernal flame. Even after over eighteen years, he couldn't be in this spot without the echoes of that fateful November night surging like a tsunami, invading his mind. He could still hear the terrible sound of the impact. Still see Jamie's form slumped behind the wheel. Still feel the terrible ache of helplessness as they loaded Jamie into the ambulance.

He tore himself from the view and restarted the big V-Twin. He hadn't told Rachel he was coming, but she would know as soon as she heard the familiar rumble from his machine.

Rachel looked up from her work as Mal entered the Two Brothers Mine site office.

'Malcolm,' she said. 'What brings you to the back-blocks? We rarely see you here these days.'

He stood and faced Rachel, who sat waiting to learn what had lured Malcolm Kincaid away from the corporate suite in Perth, with all its trappings of wealth and power.

'Lachlan,' he said bluntly, as if the name alone conveyed everything he needed to say.

Rachel waited for him to elaborate, sensing she might not like what was coming.

'You know he's doing uni part time now, as well as studying with the School of Mines. I'd like him to take on a more active role in the company.'

Rachel fixed him with a suspicious stare. Where was this heading? She wondered.

'Mal, I don't want you interfering in his life. He has responsibilities. He doesn't need you leading him from pillar to post.'

There was no one else present, so Malcolm spoke more bravely than he otherwise might have. 'He's my son. I reckon I have the right to …'

'He'll never be your son!' Rachel interjected. 'Never in a million years. You promised me you'd keep your distance.'

Malcolm leaned over the desk, his face just inches from Rachel's. She smelled the whisky on his breath and noticed his two-day stubble.

'I reckon it's time we renegotiated our deal.' He spoke slowly, evenly, with a menacing tone she hadn't heard in a long time. Suddenly, she realised she was looking at the old Malcolm, the one she once feared so much.

'If you come forward with your rape accusations now, after all these years, I don't think there's a judge in the land that wouldn't throw the case out of court. In fact, I happen to know a magistrate or two who would be only too happy to repay a debt to me by slapping you with perjury charges.'

Rachel's face was suddenly pale. This, she had not expected.

'I propose a new agreement,' Malcolm continued. 'You keep your trap shut about our little, er, misunderstanding, and I'll neglect to mention to our son just who his real father is. Meanwhile, I will take on the responsibility of guiding Lachie's career in Kincaid Mining Corporation. He needs a man's influence, not yours, and certainly not the influence of that ball-buster of a wife of his.'

He paused momentarily, catching his breath. 'She's got him at home changing nappies, for fuck's sake! And from what I can make out, you were right behind the whole damn thing!' A fine spray of saliva accompanied the last sentence.

Rachel stared, wide-eyed and too stunned to reply. How long had he been stewing over this? It was true he hadn't been a party to the new direction Lachie's life had taken, but it was Lachie's decision to make, and his alone. Rachel and her family supported him totally—but the choice had been his.

She opened her mouth to speak, to tell him as much, but thought better of it. Instead, she blurted, 'You're bluffing!'

'I never bluff,' Malcolm snarled through clenched teeth. 'You know I never bluff. Do you really want to call me on this?'

Rachel struggled to contain herself. Her hands were shaking. Her mind raced, seeking a suitable reply.

Malcolm broke the impasse. 'So I'll take that as a *no*,' he said, straightening.

Backing away from the desk and wiping his mouth with the back of his hand, Malcolm stared Rachel down one last time before saying, 'Well, that's settled, then. I'll create an opening for him at head office. He can keep up his corporate law studies, but he'll be working directly under me.'

He turned on his heels and, before leaving, spun around once more to face Rachel. 'We have a son, not a daughter. Deal with it.'

And with that, he strode outside, swung himself onto the seat of his Harley, and roared off down the access road.

Rachel sat for several minutes, struggling to contain her tears. Her headache was back, worse than it had been for a long time. She considered calling the police to report him for riding under the influence. At least that would give her some satisfaction, she reasoned, before deciding it would be a petty gesture. Besides, he probably had the local boys in blue in his pocket, anyway. It was true he held considerable sway within certain circles these days.

After washing her face at the sink in the lunchroom, she picked up the phone and dialled the supervisor's office. Her own voice greeted her, courtesy of the answering machine, informing her that James Browne, the Mine Supervisor, was unavailable, and could she please leave a message.

'Hello, Jimmy?' Rachel said in what she hoped sounded like a cheery tone. 'I'm closing up early today. If there's anything you need me for, call my mobile.'

Rachel took two Endone tablets, washing them down with a beer from the office fridge —something she normally would never do. She lay on the stretcher at the back of the building for several minutes until her headache eased, then locked up and left.

Chapter 31

May 1999

AND SO, LACHLAN FOUND HIMSELF in the position of Personal Assistant and Understudy to Malcolm Kincaid, with Special Responsibility for Legal Issues. Malcolm allocated him an office alongside his own. There was a large window separating the two, from which Malcolm arranged to have the drapes removed.

One Saturday, a month into the new arrangement, Lachie took Bronte in for a visit.

'So,' she was saying, 'this is where it all happens. The beating heart of Kincaid Mining Corporation.'

Lachie ushered her proudly into his office, ignoring her touch of sarcasm. 'What do you think?' He spread his arms to envelop the scene.

'Where does Ian spend his days?' she asked, looking around. 'I'm guessing not in here.'

'We've set up a creche on the next floor. Actually, it's pretty handy, as Uncle Mal's secretary has a two-year-old. He's hired a woman to look after them both.'

She said nothing. They'd discussed this part of the arrangement, and Bronte had made it clear she did not like the idea at all.

'You can take him out anytime you want, Bron. I mean, if you have an afternoon off or something. Maybe I could sneak off too if Uncle Mal's out. He usually disappears on Friday afternoons, by the way.' He gave her a playful nudge, and she rewarded him with a smile, of sorts.

'How are things working out between you and Malcolm?' she said.

Lachie confided that he had mixed feelings about the arrangements. He'd always wanted to be an integral part of the corporation, but didn't enjoy having to answer to Malcolm on every issue. 'The only time he really lets me have any input is if it's a legal matter,' he explained. 'And even then, he still gets an opinion from Lurie and Singh before he'll accept what I say. Sometimes I reckon he thinks I don't know my arse from my elbow.'

This rankled the younger Kincaid, but he realised he'd have to earn his stripes. Eventually, he reasoned, Malcolm would come to recognise that Lachie knew his stuff and learn to trust him implicitly.

'Well, that's Malcolm,' she replied, before asking, 'How does your Mum feel about you working here? There's not much love lost between the two of them, is there?'

'Actually, she didn't make a fuss like I thought she might. She wasn't pleased, but she said so long as I'm happy, and it doesn't interfere with my studies ...' He shrugged.

Rachel's protests, or lack of them, puzzled him. He'd expected her to refuse to let his uncle take him under his wing this way. Perhaps she was softening her attitude? There was something in their shared past that caused his mother not to trust Malcolm—that was no secret. She, and his Saba and Savta, made no bones about their low opinion of his uncle, and of his dubious business practices. Still, Lachie reasoned, now that he was a part of the inner sanctum of KMC, surely he could have an influence on management decisions. At least, that's what he told himself. Circumstances, however, would test this hypothesis before long.

There was another issue that had been causing Lachie to lose a lot of sleep: Ever since the birth of their son, Bronte's state of mind had see-sawed between euphoric highs and depressing lows. Some days, he wondered if her sanity itself was in jeopardy. She was back to using marijuana regularly, starting from only a week after she returned home from the hospital. How she kept up with her studies, God only knew.

August, 2000

FIFTEEN MONTHS into the arrangement with Malcolm, Lachie announced he was abandoning his legal studies.

'I might have known,' Bronte said tersely.

'It's just not for me—I'm not the lawyer type. I'll stay with my course at the School of Mines, but Uncle Mal keeps me so busy these days I'm barely able to keep up with that. Now he wants me to go and sort out some issues up at Skull Creek.'

'Skull Creek?' Bronte asked, 'Where the hell is that?'

'It's that new mine we took over a few months back, remember? Up near Marble Bar. Some bloke owned and operated it as a one-man show. Seems he'd been mining underground and processing on-site, but was cutting corners with the tailings.'

'Tailings? That's the waste from the processing, isn't it?'

'Yeah. He was supposedly retaining the runoff in a dam, but it's been leaking into a creek used by a local Aboriginal settlement. They complained to him, but it seems it was like talking to a brick. Eventually, the Government stepped in and for a while, it seemed the silly old sod would be out of business at best, and might even spend some time in jail. Uncle Mal heard about it and offered to help him out of his predicament.'

'Malcolm, helping someone?' Bronte said with a laugh.

Lachie joined in the mirth. 'You know Uncle Mal.' He added a chuckle of his own. 'Never let a chance go by ...

'It seems old Wally Bright ... that's his name, apparently ...'

Bronte laughed again at the hapless miner's unfortunate name before Lachie continued, 'Yeah, well Mr Bright offered a controlling interest in the mine to KMC for a song just to get himself out of the shit. He hoped that with Kincaid Mining on his side, he could sweep it all under the carpet.'

'And that's where Malcolm came in,' Bronte said. 'Mister Fixit, with all the right people on his payroll.'

'Got it in one,' said Lachie. 'Funny thing though. Wally Bright disappeared as soon as we'd completed the takeover. No one has a clue where he's gone. He was supposed to be acting as manager—under Uncle Mal's supervision, of course.'

'How odd,' Bronte said.

'Anyway, Uncle Mal has some good contacts within the Environment Ministry—as he has in most Government departments—and he reckons he can get them off our back. My job will be to liaise with the residents at the settlement while we fix the problem. He also wants Jimmy to go with me. I guess he figures they'll take more notice of what we say if we have a blackfella on the team.'

'That sounds like Malcolm's sort of logic,' Bronte said. 'Does he really think they'll be that gullible?'

'What he does think is that we need to appease them as much as possible and keep it out of the news,' Lachie replied. 'Whether having Jimmy on the team will be a help or a hindrance, I'm not sure. Jimmy's family is from the central desert people. I told Uncle Mal they don't even speak the same language, but you know how he is where Aboriginals are concerned.'

'I know how he is where most people are concerned.' was Bronte's curt reply.

* * *

It was in the first week of September 2000 that Lachie and Jimmy made the long drive up the Great Northern Highway toward the mining town of Newman, a distance of just under 1300 kilometres. They had spurned Malcolm's offer of travelling by air, preferring to treat it as something of an adventure. Jimmy had flown from Kalgoorlie to Perth, spending the night with Lachie and Bronte, before the pair set off just before dawn on a crisp Spring Saturday morning.

The whole trip, with the two lads sharing driving duties, they expected to take a little over 24 hours, including an overnight stopover. Lachie's Commodore seemed to relish the long drive, and they were soon ignoring most of the speed restrictions. They stopped briefly at Mount Magnet to refuel both the car and themselves, and also at Meekatharra, where they took the opportunity of walking around one or two local open-cut mines, rubber-necking from beyond the perimeter fences.

Later, as sunset approached, Lachie eased back on the speed a little. 'That guy at Meekatharra warned us about cattle on these roads,' he reminded Jimmy. 'The last thing we'd need right now would be a big steer coming over the bonnet and into our laps.'

'Now that might ruin our whole day,' Jimmy said with a smile.

At a little after eight PM, they arrived at Capricorn Roadhouse, just outside Newman, where they had booked their accommodation. Next morning, after a hearty 'truckie's breakfast' the two set off for the Skull Creek mine site, arriving just before midday.

'What a mongrel of a road,' Jimmy said, running a finger through the brown film of dust covering their vehicle. 'I expected the poor bloody car to fall apart.'

Lachie eyed his pride and joy with dismay. If he'd known what to expect, he would have hired a 4X4, he reflected. He was not looking forward to the return trip. Still, while they were here, at least, they could use one of the mine Land Cruisers. They'd not be any more comfortable, but at least they wouldn't have to worry about the vehicle being shaken to pieces. He'd definitely take the Commodore to his mechanic for a once-over on their return.

'I haven't seen corrugations like that before in my life!' Lachie shook his head in dismay.

After a brief tour of the workings and the tailings dam, guided by the recently appointed supervisor, Lachie phoned Malcolm.

'OK, gimme the good and bad news,' Malcolm said with little emotion.

'The dam is about a kilometre from the creek,' Lachie began. 'And yes, it's definitely been leaching into the gully and the runoff is finding its way into Skull Creek waterhole.' He paused, and when Malcolm didn't reply, he continued. 'Jimmy and I will head over to the settlement tomorrow morning and see what their chief concerns are. I'm no health expert, but I'd be expecting some serious long-term issues with anyone unlucky enough to be drinking or bathing in that water.'

'Bathing?' Malcolm spurted. 'These are boongs you're talking about. They don't bathe!'

Jimmy shifted uncomfortably. From where he stood, he couldn't help but overhear Malcolm's outburst. Lachie shot him a glance, rolling his eyes. He knew better, however, than to speak out against his Uncle Mal.

'Either way,' Lachie continued, 'we may have a major health issue on our hands. The dam looks as though it's been overflowing whenever they've had heavy rain, and we only have a month or two before the start of the next wet season.'

'OK,' Malcolm replied. 'Find out what they want to make it all go away. Just don't make too many promises, all right? I've been putting a bit of pressure on a couple of my contacts in Government. As long as we can appease the elders up there, we should be able to sail through this without too much fallout. In the meantime, I'll arrange for some earthmovers to get out there and do whatever's necessary to stop any future runoff. This was all supposed to be taken care of before now by Wally bloody Bright!'

Lachie sighed softly. Malcolm was used to getting his own way and intended that this time would be no different. He glanced across at his friend again. Involving Jimmy in something like this was not a good idea, he thought. Mal should have realised that, but as usual, Malcolm Kincaid—the Mister Fixit and Puppet Master extraordinaire—could never be expected to see anything except what he wanted to see.

The following day, Lachlan and Jimmy drove over to Skull Creek. Wirtakarrimaya—the traditional name for the collection of prefabricated buildings that made up the settlement—consisted of several dwellings arranged in a roughly circular pattern around a central building that served as a meeting place and also a communal eating and cooking area.

After making some enquiries, they were introduced to George Mitchell, a tribal elder Lachie had contacted earlier by phone.

George Mitchell was a tall man. His lithe and athletic frame belied his apparent age, which Lachie thought was probably somewhere in his early sixties. Lachie doubted that was his actual name; he would have a tribal name that only those close to him would know. George's ebony skin was wizened from many years under the harsh Australian sun, and he had the typical broad nose and dense, tousled hair of an aboriginal. The latter, along with his thick beard, carried a tinge of grey, and he was missing two of his front teeth. George's eyes, deep and dark, twinkled with a hidden intelligence that Lachie thought many might have missed.

There was something else about George Mitchell. George's gaze unnerved Lachie. It appeared to penetrate in a way he could not put into words. It was almost as if the old man could read Lachie's mind. That was impossible, of course... wasn't it?

George spoke slowly, picking his words carefully, as though he was aware he might easily be misunderstood. Clearly, English was not his mother tongue.

'When Wally Bright first come up 'ere 'e seemed a decent bloke,' George said. 'Asked if we minded 'im fossickin' around in the gully back there.' He gestured with his chin in the mine's direction. 'He'd drop by now and then and even 'ave a beer with summa the fellas. We don't allow grog 'ere usually, but 'e didn't cause any trouble.

'Once he found some pay dirt, though, things changed. Seems he filed a claim over most of the land around here, including our camp.'

'You needn't worry about your homes,' Lachie quickly interjected. 'There's no way we'll be interfering with your settlement. Besides, I reckon your rights will override ours, anyway.'

'Yeah, well, next thing we know, he's digging into that hill and dumping the rocks and stuff into the gully to build a dam. Then he set up his processing plant and before we know it, the dam's overflowing down into our creek. We tried to talk to him but he says he's got the right to do what he wants and us black pricks can go fuck ourselves.'

'Wally Bright's gone,' Lachie said evenly. 'The mine now belongs to Kincaid Mining Corporation. We'll fix things up so you'll have no more problems with tailings runoff. Jimmy and I are here to work out just what needs doing to make it right.' He gestured toward his friend.

George Mitchell looked at Jimmy suspiciously and addressed him in a language Lachlan Kincaid had never heard. Jimmy shrugged and said. 'Sorry George, I'm from Kalgoorlie. My mob are from the central desert people. I don't speak your lingo.'

'Might've known,' George replied. 'Send a blackfella up 'ere to soften us up and 'e can't even talk to us.'

'Jimmy and I have been mates for years,' Lachie cut in. 'He's a supervisor at the Two Brothers Mine, north of Kalgoorlie. Jimmy's not here to soften you up. He's here to be my assistant and advisor.'

George looked again at Jimmy. 'You work for this Kincaid Mining mob?' he asked, jerking his thumb in Lachie's direction.

'Yep,' Jimmy assured him. 'Just like he said.'

After a brief pause, Lachie spoke again. 'Has much of the runoff found its way into the waterhole? We'll have to do some testing to make certain the water's OK for your people to use.'

'Maybe a bit in the last big wet,' George replied. 'Can't be sure, though. Water tasted funny for a while, but we got used to it. Some fish and yabbies died, but not all of 'em.'

Lachie nodded. They'd be sending some water samples away for analysis, that much was certain. Hopefully, there wouldn't be excessive pollution, and they could resolve the issue before the looming rainy season.

Lachie rose to his feet. 'Well, if it's all good with you, we'll grab some samples now and send them off for testing. There are some pretty dangerous chemicals used in gold mining. I'd hate for your people to have ingested anything that can make them sick.

'After the results come back, we'll know for certain. In the meantime, do you have access to another water supply?'

'Nope.' said George, shaking his head, 'Where you gonna find any other water 'round 'ere?'

'OK,' Lachie replied. 'Tell you what—I'll arrange for a water tank to be delivered here for you to use for drinking and cooking. I reckon you'll be able to bathe in the waterhole, but tell everyone not to drink it until the results come through.'

George's face softened. Offering his hand to Lachie, he said, 'OK Lachlan. I'm thinking maybe you're not such a bad fella after all. When will this water tank get 'ere?'

'Tomorrow, I hope,' Lachie replied. 'Within a few days, definitely.'

He felt the old man's grip tighten on his. George was looking deep into Lachie's eyes for what seemed the longest time; but in reality, was barely a second or two.

'See you later, then,' said George, and the pair took their leave.

After filling two plastic bottles from different areas of the waterhole, they climbed into their vehicle and headed back to the mine.

'Sorry I couldn't be more help,' Jimmy said once they were back on the road. 'People assume that all us abos talk the same language, but there are hundreds of dialects. I can hardly speak my own people's lingo, let alone Pilbara Nyamal.'

Lachie gave him a puzzled look.

'The language he used when he spoke to me. A dialect of the Pilbara mob, I think. I'm not sure, though, and like I said, I can barely hold a conversation in Martu Wangka, my own mob's lingo.'

'Ah well, no worries, mate,' said Lachie. 'We'll need to earn their respect. The best way to do that is to fix Wally Bright's stuff-up and see that it doesn't happen again.'

After a minute, Lachie said, 'What about George—did you get a vibe from him? I couldn't put my finger on it, but there was something odd about the bloke.'

'I think he's more than just an Elder,' Jimmy said. 'I reckon he might be a Kurdaitcha. Sort of a Witch Doctor, or Featherfoot, as some call them. When I was little, my mum used to warn us kids about the Kurdaitcha Man, but I didn't believe it—until now.'

Lachie looked closely at his friend. Jimmy was dead serious. Even his pallor had lightened. 'I've heard of the Featherfoot,' he said. 'People reckon they can walk anywhere without leaving footprints.'

'Something like that. One thing I do know is that I'd rather have him as a friend than an enemy.'

Back at the mine site, the two opened a can of beer each and settled themselves under one of the few shady trees in the area. The mine had suspended operations until they resolved the pollution issue, so there wasn't much else to be done for now.

The next day, an earthmoving crew arrived and Lachie showed them what was required. After some discussion, they decided to reinforce the existing dam to prevent further runoff and create a replacement on the far side of the hill. From there, none of the waste could find its way down to Skull Creek and the settlement.

Lachie entrusted the water samples they had taken the day before to the pilot driver who had escorted the truck, with instructions to send them to Perth by Priority Post. He figured it would only be a few days before Malcolm received the reports. He then phoned Malcolm with the latest update.

'Righto,' Malcolm said when Lachie had brought him up to speed. 'I'll get you two to stay there for now and supervise the new earthworks. Make sure the job's done properly this time.

'Smart move, by the way, to organise that water delivery. That should get us some Brownie points with the camp dwellers.'

No mention, Lachie thought, of the fact that the "camp dwellers" had been using that water for ages, or of how many health issues might have been caused in that time. No, Malcolm's only concern was looking good, not necessarily doing good. Lachie wondered just what might show up in the water assessments.

'OK, Uncle Mal, I'll keep you updated on the progress here. Let me know when you get the sample results. I'm a bit concerned about long-term problems for the locals.'

'Sure, mate. When they come in, you'll be the first to know.'

The water sample results were bothering Malcolm too, though not for the same reasons they bothered Lachie. He had his thoughts focused on how to minimise any fallout. The last thing Kincaid Mining needed was the media getting hold of the story and blowing it out of proportion. He'd probably have to grease quite a few palms to get this swept under the rug. No real problem though—he'd done it before and was sure he'd have to do it again. It was just a part of doing business in Malcolm Kincaid's eyes.

* * *

Three days later, Malcolm phoned with the news. Yes, there was contamination of the water—it would have been pointless trying to convince Lachlan otherwise—but not as bad as they thought it might have been. He'd consulted a medical laboratory, and they had assured him there would be no long-term effects for the locals.

'We'll let the old tailings dump dry out, and then later we can cover it with a few feet of soil,' Malcolm told Lachie. 'Once the new dam's finished, we can ramp up production again. We've lost too much money already.

'I've also arranged for a drilling team to visit the site and sink a bore. We can use that to top up the Skull Creek waterhole.'

He assured Lachie that he'd organise continual monitoring of the billabong for safe levels of contaminants.

Lachie revisited the settlement the following day and relayed Malcolm's assurances. George Mitchell expressed his thanks, although Lachie sensed a hint of healthy suspicion.

The water delivery had arrived the day before and was being put to good use. Several naked children were happily hosing each other down, squealing with delight as they did so.

'Hey, you kids!' George shouted. 'That's for cooking and washing only. Use the trough.'

'Ahh, let 'em have some fun,' said Lachie. 'I'll order another delivery for tomorrow.'

'Thanks, but they know better than to waste water like that,' George replied. 'So you say the waterhole's OK to swim in?'

'According to the reports, yes.'

'You kids can use the creek water,' George informed the young group. 'Just remember not to drink any of it.'

With cries of delight, the naked, shiny, wet group raced to the creek and, jumping in turn from a large log, splashed about happily in the water. 'Remember, don't drink!' George called after them.

Chapter 32

LACHIE AND JIMMY made the return trip to Perth a week later. The mine was already back in production, using Wally Bright's tunnelling method for the time being. Although the operation was currently underground, plans were in place to turn it into an open-cut mine in the coming months.

Three weeks after the pair's return, Malcolm summoned Lachie to his office. Without bothering with preliminaries, he said, 'How would you like to take over the running of Skull Creek?'

'Skull Creek? I thought everything was under control up there.'

'I'm thinking we should bring forward our plans to go open-cut,' Malcolm replied. 'Tunnelling's not the answer in that type of rock, you know that. Wally should have known it, too.'

'Yeah, but I thought …'

'Well, you thought wrong. And so did John Biggs.'

John Biggs had been managing the Skull Creek mine since KMC's acquisition of the operation. Lachie knew there had been a clash of opinions between him and Malcolm and guessed it had probably come to a head.

'I need someone up there I can trust, and who knows what they're doing,' Malcolm continued. 'So I'm sending you and your coon mate, Jimmy, to take over the transition. I want Skull Creek in full production ASAP.

'You two seemed to get along with the locals, and you both know your jobs, so I figure if I send you both up on a four-week rotation each, we should be able to get it all sorted.'

Lachie was silent for several seconds. 'I'll need to speak to Bron. I'm not sure how she'll feel about it.'

'She can live without you for four weeks at a time,' Malcolm replied. 'And you can afford child care. I pay you enough.'

'I'll get back to you in the morning,' Lachie said. 'I should be able to talk her around.'

'Don't ask her, tell her!' Malcolm told his protégé. 'For fuck's sake, be the man in the household, not the resident wimp.'

*　*　*

That night, Lachie and Bronte discussed the matter over dinner. Things had been more than a little tense between them lately—she wasn't happy about Lachie working with Malcolm, nor his giving up his studies. The many recent late evenings at the office didn't help either.

She hadn't told him, but Bronte had mentioned this to Rachel recently and discovered she had an unexpected ally. Rachel hadn't gone into detail, but having a shared dislike of Malcolm had fostered a new spirit of affinity between them.

'I suppose we can work around it,' Bronte said, after listening to Lachie's proposal.

'I can leave Ian with Mummy most days,' she mused, then added, 'What about when you're back in Perth? Will you still have to go in to the office every day?'

'Probably not,' Lachie replied. 'Certainly not as much as I do now, anyway.'

'Well, I hardly see you most days as it is,' Bronte replied. 'You might as well do it. Especially if we get to spend time together when you're down here.'

This, she reasoned, might be the perfect chance to put some distance between her husband and his manipulative uncle. Hopefully, the arrangement might even become permanent.

Lachie was surprised and relieved at how easily Bronte warmed to the idea. He had expected more resistance. Bronte was not the archetypical doting mother, and she seemed to like Lachie being the primary caregiver.

The following day, Malcolm and Lachie ironed out the details. Jimmy and Lachie would each spend 30 days at a time at Skull Creek, with an overlap of two days at each end of their stints. That way, each could brief the other on any situations that might arise. An upside—one that Lachie did not mention to Malcolm—was that it would give the two friends some time together, which may or may not be spent at the mine. There was good fishing to be had around Port Hedland, and it was only a two-hour drive away.

On their breaks, Jimmy could return to Kalgoorlie, while Lachlan could spend most of his time with Bronte and Iain.

Chapter 33

June, 2002

THE SHARED MANAGEMENT arrangement had been operating for around twenty months. Skull Creek open-cut mine was in full production, with plans in place for further expansion.

They had the water situation well in hand, with samples regularly sent down to Perth for testing. Lachie and Jimmy both spent much of their time, when work permitted, at the settlement, and Lachie and George had forged a solid friendship.

Jimmy's motives for frequenting the camp were a little more personal. He'd developed an attachment with a local girl of about eighteen and sometimes took to staying overnight. Jimmy never neglected his responsibilities at the mine, though, and was always at his desk on time, regardless of what might have taken place the night before.

Around halfway through one of Lachie's scheduled breaks, he offered a suggestion to Bronte.

'Say, Bron,' he opened. 'You're not really doing much this semester break, are you? Why don't you come up to the mine with me? We can make it a family outing. I reckon Iain would love a few days in the bush.'

'Eew.' Bronte screwed up her nose. 'With all the flies, mosquitoes, snakes and what have you? I'm not sure about that.'

'Oh, come on,' Lachie chided. 'It's not all that bad. We never go anywhere together, and the weather's good up there this time of year. It'll be an adventure!'

After a bit of banter, Bronte reluctantly agreed to Lachie's proposal. 'I'm not staying up there for four weeks, though,' she insisted. 'We'll all go up together and Ian and I will stay a week or so. Ten days maximum.'

'OK,' Lachie agreed. 'There's a spare donga up at the camp. We can go up a week early, and you can fly back when my rotation starts. That way, I'll be able to show you around the area. I know of a hidden cave with aboriginal rock paintings that are hundreds, if not thousands, of years old. The countryside is amazing, Bron. You'll love it!'

Bronte wasn't so sure about the *amazing* bit, nor the part about *loving it*. She decided, though, that letting Lachlan have his way this time seemed a small price to pay for domestic harmony. And yes, it would be nice to have a trip away as a family. That would be a novelty, she thought to herself. There certainly had been no chance of anything resembling a holiday for many months. The only break from work Lachlan had managed was a few days the previous Christmas.

Lachie borrowed the motor home from his Saba and Savta. His plan was to take their time on the way up, stopping for a night or two in the Karijini Range area, then dropping the Winnebago off at Port Hedland from where Jimmy would pick them all up in one of the mine 4X4s.

Simon Rose had been adamant about one thing; the Winnebago—his pride and joy—was not to leave the bitumen. He knew all too well just what the conditions were on some of the unsealed roads in the area.

'Don't worry about that,' Lachie assured him. 'Not after what happened to my Commodore.'

His beloved vehicle had never been the same after that trip, and he'd traded it for a new Lexus IS early the following year.

* * *

The trip north, via the Great Northern and North-West Coastal Highways, turned out to be a complete eye-opener for Bronte. She hadn't realised that such scenery existed so close to home. The broad, open landscape and the occasional spectacular rock formations impressed her, especially as they drove further north. Lachie happily stopped whenever Bronte felt the urge, and she soon exposed several rolls of film with her new SLR camera—an early birthday gift Lachie had bought especially for the trip. Images of trees, hills, balancing boulders, vast chasms and gorges, quaint old buildings —all were consigned to photographic immortality via Bronte's new Pentax.

'We should do this in springtime, Bron,' Lachie said at one stage. 'The wildflowers are outstanding.'

'I might take you up on that,' she answered, adjusting her focus for another 'Bronte masterpiece'. Lachie smiled. This was the happiest he had seen her in quite a while. She seemed almost back to her old self, in fact.

Near the end of the second day, they turned west toward Mount Tom Price. This was country Lachie had never visited, and he was keen to check out the area.

'I can't believe the shape of some of these hills,' Bronte said as they drove along. 'The rocks are such a dark brown, and those mesas. They're amazing.'

'Spectacular,' Lachie agreed. 'Iron ore, that's where the colour comes from. I've heard that some ore around here is so pure you can weld it.'

They spent two nights and a full day touring and exploring the national park area before continuing northwards to Port Hedland.

They arrived in Port Hedland a little after midday on the fourth day. Lachie drove the motor home to the transport yard where he had arranged to store it, to find Jimmy already waiting.

'G'day, Lachie,' he called, as the trio climbed from the cab. 'Have a good trip?' adding, 'Bronte,' with a nod in her direction, before scooping the youngest Kincaid into his arms and spinning him around. 'G'day, Iain. You get bigger every time I see you. How old are you now?'

'Three an' a half,' the boy replied, before adding excitely, 'We saw a big waterhole. I think there was a crackerdile in there. Dad said we could swim, but Mummy wouldn't let me.'

'Well, if there was a crocodile, then I wouldn't be swimming there,' Jimmy replied. 'Did you see it?'

'No,' the boy replied, 'but I bet there was! I would've rid on his back all the way to the bottom of ...'

'All right, Ian,' his mother cut in, taking him from Jimmy's arms. 'We get the point.' Then, turning to Lachie, she asked, 'Is there a restaurant around here? I'm just dying for a decent meal.'

'We can grab a burger from the roadhouse on the way out of town if you like,' Jimmy offered. 'We need to get going, though. There's roadworks on the Marble Bar road, and it'll be a slow trip back to the mine.'

Bronte grimaced at the thought of another roadhouse hamburger. How people could eat food like that was beyond her. 'It's all right,' she said. 'I can wait until we reach the mine, I guess.'

Bronte's stomach was well and truly rumbling by the time they arrived at Skull Creek, despite the jumbo-sized coffee each had bought at the roadhouse. As soon as they settled in and washed up, the group made a beeline for the mess. Bronte ate hungrily, without complaint. The food was surprisingly good—she had to admit to herself— though she didn't say as much.

There was a donga reserved for mine visitors located a little way from the main camp. The fly-in-fly-out workers came and went at odd hours, Lachie explained, and sometimes could be a bit noisy at night. The visitors' quarters were almost a mirror image of the accommodation enjoyed by the workers, the only concession being that they had two adjoining double units instead of the single cabins allocated to the crews.

Iain thought it was exciting to be living in a mining camp. Bronte thought it beneath her and didn't fail to make her feelings known.

After breakfast the following day, Lachie took them both for a guided tour of the mine and its surroundings. He had the kitchen crew prepare a picnic lunch for them, which they dispatched eagerly by the edge of the water in a hidden gorge. Despite the seemingly harsh and arid landscape, the land around the Pilbara area often concealed deep waterholes and shady ravines. Once again, Iain begged to be allowed to swim, but this time, even Lachie insisted he stay away from the water.

'These gorges are really steep,' he said to Bronte, 'and the water's usually deep and icy cold. Even the aborigines warn about getting into trouble swimming here. I reckon that's why you never find their camps in places like this.' Then he added, 'I sure wouldn't want to be here when there were heavy rains, either. You'd get washed all the way to Port Hedland!' They both chuckled.

Then looking at Iain, he said, 'No, there are no crocodiles, but you need to stay away from the edge, OK?'

'Ookaaay,' Iain replied with a pout.

After they had eaten, Lachie took them both to a secluded cave further up the creek to show them some ancient rock paintings. George had taken Lachie to the location a few months earlier. He'd expressed concern that the area—considered a sacred place by his tribespeople—might one day be targeted in a mine expansion.

Lachie had given the tribal elders his word that the site would be off-limits to future mining.

Standing inside the rocky overhang and gazing at the ancient artwork was a humbling and fascinating experience for Lachie; one that never lost its appeal, however often he visited. He thought of how many may have stood in this exact spot—so many times, over who knows how many years—and left their mark there. It never failed to impact on his soul and remind him of the fragile and temporary existence he was living.

How anyone could intentionally destroy such a site was beyond him. And yet he knew of several instances of it happening; where, for the sake of a few thousand dollars' worth of ore—be it gold, iron, or whatever—miners reduced aboriginal heritage sites to rubble.

He shared his thoughts with Bronte, who expressed guarded agreement with his viewpoint. 'What happens if you find a rich seam that goes right under, or through, this area? Will you really be able to resist the temptation to mine here?'

'Uncle Mal knows about these paintings,' Lachie said. 'I even gave him the GPS coordinates. He's promised me the area will be off-limits no matter what.'

'And you trust him on that? Knowing how he feels about aborigines—not to mention his money-hungry nature?'

'He gave me his word. That's good enough for me.'

Bronte knew Malcolm well enough to realise he could never be trusted in anything except looking after his own interests. 'Well, let's hope the company never has to make that decision,' she said finally. 'Perhaps the gold won't extend this far.'

'Maybe,' Lachie mused. 'We're doing some exploratory work at the moment. Hopefully, we'll find enough to keep us busy on the other side of the lease.'

The next couple of days passed almost without incident. Waiting in the wings, however, was one seemingly small indiscretion on Lachie's part that was to have a profound influence on all their lives.

Chapter 34

IT WAS THEIR THIRD DAY at the mine, and Lachie had promised Iain they'd visit the Skull Creek waterhole.

'Are you sure you don't want to come along, Bron?' Lachie said. 'You spent all day yesterday here. A bit of fresh scenery will do you the world of good.'

'My tummy's still not the best,' she replied. 'I think I'll wait another day before I venture too far from the facilities, if you know what I mean.'

Lachie nodded. She might have overdone it with the curried prawns the previous night —he thought—but resisted the urge to say so.

Bronte voiced concerns about the water quality at the settlement, but Lachie insisted it would be OK. 'You know how much Iain loves swimming. And besides, the latest sample results have come back, showing there's virtually no contamination at all. And don't worry, I won't let him out of my sight.'

As they passed the old tailings dam, Brian Koss, a supervisor in charge of rehabilitating the area, waved him over. 'Stay here,' Lachie said to his son. 'I'll just be a few minutes, then you can go swimming.'

'G'day, Brian,' Lachie said as they drew near. 'Problems?'

'I would've called Mr Browne,' Brian Koss said, 'but he's over at the drilling site. We might have a problem with the dam. Looks like it's been leaking again.'

The two men walked across to the downhill side of the embankment, to where a large, damp patch of soil confirmed Brian's suspicions. It wasn't a huge breach, but enough to allow a substantial amount of liquid to seep through and start making its way down the watercourse toward the settlement.

'Bugger! We need to get that fixed, pronto. Any idea how long it's been like this?'

'I checked two days ago, and there was nothing then,' Brian said. 'Must've been that rain we had the night before last. It was pretty heavy for a while. Lucky I came to check on it, I guess.'

The pair discussed the problem for several minutes, deciding to press-gang a dozer driver as soon as possible to shore up the dam wall.

'Get onto it right away, will you, Brian?' Lachie said. 'I better get back to Iain. I'll leave it in your hands.'

As he made his way back toward the vehicle, he heard a cry and a splash. He recognised the voice immediately. Iain!

Lachie sped up the slope as fast as he could, and his heart sank when he saw Iain was no longer in the passenger seat.

He whirled around and saw his son standing waist-deep in the tailings dam, next to a platform used to collect samples. The boy was spitting water and mud from his mouth and wiping his eyes furiously. As he began to cry, he spluttered, 'It stings Daddy. It's burning!'

Lachie raced to the dam. Struggling against the heavy, sticky mud that threatened to suck him down, he finally reached Iain, who was by now screaming even more loudly.

Lachie pulled Iain from the mire and carried him up the slope, where he quickly bundled him into the cab and grabbed the first aid kit. Using whatever he could lay his hands on, he wiped as much of the foul-smelling gunk from his son's face as possible. Iain was still screaming. Between breaths, he managed a few more cries of 'It's burning! It's burning!' before reverting to hysterical wailing once more.

There were two bottles of water in the glove compartment, and Lachie attempted to rinse the boy's eyes and mouth. Iain, still crying, was struggling now against his father's efforts.

Brian Koss arrived and set about doing his best to help, holding Iain's arms still while Lachie poured water over his face and tried to remove what he could of the mud.

'Get the first aid guy on the radio,' Lachie barked. 'Tell him what's happened. Tell him to get here. Now!'

Eventually, Iain seemed to calm somewhat. There appeared to be little of the toxic goo left in his mouth and eyes. Lachie thought briefly that his crying had probably helped. The tears would have washed much of the mud away. He hoped and prayed that Iain had ingested none of the noxious cocktail, but knew he may have.

The mine's first aid officer arrived within minutes. He took over from Lachie, inspecting Iain's eyes and mouth intently.

'There's definitely some burning,' he said, applying copious amounts of cream from a tube. 'I reckon you've cleared his eyes pretty well, at least. I'll call the Flying Doctor. It'll take too long to drive him to Hedland. He needs medical attention—quickly!'

Brian Koss handed him his phone. Lachie breathed a sigh of relief at the fact that they had only recently set up a mobile phone tower on site. Previously, they would have had to travel to Marble Bar, or even all the way to Port Hedland, before reporting the incident.

With the Flying Doctor notified and Iain cleaned up and pacified as best they were able, Lachie hit the road. There was nowhere close by where a plane could land, the nearest landing strip being at Marble Bar airport. Lachie phoned the local Nursing Post.

'I'll meet you at the airstrip,' the nursing sister said once he had detailed the situation. 'It sounds like calling the RFDS was a smart move. They'll probably get here not long after you, but in the meantime, I'll do what I can.

'Do you know where the airfield is?' she asked.

Lachie replied that yes, he knew where it was.

He thanked her and signed off, knowing that the phone signal would drop out quickly once they were away from the mine.

Lachie had instructed Brian to fetch Bronte and meet them at the airstrip. She would be hysterical when she heard, but he trusted Brian could calm her fears sufficiently enough for the drive. With Mark Bain, the first aid officer, holding Iain in the back seat and doing his best to soothe the youngster, he sped off toward the Nullagine Road.

It took a little over a half-hour to reach Marble Bar airport. The nurse he had spoken with was waiting and advised Lachie the Flying Doctor was about thirty minutes away. Brian and Bronte arrived as she was checking Iain's status and bathing his eyes and lips once more.

Lachie rushed toward her, his arms wide, but she pushed him away. 'You stupid, useless prick!' she screamed. 'I can't trust you with anything, can I! What have you done to my son?'

Lachie took a step backwards, opening his mouth to speak, then reached for her again.

'Don't touch me,' she snapped, fixing him with a glare that immediately froze him in his tracks. 'I knew we should never have come to this God-awful place. And I should have known you couldn't be trusted to keep Ian safe.'

She rushed to her son's side and held his hand. 'Are you all right, baby?' she said pleadingly.

'Mummy,' Iain moaned. His lips and tongue were red and distended, his eyes bloodshot and almost swollen shut. At least, she noticed with little satisfaction, he had ceased crying.

Nurse Valerie Gray was gently applying more ointment to Iain's face when the RFDS Cessna touched down. Fifteen minutes later, the young patient was being trundled on board and the plane readied for takeoff.

'We've only room for one of you,' the pilot said, eyeing Iain's distressed parents.

'That will be me,' Bronte said without hesitation.

She climbed the steps, then stopped to turn and face Lachie. 'Don't drive in, you're needed here.' She pivoted on one heel and disappeared into the plane.

'Keep your mobile on!' Lachie called after her. 'I'll call you! Bronte? I'll call you!'

The door slid shut behind her. He wasn't even sure she had heard him.

The pilot gunned the aircraft engines, leaving Lachie standing in its wake as red dust swirled around him, stinging his eyes and filling his hair. He stood for several minutes, staring after the plane with his wife and son on board as it rose into the sky and headed northward. Even when the faint speck that was the retreating Cessna had vanished from view, he remained watching, unable to tear himself away.

'Come on,' said Mark. 'Nothing more we can do here. I'll drive you back to the mine.'

Lachie walked as in a dream. How could he have been so careless? Why hadn't he stressed more strongly that Iain stayed in the cab?

He knew Iain's inquisitive nature. He knew how he loved the water. How would he live with himself if his beautiful son had suffered permanent injury—even blindness, perhaps?

They drove back to the mine without speaking. Mark Bain had only been with the company for three months and had barely spoken more than twenty words to Lachie in that time. Now was not the right moment to make small talk, he reasoned, and certainly not the time to offer consolation or advice to his boss.

As the 4X4 pulled up in front of the site office, Lachie turned to him.

'Thanks, Mark. You did a great job back there. And thanks for not smothering me with platitudes.'

The two exchanged a brief nod before Mark replied, 'Just doing what I'm here for, Boss. I hope he'll be OK. I think we got most of the stuff off him in time. Anyway, he's in the best of hands right now.'

As Lachie alighted wearily from the cab, he paused. 'I'll see that you get a bonus. You earned it.'

'Really, Mr Kincaid, there's no need. That's what you hire me for. You get some rest. I'll write up an incident report and have it on your desk tonight.'

Lachie decided to avoid the office for now. Instead, he adjourned to his donga accommodation, poured himself a stiff bourbon, stepped out of his muddy clothes, and flopped onto the bed.

Images and sounds of his son screaming in pain, thoughts of just what the outcome might be; all this and more filled his mind. By now, he guessed, the Flying Doctor would have landed at Port Hedland and an ambulance would be rushing Iain and his mother to the hospital. He decided he'd give it about an hour, then ring the hospital for an update.

There wasn't much news to be had when he rang. Iain was 'comfortable', the nurse who took the call said. His mother was with him and had expressly asked that no visitors be allowed. The registrar had examined Iain, and a senior doctor would assess him tomorrow; there would likely be more news by then. Thank you for calling, and yes, we'll call you tomorrow after the doctor has seen the boy.

Bronte wasn't answering her phone. Lachie had received a text message telling him it was hospital policy not to allow mobile phones on the wards. Maybe that explained it. He sent her a message to let her know he'd called and that he'd be in touch tomorrow.

The rest of that day passed as if a bad dream. One perk of being the part-owner/manager of an organisation is the ability to slack off on the job. Lachie decided that if there was ever a day he needed to slack off, it was today. Besides, his shift hadn't started yet.

After briefly calling Brian Koss to make sure he'd arranged the shoring up of the tailings dam, Lachie poured himself another bourbon and drank it—a little too quickly. He looked at the bottle as he poured another. Half-full. Plenty to get him through the rest of the day. He'd sleep well tonight, he told himself.

Bronte called at around 9 am. Lachie was in the mess, nursing a hangover and a strong coffee. Breakfast had been a non-starter, and he hoped the coffee might revive him a little.

'Hi Bron, what's the news with Iain? Has the doctor been yet?'

'I've spoken with the resident doctor. He wants Ian to see a specialist as soon as possible. He's worried about arsenic or cyanide poisoning; maybe both.

'I had no idea of the deadly chemicals you were using at the mine! I mean, I guess I knew to an extent, but the doctor says ...' Lachie could sense her struggling to maintain control. After a minute, she continued, 'We're flying to Perth this morning. You stay where you are. Your rotation starts in two days and there's nothing you can do, anyway.

'God knows you've done enough already,' she added.

He was about to cut in when she said, 'Ian is being admitted to the Princess Margaret Children's Hospital. I'll call you again when we know more.'

Before Lachie collected his thoughts well enough to reply, she had hung up.

He hit the call-back button immediately, but the call went straight to voicemail. He tried three more times, over several minutes, then called the Port Hedland Hospital. After being diverted twice, he eventually spoke with the doctor who had seen his son that morning.

'Yes, Mr Kincaid,' the medico said, 'your son needs specialist attention. I advised Mrs Kincaid that we should monitor him here for 24 hours more, but she insisted we transfer him to PMH immediately.' Then he added, 'she can be quite persuasive when she has a mind to, can't she?'

'You could say that. Thanks, Doc. I'll wait until this evening and speak to somebody at PMH.'

Lachie ended the call and cradled his head in his hands. Obviously, Bronte was blaming him entirely, and why shouldn't she? Wasn't Iain in his care? Wasn't he the one who left his son, a child known for his adventurous spirit, alone in the vehicle?

Once again, the self-recriminations filled his mind. Once again, he mentally berated himself for being so stupid.

He couldn't remain at Skull Creek, though. He had to get himself down to Perth as soon as possible.

He phoned Jimmy. Yes, the news had got around, and Jimmy had heard of Iain's unscheduled dip in the dam.

'Of course, mate,' Jimmy said to Lachie's request. 'I can stay on for another week. You get yourself down there and be with your family. And give that boy of yours a hug from me.'

There was no chance of making the morning flight. He made a quick phone call and booked himself on the next available, which was the following day's early business flight. He arranged for an employee to drive him to Port Hedland that afternoon. Once there, he could spend the night in the Winnebago and catch a cab to the airport the next day. He considered briefly driving the motor home back, but decided against it. In his distressed state, he didn't trust himself to drive 1400 kilometres in one stretch.

* * *

Bronte looked up from her magazine as Lachie entered the ward. 'What are you doing here? Haven't you done enough?'

'Bron, I couldn't stay away. Not while Iain's in here. How is he?'

'Well, you may as well piss off back to work. He's in good hands. There's nothing more you can do.'

'I've been crazy with worry. What have the doctors said?'

She fixed him with an icy stare. 'He's under sedation. Tomorrow the bandages come off his eyes. Luckily for you, they say there'll be only slight eye damage, and they don't think he swallowed anything. If you want to know any more, you'd better speak with his doctor.'

Bronte turned her attention back to the magazine she had been thumbing through for the last hour. What the hell did he expect, a hero's welcome?

Bronte had hardly left her son's side since arriving at the hospital. Her parents had visited and tried to convince her to come home with them, but up to now, she had refused. Tonight, she might relent, however.

She looked up at Lachlan again. 'You still here?'

Lachie was about to leave the room when Iain's medical team entered.

'Mr Kincaid?' The doctor offered his hand. Lachie introduced himself.

'What's his condition? My wife says he's sedated?'

The doctor assured Lachie they expected no serious long-term effects. It appeared his and Mark Bains' quick efforts had saved Iain from more than minor eye damage. There may be some slight vision impairment, but it was too early to tell. He seemed not to have ingested any of the toxic gunk from the tailings, though as a precaution, they recommended he stay for a few days.

After the team had left, Lachie turned to his wife. 'I feel so guilty, Bron. I never dreamed he'd leave the cab. He must have thought that was where I was taking him to swim.'

'You should feel guilty! This is all your fault! You promised me you'd look after him. How could you let that happen?

'I hope you aren't planning to come home to the unit. You can sleep in the street for all I care, but you're not coming home with me.'

Lachie didn't want to push the issue, and he was confident Bronte would change her attitude once she'd calmed down. Figuring it might be best if he were to stay at his grandparents' house for a while, he walked to an outdoor courtyard and dialled the Roses' number.

'Lachie!' Marita Rose said excitedly. 'What can I do for you this morning—are you still up north?'

'I've got some grim news, Savta. Iain's in hospital. There was an incident at the mine.'

He heard Marita's sudden intake of breath. Lachie waited for her to catch her thoughts, then detailed the situation, including his own role in the series of events and Bronte's subsequent banishment of him.

'I'll be there as soon as I can,' Marita said when Lachie had finished. 'I'll bring some of his favourite treats.'

'Actually, Savta, I just need to ask if it's OK for me to come to your place for a bit. Bronte will stay with him as much as she can.'

'But shouldn't I come and see him?'

'Under the circumstances, perhaps it'd be better if you didn't—for now, at least,' Lachie countered. 'Maybe in a day or two.'

'I'll ring anyway,' Marita said. 'She should know we're here if there's anything she or Iain needs.'

Lachie shrugged to himself. He'd never be able to talk his Savta out of calling Bronte. In any case, Marita just might be the one to throw some oil onto what was definitely some very troubled waters.

'I'll grab a taxi and be there shortly,' he said. 'See you soon.'

*   *   *

'Bronte?' Marita's voice quavered slightly. 'How is he? I just heard from Lachlan.'

'My son is fine. Well, as fine as we can hope for, anyway.' Her tone was cool and formal. 'I suppose Lachlan told you the full story? How he left my son alone near that toxic swamp?'

Her voice trembled. 'Did he tell you the whole nasty business? It's his fault Ian is in this hospital. It's his fault he might be blind!'

Bronte's voice edged up a notch. 'The whole thing is his fault, and I don't want him or any of you coming near my son. Thank you for calling, but please don't call again.'

The line went dead. Dumbfounded, Marita stood holding the phone for several seconds before placing it back in its cradle. Obviously, Bronte was in no mood for talk right now.

After a minute, she lifted the handset again and called Rachel's work number.

'Good afternoon, Two Brothers Mine,' Rachel's cheery voice greeted her. 'How may I help you?'

'It's Mum, Rachel. Can you talk?'

'What's wrong? Are you OK? Is Dad OK?'

Marita gave her daughter all the information she had. Yes, it was serious, but Iain was in the best place and receiving the very best of care. Without giving all the details, she relayed Bronte's feelings and her own hope for a turnaround once Bronte had calmed down somewhat.

'I'll book myself a seat on the train for tomorrow,' Rachel said. 'Julie Watkins can hold the fort for a few days.' Then she added, 'I guess I'd better call Malcolm too. He probably won't be any help, but if I don't keep him in the loop, he'll spit the dummy big time.'

Once the conversation was over, Rachel called the Prospector booking office. There was a service to Perth the following day, and luckily, there was a seat available. She spoke with Julie, who was happy to help out until her return. 'Stay as long as you need,' Julie said. 'Don't worry about things here—just look after your family.'

The call to Malcolm was less pleasant.

'What the fuck?' Malcolm exploded. 'When did we start running a crèche at Skull Creek? What the hell was he thinking? Or not thinking—more to the point!'

Rachel didn't reply immediately. Everything she thought of to say would have come across as her defending Lachie, and would probably have infuriated Malcolm even more. After a few seconds, she changed the subject. 'Lachie will need to stay in Perth for a bit. Jimmy's rotation ends tomorrow. Shall I ask him to stay on for now?'

'Fuck that,' Malcolm responded. 'We need him back there to relieve Joe Griggs.' Then after a brief pause, he added, 'Call Browne, and tell him to be back at Two Brothers by Saturday, as arranged. Leave Skull Creek to me.'

Rachel opened her mouth to say more, but the dial tone interrupted her. Malcolm was already gone. She gave the phone a quizzical look before poking her tongue at it and hanging up.

She then called Jimmy and relayed Malcolm's instructions.

'How's Iain? Do they know if there will be any long-term damage?'

'Probably a bit too soon to be sure, but apparently, he's not too bad. They're keeping him in for observation, just in case.'

'OK. And Lachie and Bron—how're they holding up?'

'Lachie's with his grandparents. Bronte's …' Rachel wasn't sure how much she should say to Jimmy. 'Bronte's … upset—as you'd expect.'

'Yeah, I guess she would be. OK, tell Malcolm I'll head back as per arrangements. Thanks for keeping me in the loop.'

After ending his conversation with Rachel, Malcolm dialled Lachie's number.

'Hi, Uncle Mal.' Lachie tried to sound as upbeat as possible. 'I guess you've heard about Iain's little mishap?'

'Little mishap? I'll give you 'little mishap'! What the blue blazes were you thinking, taking him to the mine? It's not a bloody holiday camp. And why is that fucking tailings dam still there? I told you I wanted it got rid of ages ago.'

'We're waiting for the soil to dry out completely,' Lachie replied. 'If we try to remove the dam now, the runoff might end up down the creek and into the settlement waterhole.'

'So what?' Malcolm was tempted to say, but chose not to. 'I suppose you'll need to stay down here for a bit,' he said instead. 'I'll arrange someone to cover for you at the mine. How is the boy, anyway?'

He was listening to Lachie's reply, but his mind was elsewhere. Malcolm had already decided who the someone would be. 'If you want a job done properly, do it yourself' was another of his father's favourite sayings, and one that he had long ago adopted as a personal mantra.

After signing off, Malcolm gave his secretary instructions to organise an air ticket and taxi for him. 'And you'd better source some hi-vis workwear for me, too. I have a feeling I might be away for a while.'

The following day, Malcolm called a management meeting at Skull Creek mine.

'OK,' he said, looking at Brian Koss. 'What are we doing about getting rid of that bloody tailings dam?'

'Mr Kincaid, er, the other Mr Kincaid, said …'

'I don't give a flying fuck what the other Mr Kincaid said. I'm asking you. What are we doing about it?'

Brian Koss shuffled uncertainly. He cleared his throat before replying, 'I suppose we could bring in an excavator and load the contents into a couple of dump trucks, then transport it all over to the new dam. Big job, though. There's a lot of sediment—could take a while.'

'Now there's a plan,' sneered Malcolm.

Looking around the room, he said, 'I don't give a shit if it *takes a while* or not.' He emphasised the phrase with air quotes. 'I want it done, and I want it started today. The drilling reports show good ore beneath that dam. We're going to expand the pit to include all that section. Any questions?'

Those present exchanged glances. Brian Koss opened his mouth to speak but thought better of it.

'All right. That's settled then. Now get the fuck out of here and back to work.' Malcolm waved them away and turned his attention to a sheaf of papers on his desk.

Brian and the rest filed out without another word.

The job of transporting the contaminated sludge from the old tailings dam to the new location took just under a week. Mine production continued as usual, with minimal interruption.

Watching the operations, Malcom said to Brian Koss. 'Once you have most of the residue removed, use the dumpies to fetch as much soil and rock as you need from the main excavation area, and fill the hole. I don't want to see any sign there was ever a tailings dam here. Future expansion will eventually include all this area, in any case'.

'Do you think that's wise, Mr Kincaid? I mean, what if we get heavy rains? It's still part of the creek catchment area.'

Malcolm fixed him with a steely glare. 'How long have you worked for us, Brian?'

'Eighteen months.'

'You seem to like working here. Am I right?' Brian nodded.

Malcolm maintained his angry stare for several seconds. 'Was there anything else?'

Brian said no, there was not.

Chapter 35

AFTER THREE DAYS OF TREATMENT, Iain was discharged from the hospital. His face and mouth were still red and sore and his vision still blurred, but the specialist who assessed him on his release was confident there should be no serious long-term problems.

Bronte still refused to talk to Lachie, although she did allow him and Rachel to take Iain out for the afternoon on the fifth day.

'So are you and Bronte going to patch things up?' Rachel asked him, while Iain concentrated on an ice cream. 'I mean, you won't break up over this, will you?'

Lachie shrugged. 'Sometimes I've got no idea what goes on in her head. I love her, don't get me wrong, but she's been, well, difficult for quite a while now. Pretty much ever since Iain was born, actually. Some days she's on top of the world. Then suddenly, the least little thing will send her into a blinding rage. I can hardly consider this business with Iain as trivial, though, so I guess her current mood is about what I'd expect.'

'Sounds like it might be post-natal depression,' Rachel mused. 'I've never heard of it lasting this long, though. Has she seen anybody about it?'

'Her GP has her on anti-depressants, but I'm not sure how much they're helping. She's back to smoking dope regularly again, too. Says she can't sleep without it.'

Bronte had taken up the weed again almost as soon as she was home after Iain's birth. The big difference was that it didn't seem to make her horny any more. In fact, their sex life had been missing in action for some time now. He didn't confess that to Rachel, however. There are some things a man just doesn't discuss with his mother.

'It hit her hard knowing that she can't have any more kids,' Lachie continued. 'I thought she might get over it, but lately, she seems to be getting worse. This business with Iain has only brought things to a head.'

'She and I have been getting along all right lately,' Rachel said. 'Maybe if I spend some time with her?'

'Well, you'll get the chance soon if you're up for it.' he replied. 'I'm flying up to Port Hedland this weekend to bring back the Winnebago. I'll be away for three or four days, I reckon.'

* * *

Lachie's trip north turned out to be a slightly longer visit than he'd expected. As he waited for his flight to board, he called the mine office.

'Kincaid Mining Corporation, Skull Creek project,' Brian Koss' voice greeted him.

'Brian. Lachlan Kincaid here. How're things going up there? Has Malcolm reorganised the whole place yet?' He suppressed a chuckle. He was the manager, and Brian's immediate superior, after all.

'Funny you should ask that,' Brian replied. He filled Lachie in on Malcolm's new vision for the mine. The removal and back-filling of the tailings dam were almost complete, he explained, with the expansion plans well underway.

Lachie listened with growing apprehension. What was Malcolm thinking? Surely he knew the risks?

The PA crackled and the flight announcer's voice cut their call short.

'I've got to go, Brian. They just called my flight. Can you grab an LV and pick me up from the airport? I'm coming up for a while. Malcolm and I need to discuss something.'

'No problem. I'll check the arrival time. See you soon.'

Brian chuckled as he signed off. *I'd love to be there when Messrs. Kincaid and Kincaid have* that *discussion*, he mused to himself.

About halfway into the flight, the pilot's voice sounded through the PA.

'Ladies and gentlemen, please fasten your seatbelts, as we're approaching some turbulence. An unseasonal storm has developed over the Pilbara area. There will be heavy rain and thunderstorms throughout the region this afternoon. Thank you.'

Just what we need—thought Lachie,—*Mal demolishes the dam, and now it's going to piss down with rain. Why can't he leave well enough alone?*

The skies opened just as Lachlan stepped from the aircraft and joined the rest of the passengers scurrying for the terminal. Brian stood waiting and took Lachie's flight bag from him.

'Any other luggage?' he asked.

'Nope, this is it. Let's get going. I hope the De Grey River crossing is still open.'

'It should be OK for the rest of today,' Brian said. 'Tomorrow might be a different story, though.'

They arrived at the mine around four o'clock. Lachie went straight to his donga, unpacked, and headed for the mess. The meeting with Malcolm would have to wait until tomorrow. What he needed now was food, a shower, and sleep—in that order.

*   *   *

Malcolm tossed aside the folder he had been reading as Lachie entered the office and rose to greet the younger Kincaid.

'G'day, Lachie,' he said, putting as much good humour into his voice as he could. 'Leave something behind? I didn't expect you back here so soon.'

He noticed Lachie's stern expression and continued, affecting the same friendly tone, 'Hey, I'm sorry for blowing my stack the other day—I wasn't aware you'd brought the family for a visit, that's all.' He shook Lachie's hand and placed his left hand on the younger man's shoulder.

'How's Iain, by the way? I sent a gift package for the little tacker. Your Missus doesn't seem to have her phone on these days. I've been calling her for ...'

'Iain's OK,' Lachie interrupted. 'He's home with Bronte. What's this about you filling in the tailings dam?'

Lachie let the question hang between them, waiting for his uncle's reply.

Brian Koss!—thought Malcolm.—*That bloody prick! I should've known he couldn't keep his nose where it belonged. I'll talk to him, later.*

'Where did you hear that?' he asked pleasantly. 'Actually, I would have discussed it with you, but with things as they are, I reckon you've got enough on your plate.'

'The waterhole, Uncle Mal. It'll get contaminated again! Especially with this rain we're getting now.'

'Bloody rubbish!' Mal snapped. 'That dam had pretty much dried up. In any case, I had more tests done, and aside from some residue in the silt, there's no contamination worth giving a shit about. Here,' he handed Lachie the folder he had been reading, 'read for yourself.'

Lachie took the papers his uncle offered. 'Iain and I can both testify that the dam wasn't anywhere close to being dry,' he said before opening the folder.

Christoff Mineral Laboratories: Analyses of Water Samples—Skull Creek, read the cover page. Inside were the results Malcolm had commissioned.

Lachie glanced through the rows of figures. In reality, they meant little to him. Malcolm knew that, and he was counting on the attached summation to do the convincing.

These were tests that Malcolm had paid hard cash for—tests that showed exactly what he wanted them to say; that there was no health risk to the settlement, nor to anyone else exposed to the runoff.

Lachie's eyebrows furrowed as he read the last page. 'I can't believe things have improved so quickly,' he said. 'It's true. There's almost no cyanide or mercury left, according to this.'

'Well below safe levels,' Malcolm agreed. 'Once I read that report, I decided to remove it all and rehabilitate the area as soon as possible. Virtually all the sludge that remained is now over at the new location. We're backfilling with spoil as we speak. At least, we were until the skies opened up.'

Lachie handed back the folder. 'Sorry, Uncle Mal. I guess I just assumed you'd …'

'Jumped the gun and ignored the warnings?' Mal completed his sentence for him.

'Is that really what you think of me? Do you honestly expect I'd dice with people's health like that? I don't care if they're black, brown, or pink-spotted; I'm not that uncaring, Lachie.'

Lachie shuffled, glancing at the floor. 'Sorry, Uncle Mal. Maybe I was a bit hasty.'

'A bit?' Malcolm was on a roll now and not keen on giving up the moral high ground.

'OK,' he said after a long pause, 'We'll let it slide. How did you come to know what we were doing, anyway? It wasn't exactly in the papers.'

'I came up to Port Hedland to collect the Winnebago, and thought I'd pay a visit to see how things were,' Lachie lied.

'I spotted the digger and dump truck as we drove in. I asked Kossie what was going on and he said I should talk to you about it.'

Lachie made a mental note to call Brian Koss immediately after he left the office, before Mal had the chance to beat him to it. He knew what Malcolm's reaction would be if he learned Brian had spilled the beans.

Malcolm shrugged. 'OK, it's no big deal, anyway. So how long will you be here? I figured I'd cover for you for a couple of weeks, so you could be with Iain.'

'Not much point in that at the moment. Bronte's blaming me entirely and won't let me near him most days. I have to drive Saba's motor home down to Perth, but once that's done, I can come back to relieve you.' He sighed deeply and added, 'To be honest, I reckon a break might be what Bron and I need right now.'

'Righto, let me know Monday night, and we'll do the change-over on Tuesday.' Malcolm seemed keen to have him off the mine as quickly as possible. 'You better get going as soon as the river crossing's clear, in case there's more rain.'

Lachie agreed. He had to return the motor home anyway, and he'd accomplish nothing by staying any longer. A quick call—after a heads-up to Brian Koss—confirmed that the

De Grey crossing was still open, so he arranged for a worker to drive him to Port Hedland after lunch. Best if he didn't involve Brian any further, he reasoned.

Lachie spent that night in the Winnebago, and set off southward at first light, arriving at the Roses' home around nine pm.

Chapter 36

Friday, October 4th, 2002.

LACHIE'S MOBILE CHIMED. He checked the number; it was the mine office.

'What's up, Helen?' he said. 'I'm on my way back from the settlement with the latest samples. I'll be there shortly.'

'Incoming call for you, Mr Kincaid. Putting it through now.'

There was a brief pause, and a series of clicks, before he heard Malcolm's voice. 'Lachie? You got a minute?'

'Hi, Uncle Mal. What can I do for you?'

'The Diggers and Dealers Conference is on later this month. I want you and Jimmy Browne both there this year. I've arranged the tickets. You can pick them up in Kalgoorlie when you arrive.'

'But who's going to be in charge up here, if we're both in Kalgoorlie?'

'You're not that indispensable, mate—either of you. I'll arrange for Brian Koss to cover for you. There'll be someone at the event I want you both to meet, so don't make any other plans.'

'OK then,' Lachie said. 'Shall I tell Jimmy?'

'I'll call Browne and tell him myself,' Malcolm said. 'I can't chat—I'll leave it to you to book your flights, though.' And with that, he was gone.

Lachie looked quizzically at his phone. Short, sharp, and to the point. That's the way it was with most calls from Malcolm these days.

* * *

Two weeks later, Lachie stepped off the plane at Kalgoorlie and was met by Jimmy and his sister.

After the initial greetings, Lachie turned to Aretha. 'Wow, you've certainly changed,' he said cheerily. 'I could have walked right past you.'

Her warm smile quickened his pulse slightly. They shared a hug, her perfume tantalising his nostrils.

'Well, it has been three years. I'd have recognised you, though. Still suave and handsome as ever.'

He held her at arm's length for a moment. It was true; she had changed markedly from the gangly teenager she once was, with the tousled, unkempt hair and skinny limbs. In her place stood a striking, mature young woman. A woman who, Lachie realised, he found more than a little alluring.

He wondered briefly why he hadn't noticed before, but supposed their age difference was the main reason. That, and the fact he had been a married man for almost five years. He looked her up and down with admiration, then felt himself redden a little. He caught Jimmy's eye. His friend was standing behind Aretha and mouthed, 'I told you.'

The last time they had met was on his last visit to the Goldfields, just before he and Jimmy began their joint management of Skull Creek. Lachie, Jimmy, and Aretha had enjoyed lunch together at the Lucky Miner tavern, and the threesome spent the afternoon playing Kelly Pool, followed by dinner at the Browne household. Lachie found it hard to believe this was the same giggly, immature girl he had known then.

Jimmy drove them back to the Browne's Wilson Street home, where the family matriarch, Annie, had prepared lunch. 'I could have booked a motel,' he said. 'The company would've paid.'

'Nonsense,' Annie scolded. 'We've plenty room here. We never see you these days, so we're glad to have you. Marvin is at a mate's place, so his room was empty, anyway.'

After their meal, the trio sat outside beneath a salmon gum tree with a beer each.

'How are things at home?' Jimmy asked. 'You and Bron sorted your differences yet?'

'It's five months now,' Lachie said, 'and I'm still living with Saba and Savta. I can't even get her to have a proper conversation with me. I don't know where we're heading, to be honest.' He sighed, adding, 'I really miss Iain most of all. I think he misses me, too.'

They sat in silence for several minutes before Jimmy spoke. 'Wanna head in for a few games of pool at the Miner?'

The next two days passed swiftly. Lachie and Jimmy spent the days at the convention, and the evenings socialising with other attendees before returning to Jimmy's place. By sheer chance, Aretha just happened to be still up watching TV when they returned each evening.

At the end of the third day, Lachie boarded his flight and returned to Perth and his job. Before he left, however, he and Aretha exchanged email addresses and promised to stay in touch. At the airport, they hugged for the longest time before finally tearing themselves away. 'I really will miss you now,' she said, her eyes growing misty.

He kissed her gently. 'I'll miss you too, Aretha.'

February 2003

It was eight months now, since Iain's untimely encounter with mine waste, and he seemed to have suffered no long-term damage. Even his vision—at first showing some ill-effects—had returned to normal. Lachie and Bronte's relationship, however, had gone from bad to worse. Lachie was still living at his grandparents' house whenever he was not at the mine, his only contact with Bronte being to arrange for Iain to spend time with him and his grandparents. Marita and Simon Rose doted on Iain, and the four of them often went on family picnics and other outings.

On one of Lachie's home visits, he announced he planned to visit Kalgoorlie for a few days.

'That'll be nice for you,' Marita said. 'You haven't been there in ages, and your Mum will be pleased to see you.'

'Yeah, I guess I'll look in on her while I'm there.'

Lachie hadn't revealed the actual reason for the trip. Ever since the mining conference, he'd been corresponding with Aretha and had accepted her invitation to spend a few days.

Although Aretha still lived at home, she had a self-contained flat at the rear of the house, and Lachie wondered if this might turn into more than just a casual visit. He could certainly do worse, he reckoned. Aretha had blossomed into quite a beautiful young woman. She was 20 now, and studying to become a librarian. Lachie found he liked her a lot. And well, a guy can only remain loyal to 'Rosy Palmer' for so long ...

He spent the first day of his break with the Roses, then left early the following day, arriving at the Browne household just in time for lunch.

'Lachie!' Aretha had spent the past two hours seated on the front verandah pretending to read—and fooling no one.

She tossed the magazine aside and raced into the street. She pulled Lachie's door open, and as he stepped out, she flung her arms around him.

'I've missed you so much,' she murmured in his ear.

'Come on in, you two,' Annie Browne called from the porch. 'I'll have lunch on the table directly.'

'We'll be right in, Mother,' Aretha called. Annie hated being called Mother, a fact that only made it more fun for Aretha to do so. Annie snorted and retreated inside, letting the door slam behind her.

With the meal finished, Lachie looked across at Aretha.

'I'm thinking of taking a run out to Two Brothers mine. Wanna come for a spin?'

'You bet,' she replied.

'Sounds great,' interjected Marvin.

Brian Browne, the late family patriarch, had wielded his influence in the naming department here too; calling his youngest son after soul legend Marvin Gaye. Lachie and Jimmy often teased him, suggesting Brian had actually named him after Hank Marvin, from The Shadows.

'Not in a blue fit!' exclaimed Aretha. 'Anyway, you begged off work because you were sick. If you're that sick, you're too crook to come. Stay in bed.'

Annie busied herself with clearing the table as the two siblings argued noisily. Not wanting to be drawn in, Lachie offered Annie his help.

'No good getting between them two,' she confided. 'They'll sort it out, you'll see. Bin at each other's throats since I can't remember when.'

She slid a pile of plates into the sink before turning to him. 'Oh, and you give my best to your Mum when you see her, OK?'

Lachie said he would.

Annie stopped what she was doing and fixed him with a deliberate look. 'You be nice to my daughter, OK? I know what you Kincaids can be like. She's a good girl. I don't want you takin' advantage.'

'Annie,' Lachie replied. 'I give you my word: I'll never hurt her. I'm aware what sort of girl she is, and I've got nothing but respect for her,' adding with a smile, 'no pun intended.'

They both chuckled at the unplanned reference.

'I realise my Uncle Mal's got a bit of a reputation, deserved or not. I'm my own man, though, and I like Aretha. I really do. Where we end up, who knows? But I promise you, I won't hurt her.'

Annie nodded. 'OK,' she said. 'You do seem like a decent bloke, from what I've seen of you.

'Jimmy reckons you're God's gift,' she added with a grin, 'so I guess that oughta be enough for me.'

Soon, the brother and sister had settled their dispute. It cost Aretha ten dollars, and Lachie offered to take him for a spin in his Lexus later. Annie clinched the deal by suggesting Marvin should help with her grocery shopping.

After leaving the house, Lachie stopped briefly at the deli on the corner of Roberts Street to buy a couple of Cokes. As he climbed back into the driver's seat, Aretha placed her hand on his leg and said, 'I love this car. How about we go for a nice long drive?' adding with a cheeky smile, 'I know a few secret spots where no one'll find us.'

'Hmm, you fancy a run down the Kambalda road, then?' he replied. 'We'll see what she can do.'

'That's the best offer I've had in ages,' Aretha laughed. 'I thought you'd never ask.'

He swung the Lexus around in a u-turn and drove back along Wilson Street to where it gave way to the Goldfields Highway on the southern end of town.

Once clear of the populated area, Lachie put his foot down, and the vehicle lurched forward. The road here was good, and fairly straight, so they quickly passed the 110 km legal limit. The Lexus seemed to relish the chance to show what it was capable of.

Aretha whooped with joy. 'Yeah, man.' she shouted, 'Give it to her.'

She placed her hand on Lachie's leg once again, a little higher this time, and he felt a sudden urge to pull over and take her, there and then. He took her hand in his and held it, afraid that if she kept it where it was, she would surely notice the growing bulge under his jeans.

After a few minutes, they turned off onto a side road and parked under a large eucalyptus tree.

They sat in the shade, drinking their Cokes and chatting idly. This was actually the first time Lachie could remember the two of them being together without another person present. Only now, with his marriage to Bronte seemingly in tatters and Aretha seated so temptingly close—looking so mature and desirable—did he dare let his actual feelings for her rise to the surface.

Lachie knew that the sweet Aretha was not quite the good girl her mother thought she was. She'd had boyfriends, and he had no illusions about her chastity. Jimmy had kept him up to date with her frequent changes of partners over the last three or four years.

'She's saving herself for you, mate,' Jimmy once told him with a nudge and a grin. 'She reckons it's only a matter of time before you and Bron call it quits.'

'She said that to you?' Lachie had asked incredulously.

'Well, not in so many words,' his friend replied. 'I know her, though. Every guy she goes out with, she stacks up against you. And they haven't got a snowball's chance in hell.'

Lachie was watching her lips move as she spoke, thinking how much he'd like to kiss them. Without speaking, he leaned slowly toward her. Aretha's voice trailed off as she noticed his intentions.

Their lips met. Gently, tentatively, each testing the other. She pulled back, staring into his eyes. Lachie had the sensation he could get lost in the brown abyss of Aretha's gaze.

She leaned forward, and they kissed again—this time more deliberately, more passionately.

'I've dreamed of that for so long,' she said when next they separated.

'Actually, me too,' he breathed. 'I have to admit I've sort of fancied you for ages, Aretha. I mean, you were just a kid when we first met, but lately ...'

She placed a finger on his lips. 'Shh, don't say any more. Let's just see how it goes.' Then she added, 'Maybe we'd better get going before things get out of hand.'

Lachie nodded. He started the Lexus, turned around, and drove back to the highway.

Aretha finished her Coke, watching his movements with a smile.

At the intersection, Lachie stopped to phone the mine office and tell Rachel to expect visitors.

'Lachie,' she exclaimed. 'What a surprise. Haven't seen you for ages. I'll have the kettle on when you get here.'

They drove back through Kalgoorlie and northward along the Goldfields Highway toward the Two Brothers mine, each lost in their own thoughts.

Every few minutes they exchanged glances until finally Lachie could bear it no more. He pulled into a parking area and, flinging his seatbelt aside, took Aretha in his arms and kissed her deeply. She responded immediately, their probing tongues engaging in a dance of mutual delight. He ran his hand up Aretha's leg, caressing her smooth form beneath her skirt.

After a minute, they again separated, each plumbing the depths of the other's eyes.

'Sorry,' he said with a slight shrug. 'I guess I'm not big in the self-control department.'

Aretha cupped her hands around Lachie's face and kissed him again, more gently, before answering, 'Me either. But this probably isn't the time or place for this. We don't know who might come along, and besides, your mother's expecting us. Shall we pick up on this later?'

'Please,' was all Lachie could manage.

'Mum's making up a bed for you on the couch tonight,' Aretha said, 'but come to my room as soon as they're asleep,' adding in a playful tone, 'If you can stay awake, that is.'

'Oh, I'll be awake. Don't you worry about that.'

They arrived at the mine a half-hour later. Rachel raised her eyebrows to Lachlan on seeing his companion. 'G'day, Aretha, long time no see.'

'How are you, Mrs Kincaid?' Aretha extended her hand.

'I'm well, but no need for formalities; you can call me Rachel like everyone else does.'

They chatted over coffee and fruit cake; Rachel's baking speciality.

'Where's the little girls' room?' Aretha asked, 'What with the Coke and now coffee, my back teeth are floating.'

Rachel gave directions, and once she was out of earshot, turned to Lachlan. 'Are you two, er, seeing each other?'

'Nothing serious, Mum. I like her a lot, that's all. I'd appreciate it though if you'd keep it to yourself. It doesn't seem that Bron and I are going to patch things up, but we certainly don't need any more fuel on the fire, if you know what I mean.'

'I'm not sure if Aretha would enjoy being called that, but OK, your little secret is safe with me.'

She chuckled to herself and added, 'Can you imagine your Uncle Mal's face if he heard?'

Lachie almost choked on his coffee. 'Oh shit, I hadn't thought of that. Definitely keep him out of this particular loop, hey?'

They were still laughing when Aretha returned. She looked from one to the other quizzically.

'Private joke,' Lachie said, waving his hand.

'You haven't been to the mine before, have you? How about I give you the guided tour?'

Lachie stayed at the Brownes' home for four days. Each night, he would sneak out to Aretha's room once the house was silent. On one occasion, they both fell asleep, and he had to steal back just before dawn.

After the third night, he and Aretha fabricated an excuse to disappear for the afternoon and slept for three hours in Lachie's car beneath the same eucalyptus tree of their first outing.

On waking, they made love on the rear seat before driving back into town, where they enjoyed a meal together at the Lucky Miner.

'You really have to go, Lachie?' she pleaded, as they were finishing. 'Just one more day?'

'Unfortunately, I do,' he replied. 'In any case, one more day would become another, then another, and another ...'

'And the problem with that is?'

'Well, I'd lose my job, for a start.'

'You can't lose your job. You're the boss.'

'It's not quite that simple,' he said. 'Besides, there's a management meeting I have to attend at Head Office. And I've got access with Iain on Friday. It's hard enough getting her to agree to that at all these days, without complicating things.'

Aretha gave a little pout. 'Are you going to spend your last night with me?'

'Last night? I'm only going back to Perth. You make it sound like I've been given a death sentence!'

That evening, in the secrecy of Aretha's unit, they made love like possessed beings. It was well after 3 am before Lachie crept back to the lounge room.

Marvin, who had caught on to their subterfuge after the first night, intercepted Lachie as he sneaked through the kitchen. 'You two really need to learn to be a bit quieter if you don't want Mum kicking your arse from here to Kingdom Come,' he whispered. Breaking into a grin, he added, 'Don't worry, your secret's safe with me.'

Lachie imagined it might cost Aretha a lot more than ten dollars to buy his cooperation this time.

The following morning, Aretha tried hard to hide her feelings as Lachie tossed his overnight bag onto the back seat and slipped behind the wheel. She was fooling no one, however.

Annie gave Lachie a quick hug before waving him off with a 'drive safe' and heading inside.

'Yeah, take it easy,' said Marvin. He patted Lachie's arm and retreated indoors himself. Obviously, Aretha had given strict instructions.

'That's going to cost me, big time.' She smiled, before throwing her arms around Lachlan's neck through the window, squeezing tightly. 'I miss you already,' she whispered. 'Please come back soon.'

'Why don't you come down to Perth on my next break?' he suggested. 'I'm thinking of getting a place of my own. I can't stay with Saba and Savta forever.'

She kissed him fervently. 'I'll call you tonight,' she said, then stepped back, mouthing, 'I love you.'

Lachie gunned the Lexus, fearful he might be tempted to stay, and left Aretha standing in the road, wiping away a telltale tear as she watched the vehicle disappear southward.

Chapter 37

Monday, September 22, 2003

AFTER RETURNING from Kalgoorlie the previous February, Lachie went house hunting. Staying with his grandparents had its advantages; but also its disadvantages. Lachie had no idea what sort of reaction he might have received if he'd brought Aretha home, but he didn't want to find out. There are some things you just don't advertise. A serious relationship when you're recently separated and still unsure where things are going isn't seen as ideal in most family circles.

Being pressed for time, he called a friend of a friend who worked for an estate agent and secured a lease on a two-bedroom furnished unit in Marine Terrace, South Fremantle. It turned out to be an excellent choice.

Fremantle was where the diving club berthed its boat. Despite the situation with Bronte, he and Ranga remained friends and still dived together regularly. Also, he was within easy walking distance of most of the Café Strip bars and eateries.

Another plus was that his new unit was close enough to Cottesloe, where Bronte still lived, for Lachie to visit Iain, yet far enough away that he didn't have to worry about bumping into Bronte on the street.

Aretha applied for a Library Assistant position with the local council. She visited regularly for the first two months, moving in with Lachie once Fremantle Council had confirmed the appointment. By June, their domestic routine was firmly established.

Just after breakfast, as Aretha was preparing to leave for work, the doorbell rang. 'Will you get that, Love?' Lachie called from the bathroom.

'Morning,' said a tall, dark-haired man. 'Is Lachlan Kincaid home?'

'In the shower,' Aretha replied. 'Can I help?'

'I'll wait, if you don't mind. May I come in?'

She ushered him into the lounge, and he waited while she fetched Lachie.

He recognised Bruce Assan immediately. It had been almost a year since they last met.

'Bruce, what brings you here? I'm guessing this isn't a social call.'

'Not exactly. Bronte asked if I'd step up and serve this on you.'

He handed Lachie a manila envelope with 'Sleeman and Associates, Attorneys at Law' embossed in one top corner. Lachie looked at the envelope, then back to Bruce.

'Is this what I think it is?'

'Probably. It's been over twelve months since you separated, so there shouldn't be complications. Unless you choose to make it complicated, that is.' He glanced in Aretha's direction with a sardonic grin. 'Seems to me you won't be contesting the actual divorce.'

He turned back. 'She wants nothing from you—except for child support, that is. The court will decide the financial details.'

'And Iain?'

Bruce looked at him blankly. 'Best get yourself legal representation. One word of advice, though: don't rely on Lurie and Singh. You need a specialist divorce lawyer.'

With that, he turned and walked out.

Aretha ran to Lachie and put her arms around him.

'Oh well,' he said. 'We knew it was coming, I guess.' He hugged her tightly before continuing, 'Her family's firm has a hotshot divorce and family law section. I'll definitely be needing a specialist litigator; she'll be out to hurt me as much as possible. I just hope she doesn't involve you. The way she's been lately, nothing would surprise me.'

Lachie thought back over his deteriorating relationship with Bronte. From the day Iain was born, she'd had frequent bouts of depression, punctuated by violent outbursts at the slightest provocation. The only occasions she appeared close to being happy was when she was stoned; episodes that had become more frequent as time passed.

Iain's accident at the mine was merely the last straw, as far as Bronte was concerned. Sheeting all the blame on Lachie only justified her disapproval of him as a husband; disapproval that had since given way to open hostility.

Late November 2003

Lachie looked at his phone. Should he try again? Bronte had failed to answer his last three calls today—what made him suppose she'd pick up this time? He punched in her number again.

'What do you want? I told you to contact me through my lawyer.'

'And all the best to you too, Bron.' He bit his lip. *Steady*—he told himself—*don't poke the bear.*

'We need to arrange access for Christmas. I've organised time off, but I have to have dates.'

'Ian and I will spend Christmas Day with Mummy and Daddy,' she said matter-of-factly. 'You can have him on Boxing Day. Your family doesn't believe in Christmas anyway, so I can't imagine it'll make any difference to you.'

'OK,' he said after a pause, refusing to rise to the bait. 'Can I pick him up before lunch, or is that too much to ask?'

He immediately regretted the last part. Negotiating with Bronte these days was something like waltzing in a minefield.

'I'll let you know,' she said, 'it depends on whether we stay overnight. Was that all?'

Lachie considered his reply. Since the serving of documents two months earlier, all conversations between himself and Bronte had been cool, bordering on glacial. She refused to take most of his calls, any agreements being hammered out through their respective legal teams.

Might as well try for the daily double, he thought.

'The custody agreement,' he said. 'Your team hasn't supplied all the documents. Is there a problem?'

'I'm still considering my options. You'll hear from them in good time.'

'For crying out loud, Bron, I've gone along with everything you've asked for. You can have the Cottesloe unit. I've agreed to help with the repayments until you start work with Sleeman and Associates. I've agreed to the maintenance package. All I ask for is reasonable access. You owe it to Iain to grant him some stability, even if you don't give a shit about my feelings. Why the Hell can't we ...'

The dial tone interrupted him mid-sentence. She had hung up on him. Again.

'Still no joy?' Aretha frowned, seeing Lachie's pained expression.

'She's just being difficult. She seems to take pleasure in keeping me on a string,' he said. 'I've let her do all the organising. She has her family firm at her disposal, and besides, she'd never agree to anything if she thought it was my idea. And yet she insists on delaying and postulating over everything. I figured by letting her have her way, things would run smoothly, but apparently, she sees it all as a chance to make my life as miserable as possible.'

'Maybe you should go back to your lawyer,' Aretha said. 'She's just going to string it out forever if you let her. You need something in writing—something you can enforce.'

Lachlan agreed.

It was three weeks before they negotiated an interim agreement. Bronte had agreed to allow Christmas access from noon on the 26th and even consented to Lachie taking Iain to Kalgoorlie for a few days.

'At least you can make plans now,' Aretha said. 'We'll all spend the New Year with Mum, Jimmy, and Marvin. It'll be great to see them again.'

When it came down to it, however, getting Bronte to agree to an arrangement was one thing; getting her to follow through was another thing entirely.

It was around 11 am on the 26th when Lachie's phone started its merry tune. He recognised Bronte's number immediately.

'Hi Bron, we'll be leaving shortly. Should be there on time, as promised.'

'Don't bother,' she said. 'Ian's down with a nasty case of the 'flu. I'm taking him to the doctor. We're just about to leave the house with him now, actually.'

'I'll come right away,' Lachie said. 'You may need some help.'

'Daddy's here. Don't bother yourself. You get going on your little trip.'

Lachie heard something in her voice. A tone he'd become used to of late. 'OK,' he said. 'I'll call you tonight. Give him a hug for me.' He was about to say more, but Bronte had rung off already.

Lachie stood for several seconds before turning to Aretha, who raised her eyebrows in concern.

'Bron's up to her tricks again. She says Iain has the 'flu. She's probably lying, but what can you do?' He shrugged resignedly. 'It'd be no good going over there—she wouldn't be home.'

After a pause, he added, 'Might as well make tracks then, Love. The sooner we start, the sooner we'll get there.'

They drove in almost total silence for most of the trip. Aretha tried to engage Lachie in conversation, but his mind was elsewhere. It wasn't until they arrived at the Browne family house in Kalgoorlie that Lachie finally seemed to put his worries behind him.

That night, and the following morning, he called Bronte's number several times without success. By mid-afternoon, Lachie rang Ian Sleeman.

Ian greeted him warmly, wishing him a belated Merry Christmas. No, he didn't know where Bronte was. She had spent Christmas Day and the evening with them on their yacht, leaving at around 10.30 am on Boxing Day. Her mood? Just the usual—Ian informed him.

Lachlan wondered what construed the usual for Bronte these days, but offered no comment.

'How was Iain?' he asked.

'Fine,' Ian Sleeman replied. 'He had a glorious day. We sailed across to Rotto again and took him swimming at Little Parakeet Bay. He's a great kid, isn't he?'

'He sure is.' Lachie chose not to mention the failed access arrangements. 'Well, nice to talk again, Ian. Give my best to Claire.'

Over the following week, they tried several times to reach Bronte by phone, without success. It wasn't until the day before they returned to Perth that Lachie finally pinned her down.

'Ian's fine now,' Bronte responded to Lachie's enquiries. 'We spent New Year's with Bruce and Greg and the band. They've been touring the eastern states—we're in Bundaberg at the moment.'

Bruce had married about three years earlier and now had two children of his own. From what Lachie understood, Bronte had been spending most of her free time with Bruce and Angela and their respective families. Angela had fallen pregnant, and she and Greg had married at around the same time as Bruce and his wife, Holly.

The band had released an album, and the members had taken extended leave from their day jobs to do a promotional tour.

'When will you be back? I haven't seen Iain for ages, and I'm heading back to Skull Creek next week.'

'Oh, not for a while,' she replied. 'I'll call you and let you know.'

'Is he there now?' Lachie asked. 'Can I talk to him?'

There was a pause before Bronte continued. 'He's not here. Holly took him to see a movie.'

Lachie doubted that was the truth, but once again was in no position to argue.

Resignedly, preparing to sign off, he asked Bronte if she would please call and put Iain on the phone when he returned from his cinema outing. Of course, she would, Bronte assured him. She wasn't totally heartless. The underlying tone in her voice, however, told Lachie not to hold his breath.

'Bron!' he blurted. 'You can't keep blocking me like this. We have an access agreement. I've bent over backwards to appease you—the least you can do is keep your end of the bargain. He's my son. I've got the right to see him, and he has the right to stay in touch with his father.'

'Ha!' Bronte almost screamed. 'Your son? You stupid prick! You really imagine a beautiful boy like my Ian could come from someone like you? He's Bruce's you fucking fool!'

Lachlan felt the colour draining from his face. Hadn't he actually suspected that at one time? He cast his mind back to Iain's long dark hair at birth, the lack of the Kincaid 'fish-hook' on his nose—a nose that later developed into a long, aquiline proboscis—and his dark complexion. Hadn't he, in fact, deliberately suppressed these suspicions?

'I don't believe you,' he muttered. 'You're just winding me up.'

'You pathetic imbecile! Bruce always was twice the man you are. I wasn't sure until he was born, of course, but once I saw Ian, I knew. You were just the stupid, dumb cuckold who offered to take the responsibility. I guess your Kincaid ego wouldn't allow you to see the truth. And then, I had to let you suck me into marriage!'

Lachie was dumbstruck. He was about to speak again when Bronte cut him short.

'Of course, I'll deny all that, if you're thinking of reneging on the child support. Sure, you could arrange a DNA test, but do you really want to go down that track? Do you really want to admit to everyone that you couldn't even get your girlfriend pregnant without help?'

'Bron, Iain is my son. He's been my son since the day he was born, and I fully intend to honour the maintenance agreement. All I'm asking from you is that you keep up your end of the bargain.' He paused, swallowing hard before continuing. 'Iain looks on me as his father. Surely you're not going to mess with his head by telling him otherwise, are you?'

'No, I guess not. But I'll enjoy screwing with your head in the meantime.'

Lachie opened his mouth to say more, but she was gone again.

Chapter 38

Sunday, January 4th, 2004

RACHEL LOOKED UP as Lachie and Aretha entered. 'Hi there, you two. Lunch won't be ready for a while. Can I get you a drink or anything?'

'We're fine, thanks, Mum,' Lachie replied. 'We came early as we're driving back to the city later today. Aretha starts back at work tomorrow.'

Rachel took a sip from her Chardonnay. Sunday was the one day of the week she allowed herself alcohol—aside from that, she was still teetotal.

'You don't look happy,' she said, eyeing them both with concern. 'Something on your minds?'

Lachlan detailed his recent conversation with Bronte, including her assertion that he was not Iain's father. Before he knew it, he was spilling out all the details of Bronte's increasingly uncooperative attitude, her frequent blocking of his access, and her general air of vindictiveness.

'Do you believe her? I mean, about Iain?'

'I don't really know what to think,' Lachie replied. 'I have to admit, when he was first born I wondered, briefly. He's got none of the Kincaid physical traits, but Bron said he followed her side. Apparently, Claire Sleeman's father was part Lebanese, or so she said.'

'Mmm,' Rachel mused. 'So what are you planning to do—are you still going to fight her for access if she keeps on being so belligerent?'

'Yeah, I am,' Lachie asserted. 'Iain's my son and always will be. I can't just switch off my feelings after five years, can I? I love him, and I'm the only Dad he knows. I can't imagine she'd tell him otherwise—no matter how much she seems to hate me these days.'

'So is Bronte home now?' Rachel asked.

'Personally, I don't believe she ever left the state,' Lachie answered. 'It was her way of avoiding letting me have him for Christmas and New Year. I just wonder if she'll let me see him before I start back at Skull Creek next Friday.'

Rachel shook her head. 'I tried getting to know her better. You remember, when you were away that time?' Lachie nodded, and Rachel continued. 'I'm no expert, by any means, but there's something seriously wrong with her mental state.'

'Bron's been erratic since Iain was born,' Lachie said. 'I reckon her biggest issue is that she smokes too much happy weed.'

They sat in silence for several seconds. It was Lachie who broke the ice. 'So how's Graham these days—are you two planning on getting hitched anytime soon?'

Rachel laughed the suggestion away, but Lachie sensed he might have been closer to the truth than he had thought.

After lunch, they said their farewells and headed off for the trip back to Fremantle.

'I'm sure she'll let you see Iain before you go back to work,' Aretha assured him. 'Surely that's not too much to ask?' Lachie shrugged. He wasn't optimistic and told her so.

Over the next several days, Bronte refused to answer his calls—even when he used Aretha's phone. It seemed she wasn't answering her phone unless she knew who was on the other end.

Frequent drive-bys of her home produced no satisfaction either. Eventually, Lachlan had to accept she was staying elsewhere and would be until he was out of town.

* * *

A few days after Lachie had returned to his job at the mine, Bronte had a surprise encounter. As she alighted from her BMW outside her unit, having dropped Iain at daycare, a familiar figure stepped in front of her.

'Malcolm!' she exclaimed. 'What are you doing here?'

'We need to talk.'

'I've got nothing to say to you.' Bronte made to walk past him, but he blocked her way.

'You don't need to talk—you just need to listen.' The sternness of his voice stopped her in her tracks, despite herself.

Bronte fixed Malcolm with a defiant glare—yet she remained silent.

'Lachlan seems to be under the impression he has to keep you happy. That somehow you have the upper hand.' Bronte made to speak, but Malcolm cut her short. 'And before you say it—no, he hasn't asked me to step in.'

He paused briefly before continuing in a low, menacing voice, 'I don't have the disadvantage of giving a shit about you or your feelings; my only concern is that Lachlan has proper access to his son. Yes—I said *his* son.'

He jabbed her chest aggressively with his index finger. 'You ... will stop playing these stupid mind games with him; you'll pull your fucking head in and cooperate—fully. You'll allow Lachlan access to Iain as per all arrangements, and if you don't ...'

Malcolm leaned closer, to where Bronte could taste his breath in her mouth, and continued, 'I've got some pretty nasty and unscrupulous friends who'd take great delight in putting the snatch on a pretty young thing like you. They might even let you live—for a while. One thing's for sure—you'd experience things you could hardly imagine in your worst nightmares before they finished with you; before they finally fed you to the fishes in Fremantle Harbour.'

He stopped to let the menace in his voice sink in. Colour drained from Bronte's face and she swayed slightly. *He really means it!* Her throat was suddenly very dry. She opened her mouth to speak, then closed it again.

'Do we understand each other, Sweet Cheeks?' The menace was still there.

Bronte nodded dumbly, finally finding the strength to push past him, and retreated up the steps to her unit. Tears stung her eyes as she scrambled to fit the key in the latch.

She looked back as the door swung open. Malcolm stood, smiling, as he gave a little wave. 'See you then, Bron,' he said in a loud, cheery voice, for the benefit of any witnesses. 'I'll make the arrangements. Just leave it with me.'

Bronte retreated inside. Malcolm Kincaid—Mister Fixit—strode back to the rental car he had arrived in and drove off without a backward glance.

Bronte collapsed onto the sofa and sobbed for several minutes. Eventually, she rose and opened a bottle of phenobarbital, swallowing three tablets and washing them down with a full glass of shiraz, swallowed in a single draught. She might have smoked a joint as well, but her hands shook so badly she couldn't trust herself with a naked flame.

She made her way to her bedroom, collapsed onto the bed, and waited for the goofballs to take her away from the nightmare she had experienced. As she drifted into unconsciousness, the last image in her mind was Malcolm's smiling face and his parting words: *I'll make the arrangements. Just leave it with me.*

Chapter 39

Good Friday, April 9th.

LACHIE PULLED THE LEXUS TO A HALT under a shady tree opposite a public park close to Bronte's unit. From where they were, they had an unimpeded view of her driveway and front door. It was fifteen minutes before the prearranged pickup time, and Lachie sat back and turned on the radio.

'If I'm early, she'll say I'm being pushy,' Lachie explained to Aretha. 'If I'm over ten minutes late, she's just as likely to say I didn't turn up and take Iain out somewhere.'

'I thought things were getting better between you,' Aretha said. 'Didn't she tell you she wouldn't block you anymore?'

'Yeah, the last couple of visits went without a hitch. When I was in my lawyer's office the other day though, he called her to confirm this visit, and she abused the hell out of him and ended up saying she'd do anything she could to make my life miserable—her words exactly.'

'I'm so sorry, Lachie,' Aretha said. 'I know how much all this hurts you. I wish I could help.'

Lachie shrugged. 'Not much you can do, is there? Since Iain started school this year, it's been getting harder and harder to arrange visits that fit with Her Ladyship's schedule. We just have to roll with the punches these days, I guess.'

The sad truth was, Lachie confided, that Bronte's actions were becoming more and more unpredictable as time passed. What was it Rachel had called it—baby blues? Lachie put it down to the realisation she could never have another child. Bronte had looked forward to being a mother and taken this news badly. Her continued heavy marijuana use wasn't helping either, he knew. She had also let it slip that she was using other substances; antidepressants, sleeping pills, and who knows what else.

All this he had discussed with Aretha previously, but sometimes he still needed to unload. Aretha listened sympathetically, interrupting only when the time slipped past midday.

'Well, we'd best get going,' she said. 'Mustn't keep Her Ladyship waiting.'

They pulled up outside Bronte's unit at five past twelve. Lachie rang the bell and waited. After three attempts without success, he rang her number. The call went straight to voice mail.

'Hi Bron, we're at your place now. Any idea when you'll be here? Call me. OK?'

Over the next half-hour, he left several messages, resisting the impulse to sound anything other than friendly—though his actual feelings were becoming less amiable as time passed.

After forty minutes, he called Ian Sleeman.

'Hi, Lachie,' Ian said. 'What's new? Haven't spoken with you in a while.'

'I'm supposed to pick up Iain today at midday, but there's no sign of Bron. Any idea where she might be?'

No, Ian Sleeman explained amiably, neither he nor Claire had heard anything from her for several days. They were expecting her to visit that evening, though. Was there any message?

'No, I guess not,' Lachie said. 'I've left heaps of messages on her phone.'

'Well, I'll let her know you called—and that you've been waiting around,' Ian said.

Oh, she'll know I'm waiting around—Lachie thought.

'OK,' he said. 'We'll wait until one o'clock. If she doesn't show by then, we'll be on our way down south. Give my best to Claire and give my boy an enormous hug from me when you see him, hey?'

Ian said he would and signed off.

At one o'clock, Lachie made one final attempt to contact Bronte before starting the car and heading back to Fremantle to collect their things.

Atop a grassy hill just 500 metres away, Bronte smirked with satisfaction as Lachlan's car drove off. She had watched for over an hour as Lachlan Kincaid and his black whore sat outside her home and had listened to Lachlan's pathetic, simperingly polite phone messages. Messages no one would ever answer—no one would ever hear. She deleted each in turn and waited for the next with smug anticipation.

Then, of course, there was the best bit. The part where, earlier, she observed them sitting not more than a hundred metres from her, chatting away happily as if they hadn't a care in the world. They seemed to be watching her unit. What were they expecting—a bloody welcoming committee? For a moment she thought they might spot her, but she remembered Lachlan hadn't yet seen her new Audi coupé. She slumped low in the seat as she studied them from behind mirrored sunglasses. Oh, how she wished for a long-distance microphone; wished to be able to overhear their conversation.

Bronte turned to look at her son, sleeping peacefully in his booster seat. She had only given him one tablet, yet he'd been out for three hours. She'd wake him soon, she thought, before giving him the rest and attaching the hose to her exhaust as she had planned.

Oh yes, you'll be sorry, Lachlan Kincaid. You, your arsehole of an uncle, and that black slut of yours. I'll make you wish you'd never been born, you prick!

Bronte packed an appreciable amount of weed—to which she'd added some crumbled hash, for good measure—into a small glass bong. Once she'd fully loaded the implement, she set it aside and busied herself with the plastic tube. She poked one end into the car's exhaust, allowing the other end to hang in through the rear window. Once satisfied with her efforts, she woke the sleeping boy.

He stirred, and without opening his eyes, said, 'Are we home yet, Mummy?'

'No, Dear. But I've got a drink for you.'

She held the cup of apple juice, duly laced with several barbiturate pills, up to his mouth and he drank readily. Apple was his favourite, and she had added extra sugar to hide any chemical undertaste.

Bronte slipped a CD into the player and opened the bottle of tablets, swallowing the remaining pills one after another. She then lit up the bong and inhaled deeply, holding in the smoke as long as possible. She figured she'd wait until she felt the buzz before starting the engine.

There's something about barbiturates: Sometimes you notice the effects coming on, and sometimes you don't. Most often, it's the latter.

One minute Bronte was drifting in cannabis-induced euphoria—wondering just how it would feel to die—and the next she was out like a candle in a hurricane.

She might have been unconscious for hours—and indeed, neither she nor Iain might ever have woken at all—if not for John Lock.

Mr Lock was walking his Yorkshire terrier, Roger, and gave him a run off the leash. Being a Yorkie, Roger's curiosity prevailed, and he decided close scrutiny of Bronte's car was absolutely essential. One look at the hose from the car's exhaust hanging through the rear window was enough for John.

He wrenched the car door open and checked the occupants—expecting to find the vehicle had run out of fuel after delivering its lethal dose of carbon monoxide. John noted with relief that the young woman and child were just sleeping. The pungent smell of marijuana told him part of the story. The empty barbiturate bottle told him the rest.

He phoned for an ambulance and pulled both Bronte and Iain from the car, laying them in the recovery position on the grass. As he monitored his patients, both of whom were breathing shallowly, John Lock offered a silent prayer of thanks for the first aid classes taken as a gym teacher several years ago.

Lachie's phone burst into life just as they were passing the Boddington turnoff, about an hour south of Perth. He recognised Harvey's number immediately.

'Hey, Ranga, what's happening? You all set for the dive tomorrow?'

'I won't be coming, and I reckon you'll be giving it a miss too,' Ranga replied. 'Bronte and Iain are in hospital.'

'What?' Lachie hit the brakes and swerved to the side of the road, the Lexus' tires squealing in protest. 'What's happened?'

Harvey explained the sequence of events as he understood it, including the way they had been found. By the time he had given the details, Lachie had turned the Lexus around and was speeding northward back toward Perth. As he drove, Aretha called Fremantle Hospital to check on Iain and Bronte. She passed the phone to Lachie. 'They can't give me any details. I'm not family.'

Lachie took the phone, and after a brief conversation, he hung up.

He relayed the details to Aretha as they drove, heading straight to the hospital.

'Bron's parents are there, and so is Ranga,' he said. 'They're all worried as hell. What was she thinking?' He pounded the steering wheel in frustration and anger. 'What the fuck was she thinking?'

At the hospital, Harvey pulled Lachie to one side. 'We've been worried about Bronte's state of mind for a while,' he confided. 'Dad tried to talk to her about it several times, but she just brushed him off. She knows you and I are still mates, so she doesn't confide in me at all. Thank God they found her in time.'

'Sorry, Ranga,' Lachie answered. 'I don't have any sympathy for her right now. I know she's your sister and all that—but she almost killed Iain. And who knows how much damage she might have done to him in the process? Feeding barbs to a kid his age ...' He rubbed his temples with frustration. 'I'm not sure if I'll ever be able to forgive her for that—I don't give a rat's arse how depressed or whatever she was.'

Harvey nodded. 'It's OK Lachie, I get where you're coming from. We're all worried about Iain, too. Let's just hope for the best and see how things are tomorrow. They're both in the best place right now, at least.'

It was 48 hours before Bronte and Iain were released from the hospital. Iain into the care of his mother's parents; Bronte as a voluntary inpatient at a rehab centre in the hinterland an hour's drive from Perth.

Hospital staff had called in the police, and it had taken a lot of negotiation and string-pulling to avoid Bronte facing a criminal conviction. At a bedside hearing, the magistrate suspended any charges—conditional on Bronte entering a full detox program and agreeing to abstain from using any illicit drugs in the future.

Three days after the incident, Lachie visited the Sleeman home to check on his son's condition.

'He seems to be doing OK,' Ian said. 'The doctors pumped his stomach in time to remove most of the barbiturate. He was quite woozy for a while, but they say he should recover well enough. You're welcome to come and see him any time, Lachie. We're trying to stay neutral concerning your dispute with Bronte. We're both aware there are two sides to every story.'

'OK, thanks for that,' Lachie said. 'I suppose this is the best place for him at the moment —I'm due back at the mine in a few days, anyway.' He didn't mention the fact that Iain had not warmed to Aretha at all, no matter how much she tried to dote on him, and probably wouldn't have felt comfortable living with them. Lachie remained convinced this was Bronte's doing. 'How is Bron, anyway?' he asked, more for Ian's benefit than out of any genuine concern. At that moment, Lachie could hardly have cared less about her welfare.

'Once she realised what she'd nearly done, she was horrified,' Ian said. 'It seems she's been using drugs since Ian's birth. Were you aware?'

'Sorry, Ian. Yes, I knew she was smoking marijuana, but I wasn't aware of her taking anything else. I suppose I should have spoken to you, but I wasn't sure how to broach the subject.'

'Well, let's put it all behind us,' Ian said. 'And look to the future.'

Chapter 40

Monday, July 12, 2004

'SORRY WE WEREN'T ABLE TO VISIT YOU, BRONTE,' Ian Sleeman said as he hefted her suitcase and carried it to his BMW. Even with the extra clothing they had sent to her, the case was still fairly light. 'We asked, but they insisted on no visitors during your, er, stay.'

'It's OK, Daddy. I know. The staff here explained that was part of the deal. I knew from the start that I'd need to toe the line and behave myself. I'm just happy it's all over.'

She peered into the interior of the car. 'Is Ian not with you?' Her voice quavered slightly. 'Is he all right?'

'He's fine, Love. He's at home with your mother. We decided against bringing him today.'

'In case the madwoman decides to try again?' she said, making no attempt to hide the bitterness in her voice.

'Of course not,' Ian said. 'It's nothing like that. We thought you might appreciate a little space, that's all.'

Ian held the door as his daughter got into the passenger seat. She stared into the distance without saying more.

He climbed in, started the engine, and turned toward her. 'We've all missed you, Bronnie,' he said tenderly. 'Especially your mother. She's been beside herself—and Iain asks for you every day.' Bronte couldn't remember the last time he'd called her Bronnie. It was probably when she was still in primary school. She decided she liked it, despite herself.

'I've missed you all too,' she said, trying vainly to hold back tears. Ian waited while she covered her face with her hands, sobbing softly for several minutes before wiping away her tears with a tissue. She turned to face her father with reddened eyes. 'I'm so ashamed,' she sobbed, adding, 'I almost killed my own son. What kind of mother am I? What kind of person am I?'

'You weren't yourself,' Ian whispered. 'You've not been yourself for some time, but that's behind us now. Everything will be different from here on. You'll stay with us for a while until you're up to restarting your life. Don't worry about work. You can come back whenever you feel ready. For now, let's concentrate on getting you well again.'

Bronte nodded silently, still dabbing at her swollen eyes, and not trusting herself to speak at that moment. After a few seconds Ian continued, 'You'll be fine, Bronnie, you'll be fine.'

He leaned across and wrapped his arms around her, holding her close until he was sure she had regained control of herself before speaking again. 'Now let's get going so we can reunite Iain with the mother he's been missing so badly—and you can give him the hug you both so desperately need.'

She returned Ian's gaze, swallowing hard. 'Thanks, Daddy,' she whispered as Ian pulled out onto the road for the drive home.

It was several minutes before Bronte spoke again. 'How's Lachlan—have you seen him lately?'

'He calls around to see Iain every day when he's in town and takes him home every weekend. He doesn't mention you, if that's what you're asking.'

She was silent for a moment more before saying, 'I need to see him.'

'Do you think that's wise, Bronnie? I mean, there's been a lot of ...'

'I *need* to see him, Daddy. We have ... issues to sort out.'

She turned to face her father again. 'I spent a lot of time in therapy. It took a while, but I know now just how screwed up my mind was. I hated Lachlan for what happened to Ian at the mine, but what I did was worse—much, much worse.'

Ian Sleeman was silent, waiting for her to continue.

'I have to apologise to him. No, I have to ask his forgiveness,' she continued. 'If he can't forgive me, then I'll learn to live with it, but I have to try.'

Ian nodded. 'Well, let's get you home and settled first. We can contact Lachlan then, if that's what you want.'

* * *

It was two weeks before Bronte got her chance to ask for Lachie's forgiveness. She met him at the door of the Sleeman home and immediately asked if they could talk privately.

'Do we really have anything to say to each other?' he asked. 'I know how you feel—you know how I feel—the divorce is final. What's to discuss?'

'Lachlan, please give me just a few minutes.'

He shrugged. 'OK. Fire away.'

She ushered him into the sitting room and dropped into a chair opposite him.

Fearing she might lose the courage to proceed, or that he might lose the patience to listen, Bronte launched into what she hoped might explain her actions.

'Lachlan, I've had three months of therapy and soul-searching. Three months with no contact outside of an occasional call from Daddy and daily sessions with a psychologist. I'm not going to try to explain away or justify what I did, or how I've been acting lately.'

'Lately?' Lachie raised his eyebrows. 'You've been in Cuckoo Land since Iain was born!'

'I know,' she said. 'I know I have. I understand now what was happening to me. I was having a breakdown, and I should have asked for help. Instead, I tried to block it all out with drugs and alcohol. I … I don't even remember everything that happened during that time. How the hell I kept my life together at all, I'll never know.'

She looked forlornly into his eyes. 'I want you to forgive me.'

Lachie made to speak, but she cut him short. 'Don't say anything yet, please. I accept that you probably won't be able to right now, but maybe in time you might. If not, then I'll just have to deal with it.'

Lachie returned her gaze, saying nothing. At least he hadn't stormed out. That was something.

As Lachie listened, Bronte poured out everything she had held inside for so long: her profound sense of loss and anguish on learning she could never have another child. Her feeling of guilt at the fact that if they stayed together, Lachlan would never have a son of his own. The self-loathing that came from realising it was all her fault, that she and Bruce had simply got a little too stoned one night while Lachlan wasn't home and went too far. She barely remembered the event, she confessed. The knowledge that she had almost ended her son's life, as well as her own, in a drug-induced neurosis that bordered on schizophrenia.

All this—and more—she poured out, punctuated with sobbing and occasional silent pauses, while Lachlan watched, seemingly not knowing what to do or say.

Eventually, mentally exhausted, she sat facing Lachie. There were no more tears left to cry.

'If you chose to contest custody of Ian, I wouldn't blame you,' she said. 'It's too late for us, as a couple. I've wrecked everything, and besides, I've seen the way you and Aretha are. She's the one you should have married, not me.'

Lachie chuckled. 'She was fifteen when you and I got married. I probably would've ended up in jail!'

Bronte managed a snicker. 'Maybe it's just as well, then.'

'As for Iain,' Lachie continued, 'he's your son as much as mine—maybe more, but let's not go there again. I've got no intention of trying to take him away from you, Bron, so long as you can promise me he'll be safe. You're not an evil person. You just got … sort of lost, I guess.'

'I promise you, Lachlan, I'll never put him in harm's way again. And I'll never stop you from seeing him. I don't know what got into me. You're his Daddy, as far as he's concerned, and that's what's important, isn't it?'

Lachie agreed. 'Well,' he said, 'Iain and I had best be going. Aretha's waiting in the car. She'll be wondering what's keeping us.'

By mid-August, Bronte felt confident enough to return to her Cottesloe unit and to recommence her job with Sleeman and Associates. She still attended weekly counselling sessions and was progressing well. After their discussion, Lachie and Bronte's relationship thawed. It would be a long time, though, before the ice would melt completely.

Iain had started school earlier that year, so Lachie and Bronte ironed out a schedule that allowed her to work from 8 am to 3 pm when Lachie was at Skull Creek, and 5.30 other times. She delivered Iain to his daycare in the mornings, and they dropped him at school. In the weeks that Lachie was not at the mine, he'd pick Iain up from school and deliver him back home to her unit after dinner, usually around 6:30.

It was near the end of Iain's second term that his symptoms appeared.

Chapter 41

Friday, September 3, 2004

IAIN HAD BEEN IRRITABLE for some time and complaining of stomach pains when Bronte took him to her local GP. Dr Mark Patterson had attended university with Ian Sleeman and remained a family friend.

'Now then, young fella, let's see what the trouble is,' he said as he began his examination. He gently prodded Iain's abdomen, noting the way his young patient winced at his touch.

'You say he's had this tenderness for some time?' he asked.

Bronte nodded. 'And he complains of feeling sick almost every day.'

'Hmm, you told me about that incident at the mine a while back — when was it? Two years ago?'

'About that,' Bronte confirmed.

'I wouldn't expect there to be a connection, but there's definite soreness around the liver area, and I'm not happy with his yellow complexion—it suggests jaundice. I don't want to jump to conclusions, but I'd like to arrange some scans.'

Mark used the telephone to call a colleague, winking at Bronte as he dialled, saying, 'Sometimes it pays to have the right connections.'

After briefly discussing the details, he handed Bronte a referral form. 'Be there tomorrow at ten o'clock,' he said. 'Make an appointment to bring him back here next Friday. I should have the results by then.'

What followed were seven anxious days for Bronte. She kept her son home from school for the time being; the term was due to end in about a week, anyway. Bronte called in at the office each morning so she could bring work home with her. It was halfway through Lachlan's rotation at the mine, and she saw no need to inform him. She'd talk to him when there was more to know.

Doctor Patterson's expression as he ushered Bronte and Iain into his consulting room the following week was impassive, yet Bronte sensed all was not well.

He examined Iain once again, paying particular attention to his face and neck, and looking closely into his eyes. 'Well, Iain,' he said in a kindly voice, 'you are looking colourful, aren't you?' then he added, 'Why don't you go and look at the goldfish in the waiting room?'

He called a receptionist and asked her to take Iain to the creche area while he spoke with Bronte.

'It's definitely jaundice,' he said, before bringing up the scans and reports on his computer. 'There's a small mass in his liver, possibly a tumour. It seems to be obstructing the bile duct. There may also be something in the gallbladder.' He paused, still reading the report, then scrutinising the scan on his screen.

Finally, as Bronte was feeling she could contain herself no longer, he turned to face her.

'I'd like him to visit a specialist. There's a very good hepatic surgeon at the Children's Hospital. I'll make a call to see if he can examine Iain as a matter of urgency.' He placed his hand on Bronte's shoulder, seeing the tears beginning to well in her eyes. 'It's only small, and most likely benign, but we can't assume anything. The important thing is to check it out as soon as possible.'

Bronte's mind swam as she left the surgery. A mixture of shock, fear, and anger swept over her. Mostly anger. Anger at Lachlan and that damned mine. Why had she agreed to even go there in the first place? God knows she had never wanted to. Why had she stayed in that day and let Lachlan take their son gallivanting around a working mine? And why had Lachlan, the supposed caring and diligent father, left him alone within sight of the tailings dam?

Unable to even contemplate driving with such thoughts swirling in her mind, she walked to a nearby coffee shop and ordered a large latte. As she sipped her coffee—trying to still her shaking hands while Iain sucked on a chocolate milkshake opposite her—she wondered if there might still be some weed somewhere at home. Oh, how she needed a smoke right now, she thought. Oh, how …

Bronte shook her head determinedly. *No way. No way am I going back there. I'm back in control now. Ian and I will get through this together. And when it's over, I'll sue those Kincaid bastards for every penny they have!* She must have said that last part out loud, as Iain looked up swiftly. 'It's OK, Darling,' she said. 'Mummy's just a little upset. Drink up, and we'll go see a movie before we go home.' Iain squealed with delight, momentarily forgetting his stomach ache, and finished his milkshake with one long, noisy slurp.

Monday, September 13, 2004

Bronte's phone rang. It was Lachlan. She considered ignoring it, but as he would have just picked Ian up from daycare, she thought better of it.

'Is Ian all right?' she said.

'Iain's fine. What's this about him going to hospital?'

So he's told you, then—'He's got a growth in his liver,' she said, struggling to keep her composure. 'Thanks to you and your carelessness. And that damn mine.'

'Why didn't you tell me? How long have you known about this?'

Bronte relayed what details she could. She knew little more than she had on the day of that last visit to Dr Patterson. No, she hadn't told Lachie. What could he have done, anyway? He was two thousand kilometres away, working.

'I could have come home!' Lachlan almost shouted. '*That's* what I could have done.'

Bronte took a deep breath. 'OK. Sorry. I guess I'm a bit stressed. There's nothing we can do until we find out what's wrong. Which we will—next Friday.'

Lachie turned to look at Iain, who was chatting happily to Aretha. A growth in the liver? What on Earth could that mean?

He decided not to dwell on it. The last thing he wanted would be to worry Iain; he'd talk it over with Aretha later. Once the boy was briefly out of earshot, he gave Aretha a brief précis of the situation. 'And she didn't see fit to tell you anything?' She shook her head in disbelief.

'Yeah, well, we've patched things up a bit—but we're obviously not best mates yet.'

* * *

The following Friday found Lachlan, Aretha, and Bronte at the hospital, waiting for news from the medical team. Iain had been in surgery for over an hour. 'I'm sorry I didn't keep you informed,' Bronte said. 'I know I promised to let go of all the old animosity—I keep recalling that trip to the mine, and ...'

'He'll be OK, I'm sure he will,' said Aretha. She placed a hand on Bronte's wrist.

Bronte let it stay there for a few seconds before rising to her feet. 'I'm off to grab a coffee. Anyone want one?' They shook their heads.

After she left, Aretha turned to Lachie, raising her eyes. 'Well, you tried,' he said with a shrug.

When the news came, it was the best result they had dared hope for. The growth in Iain's liver was benign and had been removed without complications. It was about the size of a large marble and had severely restricted the flow of bile from his liver.

'Will there be any long-term issues?' Lachie asked.

'We're optimistic at the moment,' the surgeon said. 'Time will tell, though. I left his gallbladder in place, but there's a chance we might have to reevaluate that decision in the future.'

'Might it have been caused by the mine tailings?' Lachie feared the answer, yet still wanted to know.

'Arsenic exposure can cause hepatic tumours,' the doctor said. 'Mercury has also been implicated in similar conditions. I understand both were present in the pond Iain was exposed to, along with other chemicals, so yes, it's possible—in fact, highly likely. He's an otherwise very healthy young man, however, so I'd expect a complete recovery. I trust the source of the contamination has been contained?'

'It has,' replied Lachie. 'We're continually monitoring the area and the adjacent creek. We have to; it supplies water to a nearby settlement.'

'Well, I hope you're on the ball with that,' the medico said. 'I'd hate to be drinking water that has *any* measurable amount of arsenic or mercury in it. Your son's exposure was significant, but short-lived. Chronic, long-term exposure is something else entirely.'

'We've got a team on it at all times,' Lachie replied, hoping he sounded more confident than he felt. *Uncle Mal said it was well below safe levels. He wouldn't lie about something like that, would he?*

By the time Iain was awake enough for visitors, there was a throng of well-wishers in the waiting room. The staff allowed Iain no more than two visitors at once, and only for a few minutes at a time. Bronte and her mother went in first; Lachie and Ranga next. Aretha insisted she would wait until he felt better. 'I'm not really family,' she said. 'I'm sure he's more eager to see you than me.'

Iain, still sedated, was barely aware of who was in the ward with him anyway. It wasn't until the following morning that the cheeky boy they all knew and loved was back on deck, even if in a subdued version.

Over the ensuing weeks, Iain's health improved quickly, and before long, he had returned to his former self in almost every way.

Chapter 42

MALCOLM KINCAID was about to end a phone call with his stockbroker when there was a buzz on the intercom. 'What is it, Susan?' he asked. 'It had better be important.'

Susan Friend was Malcolm's personal secretary and had been for three years. Three years that had seen her virtually married to her role. Three years in which she had learned more than most people would ever know about Malcolm Kincaid.

She knew better than to interrupt Malcolm when his office door was closed, unless it was a matter of extreme urgency. She also knew just what would count as an emergency in Malcolm's eyes.

'We've had a package delivered, Mr Kincaid. I think you should see it.'

'A package? I guess you'd better bring it in. Oh, and get Greta to fetch me a coffee, will you? From the sound of your voice, I think I might need one.'

The item in question was a large manilla envelope, which Susan had carefully opened. The embossed logo of Sleeman and Associates was clearly visible in one corner.

Malcolm perused the contents and said, 'Better set up an appointment with John Lurie. We might need some legal input on this.'

'Three o'clock this afternoon. I've cancelled everything from one o'clock onwards.'

Malcolm smiled. 'Thanks, Susan, I should marry you, shouldn't I?'

'And lose the best PA you've ever had? I don't think so,' she answered with a smile. She turned on one heel and exited the office, as Greta arrived with Malcolm's short black. He favoured Susan's retreating figure with an admiring gaze. *She sure knows how to flaunt it*—he thought. He'd never risk losing such a valuable assistant by making any advances, but still, a man could dream, couldn't he?

Greta placed the coffee, along with a couple of caramel shortbreads, on his desk. 'That'll be all, Greta,' he said as he reached for the intercom. Depressing the button, he said, 'Get me Lachlan on the phone, will you?'

He paused briefly. 'On second thoughts, cancel that.'

If Lachie was aware of the pending lawsuit, Malcolm would soon find out. If not — well, maybe in Lachie's case, ignorance just might be bliss after all.

*   *   *

Later, in the offices of Lurie, Singh, and Partners, John Lurie looked up from the documents Malcolm had handed him. 'How much of this is provable? I mean, is that water as contaminated as they say?'

'It's a tailings dam,' Malcolm said. 'Of course it's contaminated. They're alleging criminal incompetence—and frankly, I'm inclined to agree with them, though I'll deny that if I'm ever asked.

'The thing is, Lachlan didn't have permission to take his family there in the first place. I don't care if he is the manager, the buck stops with him, and his ball-buster of a wife. Or ex-wife, to be precise. I don't see how she can sue the company for something we had no control over—something that Lachlan, the boy's father, was totally responsible for. Settle with them if you have to, but keep it manageable.'

Then he added, pointing his finger in John's face, 'And we're not covering any of their legal costs. That mob'll load their expenses to the hilt if they think we're picking up the tab.'

John smiled. 'Leave it with me, Malcolm. I agree with your stance. Sleeman and Associates are a professional firm—they know they don't have an open and shut case. In fact, if she wasn't family, they probably wouldn't be involved at all.'

He replaced the papers in the envelope. 'Any thoughts on what you'd be prepared to offer to make it all go away?'

Malcolm stared fixedly, raising one eyebrow slightly. 'So now you want me to do your job for you?'

Chapter 43

GEORGE MITCHELL looked up from his newspaper with mild surprise; nobody knocked on his door—mostly they just walked right in.

'Lachlan,' he said, on opening the door. 'Long time no see. What brings you 'ere? How's your boy, by the way? I 'eard about 'is little mishap a while back'

Lachie shook George's outstretched hand. 'G'day, George. Sorry for not visiting much lately. Things have been pretty full-on, what with one thing or another.'

He stepped into the relative cool of George's front room. 'Ian's well, thanks. We had a bit of a fright recently, though.' He rubbed his chin before continuing. 'Actually, there's something I want to talk to you about. I'm not sure where to start, so I guess I'd better just spit it out.'

'That don't sound too good,' the old man replied. 'Do I need to sit down?'

He gestured toward the kitchen. Lachie took a chair at the table, gathering his thoughts as George filled the kettle and set about making tea for them both. His wife, Irma, had passed recently and George now lived alone.

George slid a steaming enamel mug across the table. 'Somethin' to eat?' he asked.

Lachie gave a dismissive wave. George opened the refrigerator and gazed in for a minute, before deciding he didn't want anything either.

'So what's on ya mind, Lachie?'

'Tell me,' Lachie said once George sat down, 'have there been any, ah, health issues here at the camp? You know, like, er, unusual problems; things you wouldn't normally expect?'

George thought for a moment. 'Millie's boy spen' a while in Port 'edland 'ospital a while back, Can't remember what for. We've 'ad a cupla youngsters die in the past year—that's unusual, I guess. Aboriginal 'ealth Services were looking into it, but again, I dunno what the causes were.'

He swallowed hard before continuing, 'An' then there was Irma. Doctors said it was liver failure. Blamed it on booze, but you know Irma—she liked a drink when she were young, but 'adn't touched a drop in years. Not since the kids came along, actually.'

'Iain had a liver tumour,' Lachie said. 'The surgeon seemed to suspect it might have come from his exposure to the tailings.'

'Well, no one from ere's been anywhere near the mine site,' George said. He looked deep into Lachie's eyes. 'Anythin' you need to tell me, Lachlan?'

'I'm really not sure, George. I could be jumping to conclusions. We've been sending soil and water samples from the creek and the dam area away for testing every month, and all the reports have come back clear.'

What Lachie wasn't saying—what he daren't say—was that the results had been far *too* consistent. He'd spent the past two days going back over every sample report they'd received from the lab since KMC had taken over Skull Creek three and a half years ago. He would have expected some variation, especially in the wet season, yet the figures were surprisingly uniform.

'Actually, don't put too much store in what I'm saying, Mate. I reckon Iain's problem was a one-off. Maybe I'm just being a paranoid father.'

'We've all bin there,' George chuckled. 'Comes with the territory, I suppose.'

The two friends chatted for a while longer before Lachie drained his mug and rose to leave. 'I'm actually here to take this month's sample from the waterhole,' he said. 'I better grab it now so I can get to Port Hedland in time for today's post.'

'Don' be a stranger, hey?' George called after him as he left. 'I miss yer ugly mug.'

'See you again soon,' Lachie called back.

Once at the billabong, he filled the sample bottle as he always had done. What he also did, however, was to secure a second specimen; one which he planned to send to a different testing lab for analysis. He resolved to repeat this process with every test from now on until he either found an anomaly or became satisfied that all was well regarding the water quality.

It was several days before the awaited phone call. After listening intently to the breakdown of the results, Lachlan requested they be sent to him via an email address he had created for just this purpose. One which he'd fervently hoped he would never use.

He printed out hard copies and deleted the file—after uploading a copy to his personal cloud storage service.

Rachel glanced at her phone and touched the reply button on her earpiece. 'Lachlan,' she said, 'Merry Christmas.'

'Merry Christmas to you, Mum,' he replied. 'Are you at Saba and Savta's place?'

'Just driving down now,' she said. 'I'll be there in about an hour. How's Skull Creek—hot enough up there for you?'

'I'm in Perth. Just got off the plane,' he said. 'I sneaked off. I need to talk to you about something.'

'You what? Who's looking after things up there?'

'They'll be fine for a day or two. Like I said, I need to … to show you something, actually.'

'What is it?'

'Can you meet me at the airport?' Lachie said. 'I'll wait near the baggage carousel.'

'And you can't tell me what it's all about?'

'It's better if I show you, Mum. Will you come?'

* * *

Rachel stared incredulously at the two documents before her. She turned away and sipped her coffee, as if it would somehow change the figures, or offer an explanation other than the obvious one; the one they both knew to be true.

'Malcolm's been playing with these sample results all this time?' she said, almost in a whisper. 'He's been putting the health—no, the lives—of so many people at risk. For what, company profits?'

Lachie didn't answer directly. Instead, he posed a question of his own; 'But what do we do? This could ruin the company if it gets out'

'We can't just cover it up, Lachlan!' she exclaimed. 'We have to tell the people at the settlement. We have to think of the children. Didn't you say there were health issues already?'

'There have been suspicious illnesses, it's true. Nothing that we can definitely blame on mine runoff, but yes, there's circumstantial evidence. What we need to work out is how we can make things better without sacrificing KMC.'

Rachel stared, her eyes wide with incredulity. 'Are you saying we should carry on covering this up?'

'Mum, I've agonised over this for the past two days, and that's why I came to you. If we go public with this, we'll open the floodgates for litigations. Every hungry lawyer in the country will be clamouring for a piece of the action. You know how much we rely on Skull Creek for our bottom line. A class action would probably drown us, and the actual victims would end up with bugger all while the parasites in their pin-striped suits get rich.'

'I can't be a party to a coverup,' Rachel said flatly. 'You should have known that before you involved me. And I can't believe you're actually considering it!'

'I'm not saying we should dodge our responsibilities, Mum. We owe it to everyone affected to step up and fix things before they get any worse. Hopefully, we can do that without involving lawyers or the media.

'We should talk with George's people about moving them away from the waterhole. That's the most important thing. And we should cover all expenses for a completely new settlement for them, as well as making sure everyone gets the best medical care.'

'And you really think Malcolm will agree to any of that?'

'OK, Mum,' Lachlan said, 'how about this: Uncle Mal is the one who caused this entire problem; he took it on himself to cover up the pollution in the first place. Yes, he's a company director, so his actions still come back on Kincaid Mining. But what if we can somehow get him to accept responsibility and then negotiate a settlement with George's people without publicly admitting blame on the part of the company?

'At the very least,' he went on, 'we need to advise them of the actual risks. We could, for example, say that we've begun a more accurate testing method and that it's increased the risk assessment.'

'Again,' Rachel said, 'how will we get Malcolm to agree with any of this? He still holds sway in the company.'

'Uncle Mal doesn't hold the balance of power. I do.'

Rachel's mouth opened. 'What?'

'Remember that Christmas, just after my eighteenth birthday, when Jimmy and I visited Uncle Mal down south? Well, he gave me a bundle of shares as a Christmas present—on condition that I didn't tell you.' Rachel was still looking at her son with bewilderment. 'It was a tax dodge of some sort. I don't know the details.' Lachie gave a dismissive wave and continued, 'The reason he wanted it kept from you, I guess, was so he could bluff you into agreeing with any decisions he made.

'Sorry,' he added sheepishly.

'And all this time …?'

'Sorry,' Lachie said again.

Rachel sat in silence. This changed so many things. For so long now, she had experienced Malcolm bullying his way through boardroom decisions when she actually might have derailed his plans. With her and Lachlan's combined voting powers, they could have overruled Malcolm any time they chose.

There was still the matter of Malcolm's threats to inform Lachlan of his true parentage; threats he still might follow through with if things didn't go his way. She thought it unlikely, however. The trick would be to not let herself get caught alone with him before establishing the new status quo.

'And you'd be willing to vote with me if he tried to block these arrangements?' she asked.

'In the light of what we now know—definitely,' Lachlan said.

Chapter 44

Thursday, January 6, 2005

'SO WHAT'S ALL THIS ABOUT?' Malcolm demanded, once everyone was seated in the boardroom. 'An extraordinary meeting?' He surveyed the room suspiciously. 'Where's Sam—and why is Lachlan here?'

Lachie rose to his feet. Malcolm raised his eyebrows; Lachlan had never attended a board meeting before this day. Indeed—Malcolm thought—as far as Rachel knew, he had no shareholdings, therefore no reason to attend.

'Can you explain these?' Lachie said, tossing several printed pages toward the older Kincaid and ignoring Malcolm's question about Sam Bronson. The documents skidded across the table and fell into Malcolm's lap.

He picked them up and read for several minutes before casting them aside. 'Two conflicting analyses of the same samples, I assume. So someone has repeated the tests and fucked them up. What does this prove?'

Looking from one to the other, he asked pointedly, 'And who authorised these tests, anyway?'

'I did,' Lachie replied. 'I took both samples, sent both of them away at the same time, and also had the labs repeat each test, just to be sure. In both cases, the two results were exactly the same.'

Malcolm glared. Finally, he said, 'And what did you hope to achieve? What have you achieved, for that matter?'

'We know the truth; that you probably got one of your paid stooges in the testing lab to falsify the results, and that you've been doing the same since we took over Skull Creek.'

'Oh, grow the fuck up!' Malcolm yelled. 'That mine has been making us a fortune. A fortune that you were more than happy to take your share of. The soil and creek water were toxic before we took over. What were we supposed to do—walk away from one of the richest seams in the area?'

'But what about the people affected?' Rachel said. 'What about Iain?'

Malcolm fixed Rachel with a stony stare before turning his attention back to Lachie. 'Iain should never have been there in the first place. We all knew the tailings dam was dangerous. You can't dump that blame onto me.'

He pointed an accusatory finger in Lachie's direction. 'Your stupidity cost the company thousands. We had to settle with your ex-missus and her team to keep it out of the papers. I should take that out of your wages, nephew or not.'

'OK,' Lachie countered, 'but what about the aboriginal settlement? Two kids from there died this year, and George's wife, from liver failure, six months ago—probably because of arsenic and mercury exposure.'

'She probably drank herself to death, you mean,' Malcolm responded with a sneer.

He turned his attention toward Rachel. 'You do know what might be the consequences of messing with me?'

He fixed her with a vicious glare, letting his meaning sink in.

Rachel knew exactly what he was referring to and decided attack might be her best defence.

'Malcolm,' she said evenly. 'If this becomes public, Kincaid Mining Corporation will be finished. You'll end up in jail, and all the assets will be swallowed up in a black hole of litigation. Is that what you want?'

Malcolm was by now seething. He maintained his glare but didn't reply.

Rachel continued. 'Lachlan has told me about the shares you gave him.' She glanced briefly in her son's direction before continuing. 'I have thirty per cent; you *used* to have thirty per cent. What that means is that you no longer have any real say in what happens here.

'We're not threatening you,' she continued quickly, 'but you need to realise this is a family concern—not your own personal power base and money pit. There are dozens of people who rely on us for their livelihood; both at the mines and in the office. You made this mess, but it's up to all of us to clean it up.'

The trio stood in silence, Malcolm's gaze flickering from one to the other. Finally, he said, 'So no one's going to report this?'

'Relax, Uncle Mal,' Lachie said. 'This stays in-house. But only if we can agree on how to make reparation to all those affected.'

Malcolm bristled at his use of the word *Uncle*. Oh, how he wanted to spill the beans, there and then; it would have almost been worth it to see Rachel's face. Instead, though, he held back to allow Lachie and Rachel to finish. They clearly had more to add, and by now he was curious to learn what it was they had cooked up between them.

'We can't bring back Irma Mitchell,' Lachie continued, 'or any of the others. What we can do is make sure nothing like this ever happens again. We'll notify them that a newer, more accurate testing procedure has shown that we have to reassess the health risks. We'll then move their entire settlement away from the contaminated area and build a new village for them.'

Malcolm made to speak, but Lachie continued. 'And before you start with "it's only an abo camp"—this option will be a whole lot cheaper than trying to settle with them through the courts. They'll have to move anyway, so we might as well see it's done properly, without risking everything we've built so far.'

He gave his uncle a few more moments to digest everything he had said before continuing, 'If it helps you make up your mind, the recent exploratory drilling tests show good gold deposits around the area of the settlement. We can't mine while they're living there, but ...' he gave a slight shrug.

Rachel shot a look of horror at her son. Malcolm allowed himself a brief smile—she obviously hadn't expected that. 'OK then,' he said. 'Let's hear your full proposal.'

Lachie and Rachel outlined the plans they had put together. Malcolm realised he had little choice but to agree to everything, making only a few token suggestions here and there.

As for a location for the new settlement, Lachie had an idea: He told them of the deep ravine—a permanent spring-fed water source—where he and Bronte had picnicked on their visit to the mine. There was an elevated area just a half kilometre from the water. That would be an ideal site, he thought.

'How do you suppose the residents will react?' Rachel asked.

Malcolm opened his mouth to speak, but thought better of it. Neither of them would have wanted to hear his views on the subject.

'We'll have to be diplomatic with how we put it to them,' Lachie said. 'George trusts me —at least I think he does—but I'm still a white fella, and a mining executive. In their eyes, that's two negative points from the start.'

'Well, if anyone can talk them around, you can,' she replied.

'I reckon it'll help if Jimmy's involved, too,' Lachie added.

Rachel and Malcolm both agreed. *Maybe Lachie has what it takes, after all*, Malcolm mused to himself.

Lachie explained that Jimmy and Mona, a local Wirtakarrimaya girl, were in a serious relationship and there were even rumours of an impending marriage. The community held Jimmy in high regard. He could never be allowed to find out about the faked test results, of course—plausible deniability, and all that.

They closed the meeting, and Malcolm scurried off to lick his wounds. Rachel turned to Lachie. 'What's this about mining the camp area when they move?' she asked. 'Is that really a consideration?'

Lachie smirked. 'You believed that? That's good. If you did, he would've too.'

'You cheeky sod!' Rachel gave him a playful swat about the head. It seemed Lachlan Kincaid had the measure of his Machiavellian uncle, after all.

Chapter 45

Moving The Settlement

JIMMY'S TOUR OF DUTY at the mine covered most of January 2005. Lachlan arranged for the two of them to visit Wirtakarrimaya on Wednesday, the fifth.

'G'day, guys,' said George, on answering his door. 'Must be summat serious if it needs both o' you 'ere.'

'Can you spare a bit of your time, George?' Lachie said. 'And yeah, I guess it is pretty serious.'

George brewed some tea for them both and sat opposite Lachie at the kitchen table. His eyes—those same dark, penetrating eyes that seemingly had the power to examine the very depths of one's soul—burned into Lachie.

Lachie and Jimmy explained the issue at hand: The company had begun to lose faith in the testing lab and had commissioned a new analysis regimen from a different company—one with more accurate testing procedures. This new lab had discovered serious anomalies which, while not necessarily life-threatening, had required a complete rethink of the situation. The bottom line being that Wirtakarrimaya would have to be moved to ensure the well-being of the residents. Of course, Kincaid Mining Corporation would cover all expenses, and build a completely new village along with a small hospital and even arrange for a medical team to visit regularly.

'That's pretty generous of you guys,' George mused. 'What's the catch?'

'Catch?' Lachie said. 'No catch George. We've been making a lot of money out of mining your land. We've got an obligation to do right by you. Anyway, we don't want to be facing a lawsuit further down the track because we didn't take action now.'

George stared deep into Lachie's eyes again, holding his gaze for what seemed like several minutes, though in fact was probably only seconds. Lachie and Jimmy sat in silence. Finally, he said, 'OK Lachlan, I trust you, ya know that. I always reckoned you was pretty solid.' Then he added, 'Not like that other Kincaid guy, Malcolm. He came 'ere a while back when we complained about more stuff coming down from the dam up there—'is eyes never kep' still. He's a bad egg, that one. I don' care if 'e is fam'ly.'

'He's my uncle,' Lachie explained, 'and no, I don't like him much either.' Then he added, 'He doesn't run the show, though. My mother and I have shares and we can outvote Malcolm if we need to. On anything,' he added with emphasis.

George nodded and turned to Jimmy. 'I trust you too, Jimmy boy. You're OK—for a Maduwongga.'

He gave a brief chuckle and added, 'You'll be fam'ly soon anyway, I expect.'

Lachie thought his friend actually blushed, but it was hard to tell.

Looking back to Lachie, George said, 'I'll call a meetin' of elders. I'll get 'em 'ere tomorrow afternoon. You can sit in if ya like, but I'll speak to 'em first. How 'bout you come at aroun' two o'clock?'

'I'll be here,' said Lachie. 'And thanks for the vote of confidence.'

* * *

As Lachie approached George's house the following day, he could hear the heated debate long before he reached the front door. He knocked tentatively, and George ushered him in.

There were six people present besides George; three men and three women. All—Lachie supposed—aged in their late sixties. George introduced him, without mentioning the others individually. He motioned Lachie to sit at a chair near the end of the table.

Lachie looked around at the array of faces before him. Aside from George Mitchell, he only saw one he recognised—Mona's mother. The debate was on hold for now; it seemed. The elders each fixed him with their own version of 'the stare', though none had the intensity of George's. Eventually, he realised they were waiting for him to speak.

Without standing—sensing that it might be seen as intimidating—he said, 'I suppose George has explained the situation. I'm here to represent Kincaid Mining. We didn't cause the problem with the contamination, but we will accept responsibility—and we'll do what we can to fix it. If there's anything that any of you want to ask—anything you'd like us to do—please say so.'

He sat back in his chair and waited. They all looked at George.

'Nobody wants to move,' George said, 'but I've told 'em we really 'av to. We 'av to think about the kids. We all agree you're tryin' to do the right thing, but this place's bin special for a long time.'

'Sure,' Lachie said, 'I appreciate that. If you stay here, though, bad things will happen. People will get sick, maybe die.'

'Bad things 'appened the day that mine opened,' growled one of the men.

'Yep, you're right, but that's in the past. We can't change what Wally Bright did. What we can do—what we will do—is make sure nothing else bad happens to anyone here.' Lachie looked around the room, searching for a sign he was getting through.

'You wan' us to move,' said another, 'but where can we go? We got to 'av water.'

Lachie mentioned the ravine he had told Mal and Rachel about. In his mind, it seemed a logical place to resettle to, and he said as much. The group exchanged glances, several muttering in their own tongue. Finally, George spoke.

'That's a bad place, Lachlan. Bad spirit lives in that water. Kids 'av gone there an' never come back. Bad place,' he repeated, shaking his head.

Lachie thought before answering. The legend, he supposed, was probably a myth invented many years ago to frighten children out of swimming in what was actually a deep and dangerous body of water. A myth that successive generations had believed in, and that and had since become folklore. To dismiss it lightly would destroy any credibility he had built so far.

'I didn't know that,' he said.

'Only Nyamal people would,' a voice cut in. 'It part of our Dreaming.'

Lachie thought for a while. 'How close can you go to the pool?' he asked. 'I've seen cave paintings there, so you must be able to go to the ravine.'

'Men can go near,' George said, 'but we never go to the water edge.'

'OK,' Lachie said, 'how about this?'

He detailed his thoughts about the elevated area he had mentioned to Mal and Rachel. The group nodded; they knew the area well.

'We can put up a secure fence around the waterhole. That way, no one can get near the water. We'll set up a pumping station and send the water across to the hill behind the new camp area.' He waited while George translated for those whose English wasn't good.

'We can put some water tanks on the hill, so you'll have flowing water. Maybe we can also install a solar-powered chlorination unit. That way, the water will be even safer than what you've been drinking here.'

The group looked around at each other and began debating in the Nyamal tongue. It seemed all this was a bit much for some to absorb. George assured Lachie he would explain it all to them in detail, and they would debate it and make the right decision. 'Leave it with us, Lachlan,' he said. 'I'll let you know 'ow the vote goes. We 'av to agree.'

Lachie nodded. He rose to his feet, bade the group farewell, and took his leave. He knew George saw the merit in his argument. The only uncertainty was whether George could sway the general opinion of the elders' council. Lachie suspected he would. George obviously was held in high regard.

It was the afternoon of the following day, before George Mitchell called Lachie to say they had agreed to the move.

'I know how hard that decision must have been, George,' Lachie said. 'Thanks for helping me explain it. Leave it all with me for now. I'll let you know once things start happening.'

The Move

Relocating a thriving community—one that has existed in its current location for all living memory—would never be easy; nor would it happen overnight. Lachie and Jimmy knew this, and they hired a subcontracting firm to complete the task.

Mike Bloom, the project foreman, immediately arranged to fence off the Skull Creek waterhole, and for the delivery of extra water tanks.

The next step, building a high Cyclone mesh fence around the new water source and establishing the pump house, took a little over a week. By this time, the water storage tanks were in place and plumbed in.

Many of the residents were growing eager to move, and as it was still late summer—the nights not yet too cold—Lachie arranged for several large tents and a marquee for temporary accommodation.

'Looks like the circus is in town,' Jimmy said on visiting for the first time in several days.

Mike Bloom chuckled. 'All we need now are a few clowns and an elephant, and we'll be in business.'

The first of the new housing modules began arriving before the beginning of March, and by mid-April, the village was established, minus a few finishing touches.

Malcolm Kincaid neither asked, nor was informed, about the progress. Lachie, Rachel, Jimmy, and George had formed an unofficial overseeing body to coordinate the relocation. It was toward the end of May, just after Lachie had begun his rotation, when George Mitchell paid him a visit.

Chapter 46

Saturday, May 21st, 2005.

LACHIE WAS IN A MEETING with Brian Koss and another worker, discussing some recent ore samples, when the intercom buzzed.

'There's, er, a dark gentleman here. Says his name is George.' Then, in a whisper, 'What should I do?' It was Grace Willis, the office secretary.

'George?' Lachie said. *Why would he be visiting the mine?* 'Can you ask him to wait? We'll be done here in about ten minutes. Oh, and get him a cup of tea, will you? He takes it black with two sugars.'

After a brief hesitation, Grace replied, 'Very well, Mr Kincaid.'

'So what brings you here, mate?' Lachie said later, offering George his hand.

'Can we talk in private?'

'Come through to the office,' said Lachie, gesturing toward the door.

Opting not to sit behind the desk, Lachie seated himself in a chair near the window, signalling for George to take the seat opposite.

'It about your Uncle Malcolm,' the old man began. He paused, as if searching for the right words.

'You 'member 'e came up 'ere last July?' Lachie nodded. He remembered the visit; he recalled thinking Malcolm probably wanted to get away from Perth's winter for a while.

'You also know 'e came to the ol' camp a few times?'

Lachie admitted he wasn't aware of Malcolm's movements. He'd been in Perth at the time, and Bronte had been in rehab, so there were other things on his mind.

George swallowed. Lachie sensed he had something important to say, but was having trouble getting it out.

'Did you 'ear Mona's li'l sister was pregnant?'

'Marnie?' Lachie said. 'No, I hadn't heard that. Is that good news? I mean, how old is she, anyway?'

'Jus' turn' sixteen,' George replied.

'OK, but what's that got to do with Uncle Mal?'

The old man's gaze was unwavering. Finally, Lachie said, 'You don't mean—no! You're not saying …'

'She 'ad a boy a little while back. Proper fair-skinned fella. She says it Malcolm's'

Lachie pictured Marnie—a pretty girl with a sparkling personality. Surely Mal hadn't …

'She says Malcolm gave her drink. Took her up back o' the camp an'… did things.'

Lachie's jaw fell. Was there no end to what Malcolm Kincaid was capable of?

After a pause George continued, 'Marnie's father is fixin' to point 'im. You know what that means?'

Lachie nodded. He'd heard about bone-pointing, though he didn't think it was still practised. Anecdotal evidence and legend suggested that when an aboriginal 'pointed the bone' at another, the victim was doomed to die within a short time. Sometimes it could take weeks, but often days, or even hours.

Sceptics maintained it was merely suggestion amongst a very superstitious people; just knowing they had been pointed being enough to achieve the result. In many cases, however, the victims were unaware they were targeted and had still succumbed, even, sometimes, over great distances.

He'd never heard of a white man being pointed, but knew better than to scoff at such things.

'And you thought you'd better warn us?' Lachie said.

'Won't do any good, but I reckon you oughta know. Bad things in store for your uncle. Even if 'e don't die—bad things comin' to 'im'

They were both silent for a moment, before George continued, 'There's summat else, Lachlan. You bin straight with us—well, as straight as you could be, I suppose.'

Lachie raised his eyebrows.

'You done the right thing by us blackfellas. You know your mine caused sickness at the camp, an' you're doin' what you can to make it good.'

He fixed Lachie with a granite stare before saying, 'I know Malcolm fixed those tests. I can't prove it, an' I don't think I want to. Nothin's gonna bring back those kids, or Irma. But you, Lachlan, are trying' to make it right. Some fellas wanted to get Aboriginal Legal Services in, but I tol' 'em you'd do the proper thing. I'm right, aren't I?'

This, Lachlan had not expected. He swallowed hard before replying, 'George, I can't comment on that. What I can say—and this is my solemn promise to you—Kincaid Mining will do right by you and your people. What we've done so far is not where it ends, and my Mum feels exactly the same. We're indebted to you and your community, and we honour our debts.'

'I know, Lachlan,' the old man said. 'That's what I tol' the other elders. I looked in your heart when we first met, an' I saw you was a good man. I get visions sometimes, Lachlan. I get feelings about people—an' sometimes I see what 'asn't 'appened yet.'

Lachie nodded. Hadn't he known that—somewhere deep inside?

'So did you point Uncle Mal, or was it Moira's Dad?'

George turned away without replying. 'I best be gettin' back,' he said. 'Jus' mind what I tol' you—bad things comin' to Malcolm Kincaid.'

Chapter 47

AROUND THE END of that month, on a Sunday evening, Malcolm Kincaid was casually thumbing through the newspaper. The television was on, though he scarcely noticed—until a breaking news bulletin shattered his serenity.

Malcolm immediately forgot his paper and stared at the screen, wide-mouthed.

'An amateur gold fossicker, who dropped his metal detector down an abandoned mineshaft in the far east of Western Australia, received the shock of his life when he tried to retrieve it,' the announcer was saying. 'On clambering down the disused shaft, he discovered the remains of a male person on a ledge below. The unfortunate victim appears to have lain there for several years, but the body remained in surprisingly good condition. WA Police are keen to speak with anybody who might be aware of someone who had been in the area and was unaccounted for. Stand by as we cross live to Police Headquarters.'

Malcolm snatched the remote and cranked up the volume. At a hurriedly convened media conference, a senior officer addressed reporters about the recently discovered body. No further information was available and the exact location was not being released until investigations were complete. More details would be forthcoming after forensic examination of the remains, he said.

The officer continued talking, but Malcolm wasn't listening. He knew precisely where the body had been found. In fact, he knew exactly who had been lying at the bottom of that deserted shaft for the past seven years.

He poured himself a large whisky, downed it in one gulp before pouring a second, and flopped onto his couch. The images came flooding back now; memories he had almost managed to erase, at least from his conscious mind.

*   *   *

On the Friday after his coffee shop meeting with Moose, back in 1998, the two had left Perth at a little after five am. Mid-morning found them skirting around Kalgoorlie and driving north. Sharing the driving, they passed all the places where Malcolm might have been recognised and continued through Menzies and on to Leonora, where they turned right, heading eastwards toward the small mining town of Laverton.

'How about stopping at the servo for a break?' Moose asked.

'Too risky, mate. You tend to stand out a bit. If the cops post a mugshot of you as a bail jumper, someone could recognise you. It's OK though, we can pull over for a rest soon. We're making good time and I know a few spots out this way where no one'll stumble onto us.'

Malcolm had passed the word within the company that he would be on another of his exploratory trips. He regularly took time out for fossicking expeditions, so neither Rachel nor Lachlan thought it unusual.

After driving throughout the day, they set up camp at an out-of-the-way spot east of Leonora. Malcolm had packed survival food, and they enjoyed a filling—if not exactly appetising—meal. 'You can have the bed,' he told his compatriot. 'I'll sleep outside in the sleeping bag.'

Next day, after breakfast, they continued their eastward trek. Somewhere between Laverton and Warburton, however, Malcolm's real plans came to a deadly conclusion.

It was mid-afternoon, and Malcolm suggested a brief stop-off to walk around and stretch their legs. He explained to Moose that he'd spent some time prospecting the area with his metal detector and knew of a few abandoned mines nearby. He offered to show his fellow traveller what a gold mine shaft looked like up close. Standing at the edge, and looking down into the abyssal pit below, Moose hadn't known what struck him.

Malcolm placed his hand on Moose's shoulder and plunged the *skean dhu* deep into the big man's back—just below his ribs—once, twice, and once more, for good measure.

The first two blows lacerated his liver and pierced one kidney. The third struck between two vertebrae, partially severing his spinal cord. Moose's legs gave way, and he fell to his knees, gasping and teetering on the edge, before Malcolm gave a mighty shove and the big Maori tumbled headlong into the mine shaft. He made no sound; no 'Aaaaghh' like in the movies. He would have been dead before he even hit the bottom, Malcolm surmised. If he wasn't, he certainly wouldn't have survived the fall.

'Fucking Ecuador? You must really think I'm a fool,' he hissed through clenched teeth. 'Who's the fool now, you big, stupid prick?'

Nobody came near these old mines. It could be decades before anyone found the body, if ever. Meanwhile, all Malcolm had to do was to head back home and get on with his life. And, as a bonus, he had Moose's little cash stockpile as spending money! Who says there's no such thing as a free lunch?

He splashed some water into a bowl and began washing the knife. That's when he noticed the broken tip.

Gripped suddenly by blind panic, Malcolm's mind reeled. He felt confident that Moose's body would never be found, but what if it was? What if someone stumbled across it and the broken knife tip? What if, somehow, it might be traced back to him?

For a moment, he considered tossing the dagger down into the pit along with Moose, before remembering it had his family's crest on the blade. It wouldn't take Sherlock Holmes to connect the knife with the Kincaid family, and with him.

Anyway, he couldn't just throw the weapon away. It was the last connection between him and his Scottish heritage. He needed a way to keep it for posterity, yet still create separation between it and himself. And that's when he thought of Lachlan.

Chapter 48

ARETHA WAS WAITING as Lachie stepped off the plane at Perth Airport. The terminal, located north-west of the major airport buildings, served many of the smaller airlines that ferried the FIFO workers to and from their jobs on the mines.

She fidgeted impatiently as he collected his baggage. The news she had for him had already waited too long. She ached to share it with him, but she wanted to see his face when he heard. As he walked through the exit doors, she rushed forward and flung her arms around him.

'Wow,' he said. 'What've I done to deserve a welcome like this?' Then, holding her away from him in mock suspicion, he added, 'Or, more to the point, what am I going to do?'

'I have some news,' she said, beaming. Then, unable to contain herself any longer, she handed him a small plastic device with a little window showing a blue cross.

Lachie examined it with a bemused look before realisation dawned. 'Is—is this what I think? Are we pregnant?'

'Well, I'm not sure about the *we* part, but it says *I* am.' Aretha replied with a laugh, before continuing, 'Yes, Lachie, you're going to be a Daddy again!'

'Wow,' was all he could manage at first. 'Weren't you on the pill, though?'

'Yeah, and I've thought about that. Remember when I had that crook tummy a few weeks back? I threw up and must have dumped it in the loo before it dissolved. I didn't mention it, but I actually missed two days. You left around that time and we weren't having sex because I was ill, so I just forgot all about it.'

'Except for that one time,' he said.

'Yeah, I'd forgotten about that,' she said sheepishly.

Aretha searched his eyes. 'Are you pleased?'

'I was about to ask you the same, but you seemed pretty happy when you showed me the test kit,' Lachie said. Then he added, 'Yes, Aretha, I'm thrilled. You'll be a great Mum. And I can't wait to be a father again.' He flung his arms around her once again and pivoted on his heels, swinging her about in a full circle.

They talked excitedly on the way home. Aretha called Jimmy to give him the news. Keeping it to herself for the past two weeks had seemed like the hardest thing she had ever done.

'Any plans for marriage?' Jimmy asked when Aretha handed the phone to Lachie.

'Haven't thought that far ahead,' Lachie replied. 'Maybe we can have a double wedding—if you and Mona finally make up your minds, that is.'

The one thing Lachie and Aretha agreed on was to keep the news from Malcolm for the time being. He'd find out eventually, but he'd been even more volatile than usual lately, and they both knew he barely tolerated Aretha's presence in Lachie's life as it was.

Back home, Lachlan insisted on fixing sandwiches for them both. 'I'm so sick of mine food,' he said. 'I need something different.'

Aretha was watching the television when she suddenly called to him.

'Lachie, come quick! You need to see this.'

A police spokesman was discussing the item that had dominated the news lately: the 'Body in the Mine' case. He held a small plastic bag with a triangular piece of metal inside.

'We believe it may be a fragment of the murder weapon.'

'Are there any clues yet as to who the victim might be?' a reported asked.

'At this stage, his identity is still unknown,' the officer replied. 'Investigations are ongoing, and we're hoping for a breakthrough soon. I can reveal that he appears to be of South Sea Islander descent. In the meantime, we're appealing for members of the public to come forward if they feel they have any clues as to the identity of the victim or the perpetrator.'

A gaggle of voices joined in with a stream of questions. Aretha wasn't listening, though. She strode across the room and removed the skean dhu from its place in the mounting frame. She examined the broken tip before looking at Lachie.

'Is it possible?'

'Don't be stupid!' he said. 'It looks about the right size and shape, I'll admit, but you're saying Uncle Malcolm killed this guy? I know he's an arrogant son of a bitch and all that, but murder?'

Aretha looked from the knife in her hand to the TV screen. The small metal triangle had gone from the screen, and the officer was winding up the interview.

Replacing the dagger, she said, 'No, I guess not. I can't stand him—you know that—and I reckon he's capable of just about anything, but this has to be a coincidence.'

Lachie returned to his self-enforced kitchen duties. Aretha went back to watching the news but still found her gaze returning to the display case on the wall. *Was it a coincidence?*

Lachie entered with their lunch, and they dropped the subject.

Friday, May 20th, 2005.

Bronte slid on to the seat opposite Lachie. 'Well, you're the last person I expected to get a lunch invitation from today,' she said. 'Am I to assume this is business? I don't suppose you've invited me here to ask for a reconciliation?'

Lachie managed a smile. At least they could share a joke now, even if it was at their own mutual expense.

'Actually, Bron, I need some legal help.'

She raised her eyebrows. 'From me?'

'You're still a lawyer, are you not?' he said. 'And I've got something I don't want Lurie and Singh involved in. Something that's probably right up your alley, if my information's correct.'

Bronte returned his gaze, cupping her chin on the backs of her hands. 'You must really be desperate,' she said finally. 'It's nice to be on speaking terms again, but this, I never expected.'

'It does concern you indirectly, though not enough to constitute a conflict of interest. It also concerns Uncle Mal.'

He saw her eyes flicker at the name. 'Go on.'

Over the next half-hour, Lachie detailed a proposal he had been considering for some time. He needed an independent legal opinion and thought what he had in mind fell within Bronte's field of expertise. Since they were meeting as lawyer and client, he knew their discussion was confidential.

'I'll have to discuss this with Daddy, and maybe even Bruce,' she said. 'Will that be a problem?'

'Not on my part. At the moment it's just an idea, and anyway, there is such a thing as client confidentiality, isn't there?'

Bronte agreed.

'Actually, Lachlan, there's something you should know before we take this any further. Just before my, er, breakdown—I had a particularly unpleasant visit from your Uncle Malcolm.'

Bronte reached for the carafe on the table and poured herself a glass of water. Lachie watched intently as she drained the glass and sat staring out of the window for several seconds. By the time she spoke, she had worried the napkin she held into a tight, pulpy ball.

Lachie listened as Bronte relayed the details of Malcolm's visit all those months ago. His unveiled threats, his menacing speech, and the way it had finally tipped her into the downward spiral that culminated in her attempt on her own and Iain's lives. She made no apology; it was simply her explanation of the sequence of events. Lachie could see she was struggling to keep control as she recounted the harrowing experience.

When she finished, he waited a few seconds before saying, 'That must have been terrifying. I know how intimidating he can be—I've seen him in action. And you didn't tell anyone?'

'Who could I tell? For all I knew, you put him up to it—and anyway, I wasn't thinking clearly at the time. I just blocked it out. I just drank more, smoked more, and … I can't even remember what else I was using then.'

A tear ran down her cheek. Bronte dabbed at it with the remains of her serviette. Lachie placed his hand on hers.

'Well, you don't have to worry about Uncle Mal now. You've come through all that. You and I have sorted our differences, and you have your life back on track. I'm glad you could tell me about that; it must have been painful.'

Bronte nodded silently.

They finished their meal and parted with a handshake. 'I'll call you after the weekend,' she said, before stopping in her tracks, turning, and saying, 'Can I be there when you tell Malcolm about this?'

Chapter 49

Friday, June 17, 2005.

TWO DAYS AFTER Lachie had left for his next stint at the mine, Aretha again examined the knife.

If this was not the murder weapon—she reasoned—the police could tell right away, and Lachie would never need to know she had shown it to them.

But what if it was? What then?

She'd brought the subject up a few days before, when the same images appeared in the newspapers. Lachie had laughed it off before saying he didn't want to discuss the matter any further. The more Aretha thought about it though, the more uneasy she became.

Today, she finally resolved to speak with the Police when she learned they had identified the victim.

Henare Parata, also known as Henry, or sometimes 'Moose'—she read in the West Australian newspaper—had once been investigated as a suspect in the infamous 1981 'Hand of God' break-in at the Two Brothers Mine, near Kalgoorlie.

Aretha had heard of the case; it was legendary, especially in the Kalgoorlie-Boulder region.

So was this still a coincidence? Wouldn't even Lachie have his suspicions now?

Later that day, Aretha met with DC Liam Toomey, at Police Headquarters in Adelaide Terrace, East Perth

On being ushered into an interview room, Aretha was offered her choice of coffee, or coffee. She declined both.

'Aretha,' DC Toomey said on entering. 'Thanks for coming in. I believe you may have something of interest to show us.'

'I'm really hoping it's not relevant,' she said. 'I mean, I don't want to be wasting your time, but in a way, I hope I am.'

'No problems,' Toomey replied. 'All part of the job. What have you got for us?'

She showed him the knife and explained how it came to be in her and Lachie's possession.

'When we saw the news reports and the pictures of the broken knife tip, we assumed it had to be a coincidence. I mean, nobody expects to be connected to a killing, do they? It was only when I read about him being involved with the mine break-in that I decided I'd better show it to you. Even if just to put our minds at ease.'

'It's not confirmed that the victim was involved in the theft,' Toomey said. 'We'll probably never be able to confirm that, unfortunately. In fact, there might not be any connection at all.'

He examined the dagger closely. 'Beautiful piece of work,' he mused, turning it in his hands. 'We will need to keep it for a few days. Once the forensics team either confirm or deny that the piece we have came from this, someone will be in touch with you.'

They gave Aretha a receipt acknowledging she had left the knife with them and ushered her from the building. Her sense of uneasy self-reproach was palpable. Why should she feel guilty? If it wasn't the murder weapon, which it almost definitely wasn't, then no one would be any the wiser. If it was, well, surely she was doing her civic duty?

No amount of self-analysis would take away this sense of guilt, however, and the feeling was to stay with her until Monday afternoon, when the phone call from Detective Toomey finally came.

*   *   *

Wednesday, June 22, 2005.

Rachel lifted the phone from its cradle. 'Good morning, Two Brothers Mine. How may I help you?'

'Rachel,' it was Susan Friend, Malcolm's PA. 'I thought I should tell you Mr Kincaid has been taken to hospital. He hasn't been himself lately, and this morning he had some sort of seizure.'

'What? Do you know what's wrong?'

'Not sure,' Susan said. 'He's been acting a little odd for a few days. He wouldn't talk about it, but there's definitely been something bothering him. This morning, he asked for his usual coffee, and when Greta went in with it, she found him passed out on the floor.'

Rachel heard more than a touch of apprehension in Susan's voice. 'I dialled triple zero straight away, of course. He was breathing all right, though it seemed a bit shallow. I thought I should let you know,' she added.

'What hospital?' Rachel asked. She felt concern in her own voice. He was her Brother-in-Law, after all.

'Royal Perth,' Susan replied. 'He's probably in Emergency, I'd guess.'

After getting a few more details, Rachel thanked her for calling and rang Royal Perth Hospital.

Speaking with a senior staff member, she learned Malcolm was in the Intensive Care Unit. Tests were still underway, and yes, as she was a relative, someone would be sure to keep her informed.

Then she called Lachie.

'Hospital?' he said when told. 'And they can't tell you what's the matter?'

'According to Susan Friend, Malcolm's been acting strangely for a while. She thinks it might be some sort of stress problem.'

'Uncle Mal, suffering from stress?' Lachie said. 'He's usually the one causing stress, isn't he?'

'Maybe it's all caught up with him?' Rachel offered.

Malcolm's condition improved somewhat over the next two days. Malcolm being Malcolm, as soon as he could exert his authority, he insisted on being transferred to the Saint John of God private hospital in Murdoch. Public hospitals were for plebs, in Malcolm Kincaid's eyes.

He was still in the hospital when he received a visit from DC Toomey and his immediate superior, one DS Blackler.

'Mr Kincaid,' Alan Blackler began. 'Thanks for agreeing to speak with us.' he consulted his notes briefly. 'Did you, at any time, have any contact with Henare Parata, an associate of the Vulcans Motorcycle Club?'

'Why the hell would I be involved with a bikie gang?' was Malcolm's response. 'And who the blue blazes is Henarry Whatsisname?'

'You may have known him by the name of Moose. Or possibly, Henry.'

Malcolm pursed his lips, shaking his head. 'Still doesn't ring any bells.'

Blackler decided it was time to play their trump card. He held up the *skean dhu*, enclosed within a plastic evidence bag. 'Have you seen this before?'

The colour drained from Malcolm's face. He suddenly felt very faint, and the buzzing that had plagued his hearing over the past few days grew to a crescendo.

He swallowed, and whispered, 'I think I need a lawyer.'

'That might be a very smart move, Mr Kincaid,' Blackler said. 'In the meantime, it's my duty to inform you that you are under arrest on suspicion of involvement in the murder of Henare Parata. For now, you'll be confined to this room. Please tell your legal counsel that we'll be interviewing you formally tomorrow, in relation to this matter, and we may be applying to have you remanded in custody. Subject to medical advice, of course.'

'Is that it?' Malcolm said. 'Aren't you supposed to read me my rights?'

Blackler smiled. 'Sorry, Mr Kincaid. This isn't America, or the UK. We do things a little differently.' Then he added, as if as an afterthought, 'Call your lawyer, Mr Kincaid. We'll see you tomorrow.' And with that, they left. A constable who had accompanied them into the room pulled up a chair in the corridor outside and sat facing Malcolm's door.

Malcolm did not sleep well that night. He first woke at around midnight from a terrifying dream—a dream in which he saw himself on trial, with a judge and jury consisting entirely of Aboriginals. They chanted in their own gibberish, and pointed their fingers at him, while the members of his family sat in the public gallery, mocking him. Malcolm rang for the nursing staff and insisted they give him a sedative.

Despite the medication, he woke several more times in a cold sweat, convinced, on one occasion, that his accusers were there in the room with him, chanting and dancing around a huge bonfire as the flames cast flickering, eerie shadows across the ward.

By morning, Malcolm was barely coherent.

Lachie called Jimmy Browne and arranged for Jimmy to fill in for him at Skull Creek. After flying down to Perth, he met with Rachel for a hurried meeting in the KMC boardroom. Rachel had arranged for Julie Watkins to hold the fort for her at Two Brothers Mine.

'What's happening to him?' Rachel said. 'He seems to be falling apart. And what's with these charges—is Mal really responsible for this man's death?'

'It's looking that way, Mum,' Lachie answered.

Lachie filled Rachel in on the details relating to the *skean dhu*. How, if not for Aretha's suspicions, Malcolm might never have been arrested. Aretha had phoned Lachie immediately after the call from DC Toomey.

He also told her about his conversation with George Mitchell and the revelation about the bone pointing.

'But I thought that sort of thing only worked within their own people; a kind of auto-suggestion.'

'I've never heard of a white man being pointed,' Lachie said. 'I can't think of any other explanation for Uncle Mal's condition, though. And we can rule out auto-suggestion, as he knows nothing about it.'

After a minute's reflection, Lachie spoke again. 'Mum, there's something else I want to run past you. Nothing to do with Uncle Mal's illness—or his legal mess—but it's a plan I've been thinking about for a while.

'I spoke with Bronte last month—as a legal advisor.'

'Oh?' Rachel arched her eyebrows.

Lachlan had thought long and hard for some time about what he was about to propose. He didn't know how his mother would react. He knew exactly what Malcolm's reaction would have been, and that was the reason he'd not aired this idea before—not even to Aretha.

For several minutes, Rachel listened to her son's proposal; his new vision for the Skull Creek mine.

Eventually, Lachie finished and waited for his mother's response.

'We'll need to discuss this with Lurie and Singh.' she said. 'You say Bronte and her father have already done some preparation?'

'I had to talk to someone outside the firm,' Lachie explained. 'I couldn't be sure if John Lurie wouldn't go over my head and involve Uncle Mal. I only asked Sleemans for an independent opinion, and they know that Lurie and Singh are our solicitors and are happy to work in tandem with them.'

'Well, for what it's worth, I reckon this could be exactly what's required to resolve all the problems we're having at Skull Creek,' Rachel said. 'In fact, this may be the best idea I've heard in a long time.

'And I don't think we need to fret about Malcolm's opinion. By the look of things, he's going to have much more serious stuff than this to worry about.'

Relief washed over Lachie. He hadn't known how his mother would view his unorthodox suggestions. The following morning, they pitched their new plans to the corporate legal team at Lurie, Singh, and Partners. Lachie brought Bronte in as a consultant, since she had already done considerable investigation and groundwork.

After lunch, the three of them, along with Aretha—at Lachie's request—visited Malcolm in Saint John of God Hospital.

The pathetic sight that greeted them was barely recognisable as the man they knew. Malcolm's eyes were sunken and dark. His skin had a pallor not unlike Swiss cheese. His breath rattled, and his hair looked whiter than it ever had.

His declining health had forced the detectives to delay interviewing their newest murder suspect. Indeed, the prognosis was that he might not be up to interrogation for a considerable time.

Lachlan and his mother exchanged glances. Should they even broach the subject of the restructure?

It was Malcolm himself who gave them the motivation to proceed.

Looking around the room, he spotted Bronte.

'Why is she here?' he rasped, quickly becoming more alert. 'I don't want anyone except family. She's got no right …' Then, seeing Aretha, he added, 'And what the fuck is that black bitch doing here?'

Addressing her directly, he shouted, 'Fuck off, you boong slut! You'll never get your hands on any of the Kincaid assets. I don't care what you and that useless brother of yours do. Now piss off out of my room!' He waved his hand in a dismissive gesture, struggling to rise.

Aretha paled and made to leave. Lachie caught her arm, however, and pulling her toward Malcolm's bed, he spoke evenly, 'Uncle Mal, this is the woman I'm going to marry. In fact, the next addition to the Kincaid family is already here.' He patted Aretha's belly. 'And that's not the only bit of news we have for you today.'

He paused briefly. Malcolm opened his mouth to speak, but Lachie cut him short. 'Mum and I are going to turn Skull Creek into a Co-operative. Jimmy and I will continue to manage the mine, but all nett proceeds will go to the Wirtakarrimaya people.

'It's the very least we can do,' he continued, 'after polluting their water, poisoning their kids, and generally stealing their heritage. Wally Bright might have started the rot, but it was you who carried it on—and covered it up.'

Malcolm's eyes bulged. His face had lost the pale yellow cast and had taken on a dark ruddy glow.

He made to speak, but no words came out. He attempted again to rise, but fell back onto the mound of pillows on his bed.

Rachel grabbed the call button and squeezed it desperately.

A nurse rushed in and immediately ordered everyone to leave. She thumped the emergency button above the bed and began CPR.

Outside, in the corridor, Rachel looked at Lachlan as a bevy of nursing staff rushed past them into Malcolm's room.

'Should you have told him all that—in his state?'

'I couldn't help it, Mum. Not once he started on Aretha. She didn't deserve a tirade like that.'

'She didn't,' Rachel agreed.

They stood in a huddle outside Malcolm's room, each unsure what to say or how to react. It was Rachel who broke the silence. 'Is that true? Are you pregnant, Aretha?'

Aretha nodded. 'Just over three months now. We were planning on coming up to surprise you, but what with one thing and another …' She gestured toward Malcolm's door.

'Well, congrats to you both. It's such a pity not to receive the news under different circumstances, though.'

Rachel gave Aretha and Lachie a joint hug, then spread one arm to include a very surprised Bronte in the embrace.

As they separated, Lachie said, 'I guess there's no point hanging around here. Uncle Mal's obviously not going to be up to engaging in conversation for quite a while. We'll come back tomorrow and see how he's faring. Anyone for a coffee?'

They made their way to the cafeteria, where Lachie bought drinks for everyone.

'So, are wedding bells on the agenda?' Rachel said once the refreshments arrived.

Lachie and Aretha looked at each other. 'Yep,' Lachie said.

'We might even have a double wedding with Jimmy and Mona,' Aretha added.

'Any chance we could make that a triple?' Rachel said, raising her left hand to display the new engagement ring on her finger.

'Hey, so Graham finally decided to make an honest woman of you?' Lachie said. 'About bloody time!'

They shared a chuckle, and after finishing their coffees they each went their own way, resolving to meet the following day to start procedures for the setting up of the Co-operative.

* * *

Malcolm Kincaid lapsed into a coma from which he never woke. The official cause of death was multiple organ failure. Doctors were at a loss to explain the underlying origin. Skull Creek mine was renamed Wirtakarrimaya, and from July 1st, 2005, began operating as Wirtakarrimaya Co-operative Pty Ltd, with the profits being managed by a board comprising George Mitchell, Lachlan Kincaid, James Browne, and two other elders of the settlement, appointed on a rotational basis.

Twenty-five years later, Lachlan and Aretha Kincaid's son James would also sit on the board. To this day, the Hand of God break-in remains one of the great unsolved mysteries of the Australian mining industry.

****

Thank you for choosing to buy and read this book. You could have bought any book, but you bought mine. For that I'm grateful. GOLD! is Book One in the proposed Kincaid Saga series. Other planned entries include a prequel based on the life of Malcolm's father, Feargus, as well as a spin-off covering Marita Rose's early life and another about Rachel and Graham.

Reviews are important for any writer, and especially so for an independent author. As a self-publisher, I don't have the resources the major publishing houses have at their disposal for book promotion. Your honest review will make it easier for other readers to find this and other indie works.

Please take a moment to register your opinions with one of the following links:
To leave an Amazon review, try this first:
https://www.rpbook.co.uk/azr/B08N5ZVMZT
Although it's a UK link, this will direct you to your region's Amazon review page. Easy-peasy. I'm all in favour of that.

If you'd prefer to leave a review somewhere else, here are 2 options:
https://books2read.com/u/3yewpv
This covers most online retailers. Just scroll down the list until you see the retailer you purchased from and leave your review and comments.

Or this one: **https://www.goodreads.com/review/new/56165411-gold**
Goodreads is an online forum for both readers and writers. You might just find your next favourite book there. Here's my Goodreads profile link:
https://www.goodreads.com/author/show/20940426.Thomas_Greenbank

Please visit my website, **thomasgreenbank.com/join-the-tribe**, and sign up for my newsletter to receive exclusive free stories, content, and other goodies from time to time including a FREE copy of my Short Story Collection, ***The Ravine and Other Tales.***

In addition, I'll keep you informed of my progress with future books and other projects. Any feedback is always welcome.

Thanks again for choosing to read GOLD. I trust you enjoyed it. If so, please tell your friends.

Thomas.

Milton Keynes UK
Ingram Content Group UK Ltd.
UKHW020636230124
436534UK00016B/574